DELIVERANCE

Forgotten Colony, Book One

M.R. FORBES

Chapter 1

"Sergeant Card, sitrep!"

The voice came in loud and harsh through the comm in Sergeant Caleb Card's helmet. He didn't expect anything less from Lieutenant Jones. He was all business in the best of times, and these were anything but the best of times.

Caleb didn't answer right away. His response was interrupted when a demon burst out of a broken window beside him and his squad, lunging through the air toward Corporal Banks on his left. Caleb was the first to notice the attempted ambush, and he spun lightly on his heels, bringing his carbine to bear and firing. The slugs hit the demon in the chest, the impact knocking it off course and onto the street.

It didn't move again.

"Thanks for the save, Sarge," Corporal Banks said.

Caleb glanced down at the dead creature. They all called them demons, but they weren't. At least, Command said they weren't. They looked like demons, with sharp features and oily black flesh, like horror-movie bats that had lost their wings and grown spindly arms and legs that ended in razor-sharp claws. The damn things were light as bats too, their bones hollow and delicate, allowing them to jump around like they were on a trampoline.

It also made them pretty easy to kill. It was just too bad there were so damn many of them.

"Card!" Lieutenant Jones snapped again. "Sitrep!"

"Sir, we're…" Caleb paused, looking around and then at the map on the heads-up display appearing on the inside of his helmet visor. The streets all looked the same. The buildings all looked the same. Everything looked the same. Ripped and torn apart, broken and beaten, strewn with rubble, debris and bodies. Everywhere he went, there were bodies. So many and so often he hardly noticed them as anything more than a fixture of the modern landscape.

The street was a snapshot of Earth in general. It didn't matter which city they were in. New York, Chicago, Paris, London, Moscow. Everywhere was the same. Chaos, destruction and death. So much death that corpse-ridden streets had become the new normal.

Walking through this street at this time of day with this group of men and women? That was the strange thing.

He noticed a nearby wall, half crumbled. Red spray paint coated the marred surface.

SCREW THE XENOTRIFE!

He could get behind that. Screw the xenotrife.

"We're half a klick from the target and closing," Caleb finished, getting his bearings from the tactical map on his HUD.

"Roger," Lieutenant Jones said. Of course, he already knew the position of the Vultures, but he needed to make sure the squad stayed focused. "Squads six and eight are down. Four and seven are headed back to the drop point. Eyes in the sky are picking up increasing activity below, closing on your position. The bastards know they've got fresh meat in the kitchen, and they don't want to waste it."

Caleb considered telling the lieutenant his metaphor sucked. The xenotrife didn't kill people for food, or there would be a lot fewer bodies in the streets. No, they hunted humans because… well, he didn't know why.

Not exactly.

Some people said there was no motive. That it just was. How else could you explain their arrival? An epic meteor storm had created one of the most amazing light shows ever. In the morning, a layer of fine powder covered a good portion of the planet's surface. A few weeks later, people started dying. A few weeks after that, the demons began to appear.

Two years. That's how long it had been since the trife arrived. Caleb could still remember his first deployment. He wasn't doing search and rescue then. He was a Raider at the time. Marine special ops. His squad was one of the first on the scene when the trife began to appear, part of a control unit sent to New Orleans. The platoon hadn't known what to expect, and they paid for it with their lives. Only four of them made it out, clinging to lifelines and dangling from choppers.

At least the bastards couldn't fly.

Two years was a long time to survive in this mess, and he was never sure how he had made it this far. Luck? Determination? Stupidity? He had never accounted it to skill or talent. He had seen too many good men and women with so much more of both fall under the massive waves of the demons, claws tearing through the gaps in their body armor, ripping into flesh and bone and stealing their lives away in a blink.

They had survived the virus for that?

"Sir, we're at half a klick," Caleb said. "We can make it to the target."

"But can you get back out?" Jones replied. "Make the call, Sergeant. I trust you and your team to do the right thing."

Caleb's head swept across his squad. They were experienced Marines, all of them. They had watched the world burn with him, and they were still here, aching for more. There was no fear in them. Fear had been scared out of them a long time ago, and in a dozen different ways. Banks had been a civilian back then, watching his daughter die from the virus. He had been there when the first trife broke through the windows of his home and murdered his wife and son. He spent every day regretting he had used his shotgun on the trife instead of on himself. Every day, he regretted surviving when his family hadn't.

"We can make it, Sergeant," Private Yen Sho said. "In and out. You know that's how we like to do it."

"Confirmed," Corporal Banks said. "We don't do half-missions. That's bullshit. Let the rest of the platoon run back to mommy. We're the Vultures."

"Thirded," Private Habib said. "And fourthed, speaking for Washington over there."

Caleb glanced at Private Washington, who flipped Habib the finger. The private had lost his tongue and half his face to the trife. He couldn't speak but he could still fight, and these days that was good enough for the United States Marine Corps.

"Unanimous," Private Rodriguez said. "We wouldn't be out here risking our asses on this one if Command didn't think it was important."

"Finish the job or die trying," Banks said. "That isn't our motto for nothing."

Caleb smiled inside his helmet. He knew he could count on his crew.

"We're continuing ahead, sir," Caleb said. "Keep the engines warm for us."

"Copy that, Sergeant," Lieutenant Jones replied. "I'm redeploying the rest of the platoon in support. They'll be waiting two klicks out from the RV, trying not to attract too much attention. When you call, they'll come running."

"Roger that, sir. What about air support?"

"Negative. Our choppers are frozen ahead of the retreat. Command isn't willing to risk what little we have left on this one, not after the shit Valentine pulled."

"I'm sure she had her reasons, sir."

"Yeah, to force you into standing out there with a thousand trife swarming your position. You've got ten minutes at best, Sergeant. Get your team's collective asses in gear."

"Roger that. Vultures, let's move, standard column, full ahead."

Caleb broke into a run, one eye on the terrain ahead, the other on his HUD. Beyond the top-down map of the region, the Advanced Tactical Combat System connected him with every Marine within ten miles of his position through a hardened wireless mesh network, and more importantly, it linked him with his squad. Every member of the team had access to one another's vitals, camera feeds, threat monitors and sensors, ammunition levels and more. The ATCS software took the six separate Marines and aggregated the data so they could organize and fight as one twelve-armed entity. As Habib liked to joke, they could play Pac-man on the damn things in the middle of a firefight and barely break a sweat.

The ATCS was embedded into their standard-issue Advanced Tactical Combat Armor, the latest and greatest in personal trife protection out of United States military

R&D. Affectionately nicknamed SOS or *Stormtrooper on Steroids* by its wearers because of the vague resemblance, it was composed of a series of hard plates that covered most of the body. The black synthetic spider-steel weave body-suit beneath it helped protect the joints. The bodysuit also contained a light assistive artificial musculature that increased strength and stamina of the wearer by as a much as thirty percent, allowing Caleb and the squad to run faster and longer than they would otherwise.

Right now, they needed every ounce of strength and speed they could get.

The squad charged through the city, alone but not alone, dancing over piles of rubble and ash, circling burned-out cars and trying not to trip over any of the human remains. The smell was horrible, the air thick and muggy and still filled with the smoke of the smoldering fires left behind by the morning's four-bomber offensive. The bombers had dropped dozens of canisters of napalm across the area to clear the path of trife. It had been some-what successful, giving the company a window of time to attempt the extraction of some high-value assets.

But the window was closing sooner than they had hoped. Both on the Vultures, and on the whole world.

Chapter 2

Caleb's threat sensors picked up the first group of incoming trife seven seconds before they became visible. The AI of the ATCS tracked the minute changes in the feed from his helmet-mounted camera before combining that data with the feed from the drone over their heads and deciding to warn him about the incoming enemy.

Now, if the R&D folks could just make the system a little more sensitive to detect things like the trife that had burst out of the window a minute earlier. The system was good, but it wasn't perfect.

"Banks, left flank," Caleb said. "Sho, cover our rear. Washington, send 'em to hell."

Washington silently hefted his XM556 minigun, taking a moment to make sure the belt-feed was clear. The rest of the Vultures parted to give him a clear line of fire, rifles up and ready. They would need to conserve ammo, and the XM556 was enough to handle the early stages of the attack.

Caleb knew from experience that the trife would approach like sharks, sending in smaller groups to test them before they launched their full assault. It didn't matter if they had overwhelming numbers, they always always attacked the same way. First, they would send a test group in like the one Caleb and his troops faced now. Then the next few groups would be their actual test of the fire-power their enemy possessed. Then the gates of hell would open up, and the real demon horde would throw itself into the breach.

They had to be clear of the area by the time the horde showed up, or they were already as good as dead.

The trife came from the left side, a group a dozen strong. They spread out on the ground and at the side of the building closest to the Vultures. Caleb ignored them, keeping his attention on his HUD. The drone was marking more suspected trife on the map for him, showing an increasing hue of red drawing in from the northern side of the city.

The loud whine of the minigun was dulled by filters in his helmet, but Caleb still knew the moment Private Wash-ington started shooting. Marks on the map began to disap-pear, wiped out by the dozens of rounds the weapon was spitting at the demons, literally tearing some of them in half.

The shooting stopped seconds later, leaving the street clear again. Pieces of trife were strewn across their left flank, none of the creatures getting close enough to force any of the other Vultures to start shooting.

"Nice work, Washington," Caleb said. "Stay tight. Echelon left. We're almost there."

The Marines moved into position and continued forward, running through a line of thick smoke. The target came into view as they cleared the haze — a four-story stone building that had all the markings of a government installation. Old and tired before the war, with small windows and an ugly face that had some of the individual lettered tiles still attached.

U.S. DE AR   ENT O HE TH AND HUM N ERVICES

"Lieutenant Jones, we have visual on the target, sir," Caleb announced to his superior.

"Roger that, Sergeant. You're behind schedule."

Caleb couldn't help but grin. Bastard. They were well ahead of the original schedule — the one where the nearest trife were at least four klicks out of the operational zone. That's what the tactical geniuses in charge of the mission had estimated, but of course they would defend the outcome by falling back on statistical variance.

Screw statistical variance too. It was his unit whose lives were at risk. Not to mention the lives of the men and women they had entered the city to retrieve.

"Incoming," Banks said, calling the warning, his ATCS picking up the next wave before Caleb's. The trife were further back, closing from the left rear flank this time and trying to sneak up on them. The creatures didn't understand that the Marines could still see them when they weren't directly facing them. They had no concept of drones, cameras, sensors and AI. They saw humans and they attacked humans, and for every one the Vultures killed, there would be a hundred more to take its place.

That's how humankind had lost the planet. And the planet was lost, no matter how much General Stacker wanted things to be different. He was the black sheep of Command, the only one who refused to quit fighting even when the fight was so obviously lost. The only one who was trying to keep the planet instead of escaping it with whatever they could salvage.

Caleb often wished he had been assigned to Stacker's chain of command, but that wasn't the way it had all worked out. He still considered himself a Marine even though his battalion had been transferred to Space Force six months ago to perform VIP extractions similar to this one.

If he survived this last mission, he, his squad, whatever was left of his battalion and some forty-thousand civilians would be leaving Earth behind. The Deliverance was loaded and almost ready to go, and Command wanted Doctor Valentine and her team on the ship before it lifted off. As one of the top remaining genetic experts in the country, they considered her a high-value asset.

The only reason she wasn't already on the Deliverance was because she was a stubborn pain in the ass.

Lieutenant Jones had called her a lot worse than that, but Caleb didn't know her well enough to be that disparaging. All he knew was that she insisted on staying behind as long as possible to continue her work, whatever that work was.

"Washington, Sho, take them out," Caleb ordered. "Habib, Rodriguez, cover the entrance. Banks, you're with me. We're heading inside."

"Roger, Sergeant," the Vultures replied.

Caleb sprinted the last hundred meters to the front of the building. Opening Washington's camera feed in his helmet, he saw the trife approaching the big Marine, coming from across the street to limit the effectiveness of Washington's minigun.

He knew it wouldn't phase Washington. Nothing did. Washington shifted casually, rotating to the group of trife on the left, three skirting the side of one of the buildings, all of them spaced nearly ten meters apart. They weren't the demons closest to Washington, but he didn't seem to care.

Caleb might have worried about most Marines. He

didn't worry about Washington. The private hefted the minigun and squeezed the trigger, the ammo belt sliding over his shoulder as the weapon discharged into the side of the structure, blowing through one of the trife, pausing momentarily and then hitting the second.

The closer trife grew larger in Washington's feed, slightly blurry at the edges of the camera's view. They were almost right on top of the big man now, ready to attack.

Caleb heard the separate reports in his helmet and watched on the feed as the trife went down one after another, taken by surprise by Sho, who had ducked behind one of the mangled cars. Washington didn't even flinch as the last of them fell at his feet, claws reaching out toward him. He finished with his targets and swept around to the third group in the street, who were trying to use the scarred wreck of a bus for cover. Washington opened up again, his minigun rounds punching right through the sheet metal, and then through the enemy.

"Clear," Sho said.

"Roger that," Caleb replied. "Defensive positions at the entrance; we're going in." He rechecked his HUD. The larger group was drawing ever closer, and another pair of smaller groups had broken off to test them again. "Uglies approaching from the left flank, keep 'em dying."

"Roger."

"Banks, you ready?" Caleb asked. The corporal was on the other side of the shattered glass entrance, pressed against the stone.

"Ready, Sarge."

"Let's go."

They both rounded on the entrance and into a small foyer with the HHS placard hanging behind a simple desk that was slightly charred. Apparently, it had been on fire at some point within the last eight hours.

They moved into the building, sweeping the area with their carbines. There were no trife inside.

"Lieutenant," Caleb said. "Do we have a location on Valentine and her team?"

"Confirmed," Lieutenant Jones replied. "There's a hardened lab four floors below ground level. Valentine and her people are holed up in it. There should be a secured staircase around the back near the loading dock."

"Roger." Caleb checked his HUD again. Their ten minutes were draining away in a hurry.

He squinted his left eye, navigating to the building schematic that had been uploaded into his ATCS. He located the loading dock and set a marker, the AI automatically drawing a path from his location to the target.

Caleb moved to his left, through an open door and into a long corridor. He jogged along it, Banks right behind him. He turned right when he neared the end and located the loading dock on his left, through a pair of double doors. The stairwell was ahead on his right.

He squinted his eye, navigating the ATCS, checking on Washington's ammunition. He was carrying a backpack full of rounds for the minigun, but if he fired full bore he would go through the whole thing in less than twenty seconds. He had about half remaining and they hadn't even hit real trouble yet. Caleb confirmed Washington and Sho were in position with Habib and Rodriguez, and then tested the door.

Locked. He found the biometric security panel to the left of the door.

"Lieutenant, please tell me Valentine gave you a bypass for the security lock?"

"Confirmed. Triple tap to enter the diagnostic menu, navigate to manual entry, and tell me when you're there. I'll read out the hash."

"You have to be kidding me." He checked the map. Time was running out. "She couldn't have met us up here?"

"I gave you the option to leave her behind, Sergeant," Jones replied. "Don't ..."

Caleb didn't catch the last part. A trife came flying through the doors to the loading dock, coming right at him.

He turned as quickly as he could, getting his forearm up in time for the creature's claws to scrape across the thicker ballistic armor. He kept turning as it barreled into him, using the carbine as a club. Hitting it in the back of the head, he smashed it into the wall and pivoted again, putting the end of the weapon against it. Firing a single round into its skull, its head exploded while the rest of it slumped to the ground.

"Banks, cover me," Caleb said, standing over the demon and tapping on the panel. The menu came up and he quickly moved to the manual entry. "Lieutenant, I'm ready."

"4...F...G..6..." Jones started reciting the code, taking way too long between alphanumerics.

"A little faster, Lieutenant?" Caleb asked. The gunshot was going to alert the trife, and if the loading dock were open they would be on their way.

"9, 7, E, J, 1, 4, 3," Jones said quickly. Caleb kept up, the door clicking open as soon as he tapped on the three.

His helmet beeped, warning him of the trife Banks' ATCS had just identified, coming fast toward the loading dock doors. He spun around and brought up the carbine, motioning Banks to wait until the demons were on them. They couldn't afford to waste ammunition.

Three trife burst through the doors in a manner similar to the first. Banks and Caleb both opened fire, using six rounds to cut them down at their feet. The noise was still a problem, especially as the horde closed in.

Caleb and Banks moved into the stairwell. Caleb slammed the door closed behind them, and they started to descend.

Chapter 3

Caleb and Banks took the steps two at a time, quickly negotiating the narrow stairwell. The stairs were surrounded by thick stone walls, the depth and shape of the stairwell itself intended to protect the underground lab from the attacks occurring above. Not trife attacks. The trife didn't have weapons. This part of the lab had been added after the war started, hastily constructed by conscripted crews to provide a safe space for the scientists inside to live and work while the planet crumbled around them. Caleb knew from scuttlebutt that there were thousands of scientists around the globe who had been sequestered in similar spaces to work on both the virus and a means to kill the trife. After all, chemical warfare was only illegal when it came to killing other people.

It may have seemed like a bad idea to keep the scientists in the middle of a war zone, but the truth was the entire damn planet was a war zone. There were few places the trife hadn't breached, and if they hadn't, it wasn't because of a lack of trying. The demons were everywhere, literally *everywhere*, and numbered in the billions. The virus they carried had initially wiped out over half the human population, and now, after two years, the creatures themselves had taken a huge-ass bite out of the remaining half of the population. Some estimates put the surviving human numbers at one hundred million, give or take. Based on his own experience, Caleb thought it was less than ten million.

Bottom line, hidden in underground bunkers built directly on the original work-site was just as effective and a hell of a lot more efficient.

At least until the people *in* the bunkers needed to get *out* of the bunkers.

Caleb checked his HUD continually on the way down, tracking the progress of the horde above and watching Washington, Sho, and Habib work at fending them off when they came too close.

The deeper Caleb and Banks got, the worse the stone walls started interfering with the comm network. Messages were flashing in the corner of Caleb's visor, warning him of disconnection.

It didn't surprise him when the link to the rest of the Vultures went offline by the time they reached the bottom, the network reduced to just he and Banks. They hurried across a short corridor to a steel blast door, secured with the same biometric panel they had encountered above. Caleb glowered at it as he reached for the door's handle. If Valentine had left this door locked, he was going to give serious consideration to bugging out and leaving her there.

He turned the handle and pulled. The door slid open. Banks ducked into the space, carbine up.

Caleb joined him a moment later, finding himself face-to-face with Doctor Valentine. He spent a moment giving her a critical once-over. She was petite, with sharp eyes, brown hair tied back in a ponytail and worry lines etched deep into her small face. She was in good shape and dressed smartly in a pair of yoga pants, sneakers, and a fitted top under her white lab coat.

"Doctor Valentine," he said, recognizing her from the photo Lieutenant Jones had shared during their mission briefing. "It looks like you're ready to go."

"We're ready, Sergeant," she replied.

He glanced past her to the rest of her team, nearly a dozen scientists in all. They were a mix of men and women – both young and old – in various states of exhaustion, anxiety written plainly on their faces. They were also dressed in exercise gear. It was easier to run in, and that little bit of extra mobility might be what saved their lives.

"So why are you down here instead of up there?" he asked, returning his attention to her.

"We had to finish packing."

"Packing? We're not taking any more than what you have in your hands right now. The xenotrife are coming on hard. A lot of them."

"Wrong, Sergeant. Why do you think Command sent you jarheads in on the ground instead of airlifting us out?"

"I don't ask questions about the mission parameters, ma'am."

"Because the delivery won't fit on a chopper. Anyway, you'll take what I tell you to take. Unless you want to stand here and argue?"

Caleb glanced at Banks. What the hell was this? He was already pissed at Valentine for making them come to get her and her people. Now she was making demands?

"All right, look…" He couldn't stand here and argue her point. There was just no time. "…if it won't fit on the chopper, how do you expect a pair of jarheads to move it out?"

"It's already loaded onto a truck upstairs. We brought

it up through the secured service elevator right after the bombing run when we were sure it was clear. The bugs don't care about science. If it isn't alive, if it isn't human, they aren't interested."

"Right," Caleb replied. "But there's nothing insect about them. No antenna, no thorax."

"Don't be a smart ass, Sergeant."

"If the package is already loaded, what the hell are we doing down here?"

"It's safer down here. We loaded the package into the truck, but the west wall of the loading dock didn't make it through the fighting. No offense, Sergeant, but we're scared shitless of the trife."

"So are we," Banks said.

"You wasted almost two minutes of our time getting down here," Caleb said. "If we die two minutes before we make it, I'm blaming you."

Doctor Valentine's face flushed, and she looked like she wanted to tear his head off. Caleb glared at her. He didn't care. If his team members died because of her stupid arrogant demands...

"Banks, take the rear. Let's see if we can make up some time."

"Roger that."

Caleb turned back to the doorway, rechecking his HUD. He needed to ascend faster than the rest of the group, to get in contact with the rest of the squad.

"Banks, I'll meet you at the top. Keep the civilians moving."

"Roger."

Caleb started up the stairs, rounded the first corner and threw himself backward, barely avoiding the claw that slashed at his face. He didn't avoid it altogether. The needle-sharp tips slid against the edge of his visor, leaving light scratches in the laminated glass.

His back hit the wall of the landing, keeping him from falling over completely. The trife came around the corner, mouth opening wide and revealing its multiple rows of sharp teeth. Caleb didn't panic. He had been through too much of this kind of thing to panic. He brought the carbine up and fired a single round into the demon's head.

"Banks, the trife are in the stairwell. Move up to the front and back me up."

"How'd they get in the stairwell? Didn't you close the door, Sarge?"

"Yeah, but it doesn't matter. They're here. Just do it."

Caleb went up a little slower, continually checking the HUD, waiting for the ATCS network to reconnect to any of the Vultures on the surface. He could hear the trife on the stairs now, their claws scraping the metal risers as they made their way down. He should have sent Washington and Sho to the loading dock to cover that entrance.

Banks caught up to him at the base of the second platform, moving beside him with his carbine up and ready. The scientists were still further back, moving too damn slow.

"Maybe we should let one past," Banks said. "That might hurry them up."

"Tempting," Caleb replied with a smile, just as a pair of trife moved into view ahead.

They each fired on the one closest to their side, two rounds to kill two trife. Caleb would never argue that the minigun Washington carried wasn't inefficient overall since its bullet-to-kill ratio was so much higher than the carbine's standard one-to-one or at worst three-to-one, but sometimes that quick stopping power made a life or death difference.

He rose another few steps, a quick moment of elation triggering when the ATCS showed the rest of Vulture suddenly reconnecting. Once the mesh network had one of them, it had all of them, and from them it was able to stretch out back to the transport, and from the transport back to Command.

The elation only lasted as long as it took for his map to update. In the two minutes they had been underground a new trife mass had moved in from the south.

And it was already on top of them.

Chapter 4

"Sho, sitrep!" Caleb snapped into the comm, immediately quickening his pace up the stairs. Banks didn't miss a beat, staying shoulder-to-shoulder as they rose.

The first corner revealed three more trife, and they didn't spare their ammo this time, each firing a burst that knocked the demons down.

"Sarge!" Sho said. "Bastards came up fast from the south at a full run. The lieutenant barely had a chance to send the warning before they were up on the grid. We had to fall back into the building. We used a charge to seal the corridor leading back toward the door you marked on the ATCS, but there's a massive hole in the loading dock wall, too big to seal."

Caleb found the Vultures on the grid, inside the building near the twin doors leading out to the loading dock. He checked Sho's ammunition status, noticing she was at fifty percent already. He squinted over to Washington. The minigun wasn't using rounds. The big man had switched to his sidearm for now.

"We're two floors down," Caleb said. "A few of the trife got through."

"Before we got here," Sho replied. "You should be clear now?"

Caleb's tactical showed they were, at least until they reached the top of the stairs. "Do you see a truck inside the loading dock?" Caleb asked.

"Yes," Sho replied. There are four of them in here."

"Any of them clearly packed with something?"

"One has a heavy canvas tarp over the bed, why?"

"Rodriguez," Caleb said. "Find your way to that truck and get her started. Vultures, your new directive is to defend that truck."

"The truck, Sarge?" Sho asked.

"That's the reason we're here, Marine. It also might be our best chance of getting out of this shit alive. Lieutenant Jones, do you copy?"

"I copy, Sergeant. I've got my eyes on the feed. You need to hurry."

"Yes, sir. Working on that. Can you spare any support?"

"Negative. All other teams are pulled back to the transport, waiting to cover you if you make it inside the safe zone... I'm sorry, Caleb, we just can't risk them out there."

"Yes, sir," Caleb replied. "Understood. We'll make it to you."

"I know you will."

"You heard the lieutenant," Caleb said. "We're on our own."

"What else is new?" Habib said. "Typical Space Force bullshit. Go clean up our mess, will you?"

"Cool it, Anaya," Caleb said. "Stay focused."

He and Banks climbed the last two flights of stairs, bursting out into the corridor. The rest of the vultures had already abandoned the hallway, moving out into the loading dock and doing their best to keep the trife out of the area.

He heard Washington's minigun open up again, at the same time he heard the roar of the truck's engine. He checked the HUD. The red mass was all around the building, and the eastern group was only a couple of minutes away.

"Please, for the love of all that's holy, let them be from competing nests," Caleb said.

If the trife were bound to two different queens, they would just as soon fight one another. It might be their only chance to escape.

Caleb stood at the entrance to the underground bunker, waiting for the scientists to arrive. Doctor Valentine was the first one out, and she barely flicked her eyes over to Caleb before running straight to the doors ahead and through.

"Banks, make sure she doesn't get herself killed, I guess," Caleb said.

"You got it," Banks said, his grin almost visible through his visor. He chased after her, and a moment later Caleb heard Banks' carbine start firing.

"We can't hold them much longer," Sho said.

The rest of the scientists were moving out, and Caleb windmilled his arm, trying to hurry them through the doors and to the truck. The engine was rumbling steadily, ready to go.

Caleb counted the scientists coming through, following the last one out through the doors and into the loading dock.

It was like stepping through the gates of hell.

Four trucks were spread across seven loading bays, each with their backs against the raised platform leading to the doors. Ahead of each bay was a metal roll-up door, all of which were surprisingly still intact. The hole in the wall was on the right side, eighty feet away and large enough for a dozen trife to fit through at one time, while their target was on the left side, furthest away from the damage.

At least Valentine had made one smart decision.

Washington was standing at the edge of the platform on the right side, a near constant flame pouring from the minigun, empty shell cases falling to his right like rain. There were already nearly a hundred trife carcasses piled at the hole, the heavy weapon in its element when a single round could cut through three or four of the enemy.

But more of them were still coming in, and some had taken to the top of the hole, climbing in and up the side of the wall, crawling along the ceiling. Some dropped to the floor. Some landed on the other trucks and tried to leap the gaps from there.

They swarmed into the space, more dense that Caleb had ever experienced.

Habib was standing halfway down the platform, trying to keep up with the incoming demons, her rifle sweeping across the room, firing single rounds whenever the targeting reticle on her HUD turned red, the rounds punching into shoulders and legs and heads and chests, knocking the demons down but not always out. Banks and Sho were standing on the hood of the running truck, a large open-bed hauler normally used to transport dirt or debris. They shot at the trife who came too close, managing to keep the immediate area clear.

The scientists were climbing onto the truck too, careful where they positioned themselves near the green canvas tarp covering whatever it was they had loaded into the vehicle.

"Washington, pull back," Caleb ordered, raising his

carbine and firing a pair of rounds that cut down a demon approaching the Marine. He pivoted and fired again, taking out another one. He paused a moment to check Washington's ammo levels. The minigun was at ten percent. "Now!"

Washington stopped firing and started charging back down the platform. His assault was keeping the trife honest, and now that it had stopped they crashed through the hole like water breaking through a dam.

"Vultures, fall back to the truck, now!" Caleb shouted into the comm. "Rodriguez put it in gear."

"Roger," Rodriguez said.

Caleb heard the truck shift gears. It hissed and whined, the engine roared, and it started rolling forward.

"Habib, let's go," Caleb said. Habib was lingering, trying to stave off the entire horde herself. "Habib!"

She turned to retreat. At the same time, a trife dropped from the rafters over her head, coming down toward her. Caleb shifted his carbine, firing into the creature. The rounds hit it, but momentum still carried it to Habib. Its claws slashed at her, finding the weakest spot on the armor, the small gap between the helmet and the body.

Time seemed to slow as Caleb watched the claws rake across Habib's neck, one of them finding purchase and digging in deep, ripping through the edge of the spider-steel bodysuit, blood spraying out behind its fingertip. Habib's head twisted awkwardly, and then the trife landed on her, its weight not enough to knock her down. It hissed once and fell off, dead.

It didn't matter. The damage was already done. Habib dropped her carbine, reaching up to staunch the flow of blood from her neck. It only took Caleb two seconds to reach her, but the blood was already running past her hand and down her armor when he did.

He grabbed her shoulders to keep her up, trying to help her back to the truck. It was accelerating slowly, giving him time. A warning had popped up on every Vulture's screen, informing them Habib was injured. He kept her upright with one hand, firing the carbine with the other, killing two more trife that were coming their way.

"Sarge. Caleb, go," Habib said. "You don't have time to help me, and I don't want you all to die because of me. I know you would."

"Shut up. I'm getting you out."

"You aren't." She reached up with her other hand, yanking off the helmet to reveal her face. She didn't look like a Marine under the SOS. She should have been an actress or a singer or something. "Don't worry about me, Sarge. I didn't want to go to space, anyway. I belong here on Earth with my family. I'll see them in Heaven."

Caleb was set to argue, but her eyes glazed over and she got heavy in his hands. It didn't matter if he wanted to save her, she was already dead.

He lowered her body, shooting three more trife and then quickly ejecting the magazine and replacing it. The swarm was so thick their hissing sounded like a constant hum, and they were seconds away from overtaking the truck.

"Rodriguez, floor that thing as best you can," Caleb said, turning and dashing across the platform toward the escaping vehicle.

"Sarge – !"

"I'll make it."

The truck's engine echoed in the space, and it lurched ahead, gaining speed. Caleb ran toward it, rolling to the side as a trife landed in front of him, avoiding its lunge and getting back up to continue the sprint. Another tried to take him from the side and he whipped the carbine around, smashing it in the face with the stock. The third dove at him from behind, but Banks cut it down from the rear of the truck.

"Come on, Sarge!" Banks yelled.

Caleb reached the edge of the platform and jumped, heading full speed toward the back of the truck. He dropped the carbine to his side, slamming into the metal rear and grabbing onto the ladder there, losing his grip with one hand and dangling from it. He gritted his teeth, holding on as the truck reached the metal door in front of it, slamming into it and breaking through, the sound of rending metal echoing loudly in the space.

The trife seemed to sense their quarry was escaping, and they hissed louder, becoming more desperate to reach them before they disappeared. They dove at the back of the truck from wherever they were. From the floor. From the ceiling. From the tops of the other vehicles. The Vultures did their best to manage the sudden flow, but it was impossible to catch them all immediately.

Caleb heard cries and shouting above as the trife landed on the truck and attacked the scientists. He cursed and started up the ladder, grabbed suddenly when one of the demons fell on his back. He rocked beneath it, pushing it back and kicking out. He hit it in the chest, knocking it to the ground. The truck made it out of the building, and Caleb leaned around the edge of the trailer to see into the street ahead.

They were all going to die.

Chapter 5

The map on Caleb's HUD was frightening enough. A sea of red surrounding the Department of Health and Human Services, an apparently never-ending slick of the demonic alien trife surrounding them.

The real visual was more terrifying. The trife ahead of the truck were like a roiling sea stirred up by a massive storm, a line of creatures that spread back into the dark and smokey haze, churning as if they were a single entity.

Caleb pulled himself up the ladder as quickly as he could, jumping into the back bed of the truck. There were three scientists down, two of them motionless and the other groaning. Banks was injured too, with a gash in the joint of his elbow. They hadn't all seen the road ahead of them, so they didn't all know how scared they should be. Caleb had seen though.

"Rodriguez," Caleb shouted into the comm. "If we're going to have to go through the bastards, at least get us moving in the right direction and step on it."

"Roger that," Rodriguez replied. The truck slowed, approaching a corner. "Hold on."

Caleb crouched low, leaning on the tarp and whatever was under it. The brakes on the truck squealed as it slowed harshly, the cab turning down an adjacent street and back toward the waiting transport. They only had to cover about three-quarters of a mile to make it to what Lieutenant Jones called the safe zone.

It was going to be the furthest three-quarters of a mile of their lives.

The truck picked up speed and shuddered slightly as it started hitting the trife, who were either too stupid to move or thought they could stop the heavy vehicle if enough of them sacrificed themselves to it. They were pulled under the wheels and flattened, thrown aside by the fenders, and left broken and bent by the truck's front nose.

Crashing through the trife in front also meant driving down the middle of the rest, putting healthy trife on both sides of the truck. The Vultures spread out, two on either side, aiming their weapons and waiting.

A trife jumped from the sidelines, easily able to get its fingers around the top edge of the bed to pull itself up. It didn't have a chance. Washington aimed his pistol and fired, his round snapping its head back and knocking it from the truck.

Another made an attempt, and Sho took it out just as easily. On the other side, where Caleb and Banks were, three more tried to scale the truck, and a burst of rounds pushed them back.

"Sergeant!" one of the scientists shouted. Caleb looked to the back of the truck as a trife climbed over the side and rushed the scientist. He screamed and fell backward onto the tarp. Caleb aimed and fired, and the trife fell.

More replaced it as the larger group started climbing up the sides of the truck. Caleb didn't have enough Marines to stand at every possible entry, and it was only a matter of time before they would be overwhelmed. "Rodriguez," he said. "Cut back to the west."

"West?" Rodriguez replied, confused. "We don't have enough of these assholes to deal with already?"

The second mass of trife were coming in from that direction, closing fast but not fast enough.

"Not really, no," Caleb replied.

Rodriguez laughed into the comm. "I ever tell you that you're one crazy son of a bitch?"

"Not in so many words."

"Consider it done."

"Noted." Caleb activated his external microphone. "Hold on!" he shouted for the benefit of the scientists.

A moment later, the truck started to turn again. The maneuver surprised Caleb too because they hadn't reached the end of the street.

"And he thinks I'm crazy?" he said to himself. The truck was headed right toward the blown out face of a diner, cutting the corner too soon to confuse and slow down the trife.

Caleb heard a shout behind him, and he turned around to see a trife had gotten to Banks. The demon had its arms around his shoulders, its legs wrapped around his legs, and its mouth trying to find a weak spot to bite.

"Get the hell off!" Banks roared, the contact too close to bring his carbine around. Caleb charged the demon, rushing to help.

The truck hit the curb, bounced up and slammed into the diner. The sudden change in momentum sent Caleb off his feet. It sent Banks off his feet too.

Right over the edge of the truck and into the horde.

"Banks!" Caleb shouted, rushing to the other side of the truck. They were pushing through the walls of the building, smashing through the counter and the tables toward the broken adjacent window. "Rodriguez, we have to stop."

He found Banks standing in the middle of the group, not even looking back at the truck. He had his carbine in one hand and his pistol in the other, and was shooting trife as quickly as he could.

"No," Banks said. "You keep moving damn it. You get back to the Deliverance."

Caleb's heart pounded, his body tense. He kept his eyes on Banks as the trife fell in front of him, shot down in his blaze of glory. Then the demons took him from the rear, first one, then another, then three more.

Banks made sure to turn off his comm before he started screaming.

"Damn it!" Caleb shouted.

The truck cleared the corner, gaining a few seconds of respite from the attack. Caleb turned his head, finding a trife on top of a scientist, claws covered in blood. He shot it, needing all his resistance to keep from emptying his magazine into the hellish creature. His Vultures were dying. Banks had been a close friend.

This was all Valentine's fault.

If she had left the bunker earlier. If she had been waiting at the top of the steps. If she had moved up the stairs faster. He stopped himself. There was no value in blame. It wouldn't make Habib or Banks any less dead. He had to get the rest of his team and the rest of his scientists out of this disaster alive.

He checked his HUD. The truck had maneuvered into a short space between the two groups of trife. The area around them was evident. They had entered the eye of the storm. A harsh silence descended on them, and he had a moment to scan the truck and find each of the survivors.

Washington and Sho remained on top of the truck's

cab, manning each side. The minigun dangled from Washington's chest. Sho kept her carbine shouldered and ready. There were eight scientists still in the back of the truck, including Valentine. She had found a spot in the corner near the front, and she had her eyes fixed on the tarp.

What the hell was in there that was so important?

He wanted to ask her, but the eye of the storm wasn't all that big.

"Here they come," Rodriguez said, his voice quaking. He was a tough man, but even tough men struggled to deal with the truth about the trife.

Earth wasn't humankind's anymore.

It was theirs.

Chapter 6

Caleb ran to the front of the trailer, looking over the cab to the trife ahead. They were identical to the group behind them, human-sized, ugly, and ferocious. They were slightly smarter than the first group though, because they moved aside as the truck neared them, choosing instead to jump at the doors of the cab to reach the driver.

"Little help," Rodriguez said, as three of the demons made it to the door, and another two leaped onto the hood.

Sho was there in an instant, firing down at them, knocking them away one at a time while Washington covered the opposite side. Caleb watched the carnage, then traced the trife back as the truck started past them. He couldn't manage both sides alone.

"Sergeant!" Valentine shouted. She was on her feet now, coming toward him. "Give me your sidearm."

"What?"

"I used to be a Marine too," she said. "That's how I covered my doctorate. I know how to shoot a gun, and you need someone to cover the right flank."

He didn't waste his breath arguing. He handed her the

carbine instead. "You don't need to be as accurate with this."

She took it. He handed her an extra magazine to go with it, and then returned to the left side of the truck. Things were getting dicey again, the trife building up around them. He fired down at the demons, and he heard the carbine going off on the other side.

"Rodriguez cut left again ASAP," he ordered, noticing a cross street approaching.

"Roger," Rodriguez replied.

Caleb turned around to look over the rear of the trailer. The first group of trife was closing on this one. He kept staring, waiting for the first of them to interact. He had been part of this war since the beginning. He knew how the demons worked, how they reacted, and he knew what to expect if the two groups were from separate nests.

"Come on," he said, interrupting his observation to shoot a trife that made it into the trailer, right before it lunged at a terrified scientist. "Come on!" He ran to the back of the trailer, firing into the trife. "For hell's sake, come...*on!*"

He shot another trife. It spun and hit the trife right behind it. That trife caught the body, and for a moment they stood there, reminding him of a picture he had seen once of a sailor kissing a woman in the middle of a crowded New York street. Only the first trife didn't kiss the second. It dug its teeth into the opposite demon's neck, tearing it out.

"Yes!" Caleb shouted, spinning around again.

A trife hit him, slamming into him and pushing him back. Then he was falling, claws scraping against his armor as he stumbled toward the rear edge of the truck. He couldn't believe this was how he was going to die.

He went over the edge, dropping the pistol and

stretching desperately for the ladder. He got his hand on it, wrapping his fingers around it and holding tight. The trife that hit him fell into the scrum behind, screaming as it was attacked. Caleb regained himself, reaching up with his right hand to grab the next rung.

He tried to grip it but couldn't find the strength. Blood was pouring from a deep wound on his wrist, the tendons likely severed by the claw he hadn't felt cut into him. He grunted, planting his feet and wrapping his arm around the rung, pulling himself up. Another trife leaped at him, and he kicked out at it, catching it in the face and knocking it back. He grabbed the next rung and lifted again, rising to the edge of the trailer. He held on tight while Rodriguez turned, bringing the truck around the next corner and heading back toward the transport.

Two seas of inky black leathery flesh crashed into one another in a din of flailing claws and hissing. The two groups turned one kind of chaos into another as they began to attack one another in addition to the truck, each eager to be the one that killed the humans, as though the whole thing was one big competition, one big game to see which queen could score the most points.

Caleb pulled himself up over the edge and fell into the truck bed. He dragged himself up enough to grab an emergency med-kit from a hardened container on his armor. He jabbed a needle into the wound to numb it. Then he slapped a large patch over it. The patch reacted to the blood, shrinking tight against the damage and stopping the flow in an instant.

"Sarge!" Sho shouted at the front of the truck.

Caleb checked his HUD. Rodriguez's vitals had shifted, indicating a wound to his side. He looked ahead, seeing Sho leaning over the cab, throwing punches down toward the demon that had to be clinging to the side. He rushed forward while checking her ordnance levels. She was out of bullets.

The truck shifted slightly, losing control for a moment while Rodriguez dug out his sidearm and shot the trife through the door. They straightened out again just as Caleb made it to the cab.

"Sarge, are you okay?" Sho asked, noticing his wound on her HUD.

"I've been better," he replied. As soon as the adrenaline wore off the wound would hurt like hell. It would be worth it if it meant they survived.

He checked his HUD. They were closing on the safe zone, the opposing trife evening out the odds for them and helping them turn the balance closer to their favor. The trailer was littered with dead, both trife and scientists. Doctor Valentine hovered on the right side of the truck, still aiming down and watching for more interlopers.

"Lieutenant," Caleb said. "We're closing on the safe zone. Are you ready to receive?"

"Locked and loaded, Sergeant," Jones replied. "Come on in."

"Hold on!" Rodriguez shouted.

Caleb threw himself down, rolled into the side of the trailer as the truck smashed into something ahead of it. The impact tossed the trailer, pushing it sideways, and Caleb felt it teetering, ready to roll. Then it dropped back down with a loud bang, bouncing everything in the back as its shocks tried to absorb the blow.

Valentine left her position and climbed over the tarp, lifting the edge to check on whatever was underneath. When Caleb tried to get a peek, she lowered the cover and glared at him. "None of your business, Sergeant," she growled.

"Two of my people are dead for that thing," he hissed

back. "Two more are wounded. You lost half your people. It is my damned business."

"Need to know, Sergeant. You don't rank."

He had gone from wanting to strangle her, to almost respecting her, to wanting to strangle her again in the span of a few minutes. He dropped the subject as Washington hopped down off the cab and made his way to the back.

"Wash?" Sho said.

Washington glanced back and smiled grotesquely. Then he picked up the minigun and started firing, ripping through fifty trife in five seconds, which was all the time it took for the gun to run dry.

"What the hell, Washington?" Caleb said. Then he checked his HUD. The truck was suddenly surrounded by green marks, the rest of the battalion closing in to defend it on the last leg of its journey. Not that it mattered anymore. The trife had found something else to worry about.

Each other.

"We made it Sarge," Rodriguez said. "Hell's bells, I can't believe we made it."

Chapter 7

"Hell's bells?" Caleb raised an eyebrow toward Rodriguez.

"It was the first thing that popped into my head," the Private replied, smiling.

Caleb could sense the tension behind the smile. He felt it too. Maybe they had survived. Habib and Banks hadn't. He had been fighting the trife long enough that he was used to losing people. At least, he liked to tell himself that. No matter how many friends died, it hadn't gotten easier. In some ways, it got harder. He had memorized a list of all of their names, and he mentally added the two newest dead to it. Three hundred and seventy-eight names, and those were just the people who were close to him.

His family, and his Vultures.

Rodriguez's smile faded as he watched Caleb's face. Caleb knew he realized what he was thinking. That they were thinking the same thing.

Three hundred seventy-eight names.

Caleb's parents were the first two. The virus had killed them both. He often wondered why it had taken them and not him. They said the outcome had a genetic component,

38

and his family didn't seem to have the genes to resist. It wasn't just his folks. His drug-addicted brother who he had hardly seen and barely knew was gone. His aunts and uncles were gone. So many. For some reason he had survived. He knew his father would have told him it was because he was too damn stubborn to die.

He wasn't that stubborn.

He was standing beside the truck with Rodriguez. Sho and Washington were still on it, keeping an eye on things from the top of the cab. Washington had handed off the empty minigun, trading it with one of the other Marines for a new carbine. Sho had collected two new magazines. The sound of gunfire still echoed at the front of the line. The fight was hardly over, but the Vultures had finished their mission. Now they were on guard duty while the truck was unloaded.

The scientists were looking pretty ragged around the edges, their faces stained with tears and sweat and in some cases blood. The injured had already been pulled aside and loaded onto the transport behind them, a large, boxy craft with powerful thrusters and no armaments to speak of. It was based on the same starship designs that had bred the Deliverance, scaled down for medium-distance hops from one site to another. In the beginning, the military had used the Hoppers to transport troops to the front lines to try to beat back the trife. When beating them back with infantry didn't work, they switched to conventional bombs. When conventional weapons didn't work, they went to nukes.

The nukes made everything worse.

The trife fed off radiation. All kinds of radiation. The vaporizing heat of the initial blast did okay, but within a week the bastards were back in far more significant numbers, the energy of the radiation allowing them to expand their forces through faster breeding.

When it came down to it, humankind had lost the war because they turned to all-out war against an enemy they didn't completely understand. It was a desperate, panicked act, and it had cost them everything.

The Hoppers had been put back into use, only by then their role wasn't to deliver multiple battalions of troops and equipment to an area. It was to send in maybe a single company, fifty to a hundred Marines or less. Sometimes they hopped in a single squad like the Vultures. Search and rescue. That's what they called the mission parameters. Find the people Command thought they needed to bring to their new world and pull them out of the war zones.

That's why Caleb had named his squad the Vultures. They picked out the carcasses of the people who were dumb enough to have stayed alive.

"Be careful with that!" he heard Valentine snap near the back of the truck. He glanced up and saw a team of Marines had brought a forklift out to help manage what-ever was under the canvas tarp. Hadn't her team carried it from the secured elevator to the truck on their own?

He started toward the scene, Rodriguez following. The private had a nasty gash in the space between the chest plate and the backplate of the SOS, but he had patched it, and he refused to get further treatment until they were out of the combat zone. Caleb appreciated the Marine's toughness and desire to see the job through to the very end.

"Sergeant Pratt," Caleb said, getting the attention of the loading crew's commander. "These people carried that thing by hand. The lift may be overkill?"

"Do you think you know everything, Card?" Pratt replied. He looked tougher than he was, tattooed and muscled beneath his fatigues.

"I know that much," Caleb replied. "Besides, Doc

Valentine here is pretty protective over her bouncing bundle of joy. You break it; you buy it."

Pratt laughed. "Affirmative." He looked at Valentine and whistled to his team. "Leave the lift, take it by hand."

"Roger that," they replied.

"And be careful to keep it covered!" Valentine shouted, following after them to make sure they didn't sneak a peek.

"What the hell did you bring back with you?" Pratt asked.

"Do you mean the doctor or the package?" Caleb replied.

Pratt laughed again. "Both? Seriously, I get the feeling we came out here for whatever's in that truck, not the scientists it belongs to."

"No. We came for Valentine at least. I'm not kidding when I say that thing is her baby."

"If you'll excuse me," Pratt said, rushing over to help his team as they lifted the delivery and started bringing it over the side of the truck. It was about four meters long and three meters wide and shaped vaguely like a missile. It was lightweight enough that four Marines up top and four on the ground were able to control it despite its overall size.

Of course, no part of it was visible. Valentine had cloaked it expertly, keeping it out of sight of the crew.

"All hands," Lieutenant Jones said, his voice cutting into Caleb's comm and echoing out through the Hopper's external loudspeakers. "All hands. Fall back. I repeat. Fall back. Mission complete."

A few scattered cheers went up from the Marines closest to the Hopper. Pratt's team was carrying the package now, running it back to the craft. The Marines guarding the area were backing out with it.

"Vultures," Caleb said. "We don't get on that Hopper until every other Marine in the Sixth reaches that truck."

"Roger that," Sho and Rodriguez replied. Caleb didn't worry about Washington. He knew the big man had the order.

They weren't required to stay behind. All four of them could have retreated to the ship, climbed the ramp into the massive open space of the hold, buckled into the restraints lining the walls, and called it a job well done. Lieutenant Jones wouldn't complain, and nobody would blame them.

Caleb would blame himself if another Marine died because he wasn't out there helping them retreat. Search and rescue didn't end when they retrieved the target. His fellow jarheads needed rescuing too.

He returned to the truck, climbing onto it. The four remaining Vultures crouched in the back of the trailer, using the iron side as both cover and a rest for the ends of their guns. Caleb could see the other Marines pulling back ahead of him, laying down alternating lines of fire to keep the trife honest.

The demons had lost a lot of their steam and were barely giving chase. They were too busy with one another, engaged in a massive skirmish that would only end when all of one side was dead. It didn't matter. Staying out there wasn't a function of need. It was more important when the danger wasn't as severe, a show of support for the rest of Sixth Company, even if they had fallen back while the Vultures advanced.

They were all in this together.

He noticed the others noticing him and his team as they reached the truck. The Vultures fired on the few trife who were still tailing the Marines back to the hopper. Once the last of the group had come even with them, they rose and jumped down on the other side of the vehicle, running with their company-mates up the ramp to safety.

The last group into the hopper had the job of turning

around and continuing the cover fire. The thrusters flared, a loud whine and hiss preceded the ship starting to rise. Caleb continued shooting down at the trife, only a few dozen still coming after them. Once the ship was high enough, the ramp began to close. Caleb only dropped the carbine from his shoulder once it had banged shut, clanged locked, and sealed with a loud hiss.

Now the mission was complete.

They had made it.

Chapter 8

"Sergeant Card," Lieutenant Jones said.

Caleb turned his head. The Lieutenant was approaching from the front of the hopper, where the mobile CIC was located. He was a tall, wiry man, with short, prematurely white hair. A neatly trimmed mustache and beard covered a long scar across his chin. Caleb had served under many officers in his career, and Jones ranked at the top of the list for the men he respected the most.

"Lieutenant," Caleb said, prepared to stand at attention.

"As you were," Jones said. "No need to stand up. I'm sure you and your team are exhausted." His eyes flicked to each one of the Vultures. "I want you to know; I'm going to submit a commendation for what you did out there today. General Watkins stressed the importance of getting Doctor Valentine and her team back safely multiple times."

"We didn't get them all back safely, sir," Caleb replied.

"Considering what you were up against, saving half of them is more than impressive." His expression shifted. "I'm sorry about Banks and Habib. They were both good Marines."

"Two of the best," Caleb agreed. "They sacrificed themselves for the rest of us."

"I'll be sure they receive posthumous commendations for their bravery. I know it isn't much, especially considering the circumstances."

"We all do what we can, sir."

"I know Banks didn't have any family on the Deliverance. But Habib's husband is on board, isn't he?"

Caleb nodded. "Yes, sir. And their son."

Lieutenant Jones nodded, his face pained. "I'll be sure to inform them as soon as we get back."

"No, sir," Caleb replied, sure his expression was the same. He hadn't even thought about Habib's family until now. Damn it. "I'll tell them."

Lieutenant Jones didn't argue. Caleb had broken the news every time the situation had arisen. It was another thing that never got easier, and he was grateful for that. People deserved to see sincere regret from someone who knew the person they loved, in some cases better than they did.

"Sir, what happens now?" Rodriguez asked.

"Ours was the last search and rescue mission," the lieutenant replied. "Once we get back to the Deliverance, we'll have twenty-four hours to get everything settled and all the pre-flight checks completed, and then we're gone. Eight ships have already launched successfully, so I think as long as our luck holds out and the hopper makes it home, we're going to be alive for a long time after this."

"Alive and holed up on a giant tin can," Rodriguez said. "I'm going to miss open spaces."

"Not once you get used to not having to fight for your

life you won't," Sho said. "I'm looking forward to it. I heard they have atmospheric generators on board that simulate weather. Light, dark, sunshine, rain, thunderstorms, blue skies, clouds. It's like being outside without actually being outside."

"And best of all, no trife," Jones said. "None of you have been in the city yet?"

"No, sir," Caleb said. "We've been too busy trying not to die."

Jones nodded. "I've been with you on most of those missions, Sergeant."

"Yes, sir."

"In any case, Metro is a wonder to behold. Hell, the Deliverance is a miracle of its own. From an empty hangar to a generation starship in less than two years? I would never have thought it would be possible."

Washington tapped Caleb on the shoulder. Caleb glanced over, and the big Marine spread his hands in apparent frustration.

"And now we tuck our tail between our legs and run away?" Caleb said, translating the gesture. Washington nodded and flashed him a thumbs-up.

"Nobody is happy about that part," Jones said. "We're leaving a lot of people behind. What else can we do? This isn't a fight we can win, we all know that."

Washington dragged his finger across his throat.

"Not me," Sho said in response. "I want to live. I want to have a family, maybe make a few babies."

"You'll get your chance," Jones said. "Once the Deliverance reaches space safely, we'll be reducing the number of military by a factor of ten. We don't need Marines in the middle of the black. Metro will need law enforcement, and of course as a generation ship we'll need to provide the future generations."

"I don't even have a boyfriend," Sho said.

"There are protocols in place to arrange for women to be paired off. Not an arranged marriage, but as a genetically healthy woman you'll have your pick of the litter, so to speak."

Sho smiled. "Sounds good to me." She looked over at the other Vultures. "What about you guys? Sergeant Card, if you're looking for a wife, I would definitely consider you."

Caleb smiled. "I'm honored, Yen. But I'm not ready to make any decisions like that just yet."

"I'll marry you," Rodriguez said. "Why not?"

Sho wrinkled her face. "I didn't ask you, Taco."

"Why do you have to go there, Dumpling?" Rodriguez replied, making his accent thicker. "Seriously. I was trying to be nice."

"You make it sound like being with you would be a good experience."

Caleb glanced at Lieutenant Jones, who was shaking his head and smiling. "Sergeant Card," he said, causing Sho and Rodriguez to quiet their banter. "I'll leave you and your team to relax for the rest of the ride home. When we get the hangar, get cleaned up, head to medical to get that wrist of yours looked at, and then meet me in my office." He raised his arm, revealing a gold watch. "Let's say, thirteen-hundred."

"Yes, sir," Caleb said.

"Again, excellent work, Vultures. I'm proud of each one of you."

"Thank you, sir," they all replied.

Lieutenant Jones turned and headed off toward another of the squads to offer praise for the job they had done. Sho and Rodriguez went back to insulting one another. Washington made knowing eye contact with Caleb, who leaned back against the bulkhead.

Washington knew what the others didn't because he was in the same boat.

Caleb wouldn't be joining them in Metro.

Chapter 9

Caleb closed his eyes, letting the hot water of the shower pour down on him, the rivulets smacking his face in a soothing cadence. He was thankful to be out of the SOS. Thankful to be back in the barracks and washing off the dirt and sweat and grime. Knowing the last mission was done, knowing it was a success made it easier to enjoy, bittersweet as it was.

There were Marines at all of the showerheads around him. Sho was on his left, Rodriguez next to her, and Washington to his right. Other squads were positioned beyond them, each of the people in them likely just as grateful to be out of their armor or fatigues, away from the battlefield, back home and getting cleaned off. Most of them would head right to their bunks when they were done, exhausted from the mission.

Not Caleb. He had orders to get his wrist looked at, and then to stop by the lieutenant's office. He had no idea what Jones wanted to talk to him about. He was sure it wasn't anything terrible. He had done what Command tasked him to do. As far as he knew, both Doctor Valentine and her valuable equipment were safe.

The other Vultures finished their showers within a few minutes, turning off the heads and retreating from the space in silence. He wasn't sure when or how, but treating the shower like a church had become a custom for the United States Space Force D-Battalion. Men and women alike stood naked under the water and prayed to whatever god they believed made them, or to whatever kind of fate they put their trust in. They were silent and reverent from the moment they entered to the moment they left. It had been that way before the Vultures had been transferred to the unit, and he had come to appreciate it during his stay. It wasn't uncommon to see fellow Marines break down in tears in here. It wasn't unusual for them to receive silent and understanding support. There was something about the water, the silence, the unified experience that made the experience therapeutic.

Caleb needed the therapy right now. Not only for the past. For the future too. Lieutenant Jones had said they were cutting the military presence on the Deliverance by ninety percent. He was one of the ten percent that would remain, keeping watch over the people of Metro from the outside. He wouldn't be living in the city. He wouldn't be mingling with most of its residents. The protocols had all been developed by a team of highly regarded social psychologists, tasked with writing the rules for how to survive a two hundred year trip across the universe without going insane.

What they had come up with covered three thick volumes of paper manuals, though Caleb skimmed over it on his tablet whenever he couldn't sleep. He had found that the dry material was an excellent cure for insomnia. The bottom line for him was that he wouldn't have much contact with anyone who wasn't a Marine, and having a family was out of the question. There was nothing worse than an absent father.

He lingered under the water until he was alone. Only then did he let the tears come, lowering his head and putting his hand over his eyes. He didn't think he had PTSD, but how was he supposed to know? All he knew was that he needed to get all of the horror, all of the pain, all of the tension out sometimes, and this was how he had learned to do it. It eased his mind. It renewed his clarity and his soul.

Only for a minute. Then he turned off the water and backed out of the shower, grabbing a towel and drying off. He went from there to a locker along the wall, lined with the same gray shirt and shorts in enough sizes and quantity for everyone. He grabbed the clothes and slid them on, then stood in front of the sink to shave.

He looked at himself in the mirror. A tired and worn face stared back at him. Sharp blue eyes, an equally sharp nose, brown hair was getting a little long at nearly half an inch. He would have to get it trimmed before they left.

He grabbed his razor and quickly shaved the stubble on his face. Then he headed out of the head and into the main barracks, walking down three doors to his squad's bunk on the right. He walked in, his eyes heading instantly to Banks and Habib's racks. They had already been stripped, their personal effects boxed and removed. It hit him like a punch in the gut.

Sho looked up at him, her expression sad. She held up the tablet she was looking at. "Newswire says the Russians got another ship out."

"Shouldn't you be sleeping?" he asked. Rodriguez and Washington were both in their racks, out cold.

"Couldn't sleep. Not when I saw the empty beds. It feels worse because it was the last run, you know?"

"All too well," Caleb agreed. "Banks was with me almost from the beginning. Habib, over a year. They were more than squad mates."

"They were family," Sho said.

"To family," Caleb said, pretending he had a drink to toast with.

"To family," Sho replied, raising a mock glass of her own. She paused, staring at him. "Permission to speak freely?"

"You don't have to ask."

"Just following protocol." She paused again, hesitant. Then she stood up and approached him. "I know we were joking around before, on the hopper. I really would be your wife if you were interested. I have a lot of respect for you, and we already make a good team." She smiled. "I don't mean to be too forward, but the trife beat all the submissiveness out of me."

Caleb stared at her. He had been hoping she would drop that particular line of thought once they got back to base. No such luck.

"Yen, you're a damn good Marine. And a good friend. And like I said before, I'm flattered that you would even consider me. You're a good looking woman, you're intelligent, and you can kick pretty much anybody's ass in a fight. What's not to be attracted to?"

"I can feel the but coming up from a mile away."

He held his breath for a second. If not now, then when?

"I'm not going to Metro. I'm staying outside the city as a Guardian."

She froze for a moment, unsure what to say. She pursed

her lips. "I should have guessed that, huh? That's the only reason you wouldn't want to be with me, right?"

"Of course."

It didn't matter if he was honest about that or not. She knew what his decision meant. "I'm surprised you volunteered for that. Don't you want a family? Don't you want to continue your line?"

"I want to make sure the people in Metro like you get there safe. That's more important to me."

"There are other volunteers."

"I don't want to sound arrogant, but they aren't me."

"You sound arrogant."

"I do." He smiled. "Washington already knows. He volunteered too. But don't tell Rodriguez, okay? I'll tell him before we leave."

"You should have told him already."

"Not until after the mission. No distractions, right?"

"We did good today, didn't we, Sarge?"

"We did. If you'll excuse me." He held up his arm, showing off the patch on his wrist. "I have to get this thing checked out."

"One more scar for the collection."

Caleb absently touched his side. He had a fourteen-incher that ran across his abdomen. That one was the closest he had come to dying. "I've heard women think scars are sexy."

"Some of us," she replied. She returned to her rack and picked up her tablet. "See you later, Sarge."

Caleb turned and headed out of the barracks, still thinking about scars. He had seven physical ones across his body. But the deepest, most painful ones were all emotional.

Screw the Xenotrife.

Chapter 10

Lieutenant Jones' office was in the heart of the command center, a short walk from the enlisted barracks. That wasn't saying much. Everything was a short walk away, the living area inside the Deliverance hangar intended only for short-term use.

A term that was almost up.

Caleb reached the lieutenant's office at precisely thirteen hundred hours. He hung back near the mess for a few minutes making small-talk with Sergeant Pratt ahead of his meeting. He had asked Pratt if he knew anything about the equipment his people had brought off the hopper. The only thing the sergeant had to say about it was that it was too light for something of its size, and he had no idea what could be under the tarp — unless it was a hardened aluminum frame filled with air.

Lieutenant Jones' door was closed when he arrived. He raised his fist, but didn't knock as he heard a voice on the other side. Doctor Valentine. Caleb cringed slightly, wondering if he was wrong about not being in trouble. Valentine didn't sound happy.

"There's more at stake here than a few jarheads, Adam," he heard Valentine say. "And you damn well know it."

"I used what Command gave me, Riley. And by the way, you and your team were picked up by the best search and rescue squad I have. If you don't like how the situation was handled, you need to talk to General Watkins."

"I've already put in the request."

"By the way, you could be a little more respectful of the Marines that saved your life, and your precious cargo."

Caleb heard her literally growl, and then the door to the lieutenant's office was swung open violently. Doctor Valentine glared at him as she stormed past.

"Hi, Doctor Valentine," he said, smirking. He expected an epithet in response, but she just kept heading away without reacting visibly.

He turned back to the doorway and entered Lieutenant Jones' office, coming to attention. The room was small and spartan, a simple metal desk with a tablet on the left side and a display on the right, with Lieutenant Jones sitting in between on a simple steel stool. It hardly looked like an office at all.

"At ease, Sergeant."

"Woman trouble, sir?" Caleb said.

Jones shook his head. "I wouldn't classify it as a problem specific to any single gender. Doctor Valentine is upset that six members of her science team didn't survive the extraction."

Caleb looked back at the open door, tempted to go back out and tell her what he thought of that sentiment.

"I know," Jones said before he had a chance to comment. "I agree with you."

"Sir, she was a Marine. She ought to know better."

"She's been a scientist longer than she was an officer. She cared about those people."

"I cared about Banks and Habib, sir."

"No argument from me. She's hurting. You know how that is."

"Sir, I don't take that hurt all the way to Watkins."

"It'll blow over by the time we're all on the Deliverance and all systems are go. I'm not concerned. Anyway, that's not why I asked you to come over."

"Am I in a different kind of trouble, sir?"

"Not exactly." Lieutenant Jones stood up and circled the desk. "You said on the hopper you hadn't seen Metro yet."

"That's right, sir."

"Come with me."

"Where are we going, sir?"

"To see Metro."

"Sir, I don't understand?"

Lieutenant Jones stood in front of him. "Caleb, you're a good Marine. A great leader. You've been in the Marines for six years. Do you know how many of your fellow Marines have seen as much combat as you and haven't died?"

"No, sir."

"I can show you the whole list on my tablet without scrolling."

"What's your point, sir?"

"I know you volunteered to become a Guardian. I want you to see Metro. I'm hoping I can change your mind."

"You want me to stop being a Marine, sir?"

"Confirmed. The Guardians aren't going to have anything to do. There's no threat out there, and if there is it's going to hit us from outside the ship where there isn't a damn thing we can do about it. You'll be spending the next two centuries cycling through years of stasis and active duty, and when we get where we're going you're going to be an old man with no war to fight. Everyone you knew will be long gone."

"Washington won't be gone, and everyone else I cared about is already dead. I'm a Marine, Lieutenant. That's all I know how to be anymore. Even if I do have nothing to fight."

"Then humor an old man who thinks of you like a son," Lieutenant Jones said.

"You're only eight years older than me, sir."

"So I'm a young father. I want you to see Metro. If it doesn't change your mind, then I'll let it go."

Caleb didn't have the will to fight Jones on his request. "Okay, sir. Lead the way."

Jones headed out the door with Caleb beside him. They started walking. "What do you know about the generation ships, Sergeant?"

"Sir, I know the components were in development before the war started," Caleb replied. "I know the Department of Defense was paying Lockheed a shit-ton of money to develop the thrusters and…" he paused. "I can't remember who was contracted to do the fusion reactors or the gravity generators. The tech was certified six months before the trife showed up."

"Originally designed to be used for crewed space stations and high-altitude space fighters, part of the new Space Force. Nobody was thinking about combining the two technologies to launch starships that could travel up to point five cees with enough fuel to last two centuries."

"Sir, I thought there was one group pushing for access to purchase all of the associated components? They wanted to develop a long-range exploration vessel."

"That's right. You know more than I thought."

"I hit the news feeds when I can, sir. I was interested in space before I became a Marine."

"Some people think an extraterrestrial intelligence sent the trife to stop us from leaving our solar system. As if they knew we had advanced enough to build the vessels to do it. Other people think it was just a crazy, cosmic coincidence. What do you think?"

"I haven't given that much thought, sir. The trife are here. Who cares why? If their goal was to keep us from leaving the planet, they failed, right? If that was the case, the joke's on them."

"No winners," Lieutenant Jones said. "Not them. Not us. Just a lot of suffering for nothing." They turned the corner. The wide twin blast doors out to the main part of the hangar were ahead of them. "Once we saw we were losing the war, every government came together to work on the designs and to plan a way to build the generation ships, as many as they could with the resources they had. It's sad it took an apocalypse to get us to realize what was important and stop the petty attacks against one another. Unity in agony. But here we are."

They reached the end of the corridor, and the twin doors slid open ahead of them. They stepped out into the hangar and Caleb looked up. He had seen the Deliverance plenty of times before, but he had never stopped being amazed.

"A lot of suffering," Lieutenant Jones repeated. "It's our job to make sure it wasn't for nothing. Starting right there."

Chapter 11

Caleb continued to stare up at the starship. He could only see a small portion of it from his position near the hull, but even what little he could see was impressive, if only because of the scale.

There was a printed model of the ship against the south wall of the mess, right next to the chow line. It had been put there to remind the Marines what they were fighting for as if the real deal in the hangar wasn't enough of a reminder. Maybe Command didn't think it was because only a chunk of it was visible at any given time -- a dull metal monolith hidden inside one of the largest human-made caverns in the world.

He knew from the model that the Deliverance was almost four kilometers long, two kilometers high, and had over thirty decks from top to bottom in both the fore and aft. The center of the ship was different in that it was practically hollow, containing only six decks. The center of the ship had been hastily designed as a massive hold, which had been further engineered into the outer shell of the city they called Metro.

On the whole, the Deliverance was blocky and ugly, the outside mostly just metal plates lined with all kinds of sensors and more than five thousand mounted cameras to provide a view of the black beyond the hull. He had only been inside the ship once before, and he had declined to go anywhere near Metro. He had been more concerned with his role as a Guardian, which was limited to the outer portions of the ship beyond the city. He knew they had loaded a lot of equipment into the secondary hold and the vessel's main hangar. Special modules had been designed to be easily transported to the site, carried down the huge industrial elevators, and pieced back together inside the superstructure. There was an entire module dedicated for the Guardians, containing weapons and equipment, a mess, a workout area, clothing, and everything else they would need to fulfill their end of the mission.

He had seen the stasis pods where they would be put into what was almost literally cold storage, their bodies frozen in state for years at a time. The volunteers would cycle through the journey so that they would all make it to the other end of the line still young enough to help found the colony, but too old to ever start a family or be more than an advisor to the effort. There were a hundred Marines who had been accepted into the program, plus two hundred more who had applied but had been turned down for various reasons. Other than a few of the high-ranking officials like General Watkins and the ship's engineers, they would be the only ones who would ever have lived on both Earth and their new home almost a hundred light years away, a planet the scientists were calling New Earth.

Scientists weren't known for their creativity in naming conventions, but he supposed it was better than referring to it by its star coordinates.

In any case, it promised to be a lonely and dull existence. Like Lieutenant Jones had said, there was no reason to think the Guardians would have much to do. Only ten of them would be awake at a given time, on a one-year duty cycle that would mainly consist of making sure everything stayed the same. They weren't there solely as peacekeepers, because only a limited number of the civilian population would even have access to the areas beyond the city. There was just no reason for most people to wander out into the less refined portions of the ship. But if anything broke, they were authorized to contact Metro's engineering department to send a unit out to work on the fix.

A lonely and dull existence, but an important one. That's why there had been so many volunteers. Getting the civilians from Earth to New Earth successfully was for men like Caleb the reason they had joined the military to begin with. Protect the innocent. Secure their freedom. For the love of country. It sounded hokey or idealistic, and maybe it was. It was a motivation that worked for him. He really believed in it, from soul to skin.

Men like him. Women were excluded as Guardians, both to limit any unforeseen complications outside of the city, and to ensure the city had as many potential mating pairs as possible. The scientists weren't sure how space travel was going to affect virility, and they had protocols that went in either direction, either to boost or limit reproduction rates. But every woman was more valuable than any man. A man could impregnate multiple women if it came down to that. The same process didn't work in reverse.

"Let's go up to the civilian entrance," Lieutenant Jones said, breaking Caleb out of his thoughts.

"Yes, sir," Caleb said.

There were a number of electric carts parked near the entrance to the living area, and Lieutenant Jones and Caleb claimed one of them, using it to drive the two klicks across the massive hangar to the other side. There were two elevators located there, a few hundred meters apart from one another. One was smaller, intended to ferry people up and down inside the complex. The other was gigantic; a huge industrial elevator used to transport the heavy equipment being loaded into the starship. Everything from the prefabricated modules, to heavy machinery intended to help tear down and rebuild Metro on the surface of New Earth, to drones and armored personnel vehicles and other military equipment they were all hoping they would never need for anything beyond exploration. The science teams had made educated guesses about New Earth, but until they got there it was impossible to know if the indigenous life was dangerous or not.

They stopped with a few other carts near the personnel elevator. It was already at the ground level, and they boarded it and Lieutenant Jones called for it to rise to the only other stop before the surface. They stepped out a moment later, walking from the lift past a small operations building manned by a pair of Marines. The Marines came to attention as Lieutenant Jones and Caleb went past.

They stepped out onto a metal bridge that crossed the gap between the excavated side of the cavern and one of the higher decks of the Deliverance. More of the ship was visible from this perspective, the port side stretching off into the distance to their left, disappearing into darkness before it reached the bow.

Caleb looked up at the layer of stone over their heads. When the Deliverance was ready to launch, the entire top portion of the underground cavern would be removed with a series of perfectly calculated blasts that would cause a controlled collapse of the rock above, bringing the rubble down around the sides of the ship or blasting it out beside the resulting hole. It was a one-time action, but they had no intention of keeping the ship underground forever.

They walked across the bridge and into the side of the ship. Another Marine was standing guard in the airlock, and he came to attention as Lieutenant Jones entered.

"Corporal Styles," Jones said. "Is General Watkins on board?"

"Yes, sir," the corporal replied.

"Good. Thank you, Corporal."

"Of course, sir."

They moved beyond the airlock and into one of the corridors. There was a smell to the place that was familiar to Caleb and always reminded him of a new car. Everything was so fresh and new and clean.

"Are you taking me to General Watkins, sir?" Caleb asked.

"What?" Jones glanced over at him. "Oh. No. I have an appointment to meet with the general. I told you, I'm taking you to Metro. I'm going to leave you there for a while."

"I didn't volunteer for that, sir."

"I'll order you to stay put if I have to."

"Sir, I don't understand why you're taking such a personal interest in my decision?"

"I told you, you're like a son to me."

"It has to be more than that, sir."

"Caleb, I've read your file. Before you joined the Marines, you were a student at Stanford, completing an engineering degree on a football scholarship. You set a couple of rushing records in your freshman year."

"I'm not the first person to leave school to become a Marine, sir."

"Your sister was killed in a terrorist attack."

"Yes, sir. And I promised myself I would do whatever I could to make sure that didn't happen to anyone else."

"And you did. Before you joined Search and Rescue you were with the Marine Raiders, First Battalion. That's no easy feat."

"I still don't see your point, Lieutenant. Because I was going to an Ivy League school, that makes me special? I don't think it does. Because I was good at football? That only helps me run from the trife faster. Because my sister was killed before the trife came? I'm not the first grunt who lost a family member to evil doers. Because I was a Raider? I worked my ass off to get there. Anyone can do that if they're motivated enough."

Jones smiled. "Look at it from a generational perspective. Your genes are valuable."

"Then why was I accepted as a Guardian when so many others were turned down, sir?"

"The program wasn't allowed to use genetic quality as a factor. I'm not trying to stroke your ego, Caleb. As your commanding officer, you aren't any more important than anyone else. But, I believe in doing what's best for the mission, and for the colony that comes out on the other side. That's why I'm trying to convince you to join me in Metro."

"You, sir?"

He nodded. "I'll be the first vice-governor of Metro, under Colonel Lin. If you want it, I can make sure you're installed as the first Sheriff. The top position in internal law enforcement, one of four in the city, even though you aren't commissioned. I've already discussed it with General Watkins, and he's on board. You'll still be protecting people, but from the inside."

Caleb was silent as they kept walking, heading to one of the banks of elevators nearby.

"Just experience the city first, and then tell me what you think," Lieutenant Jones said. "I've only done this recruitment speech for a few Marines so don't turn me down too quickly."

"Your pretty persuasive, sir," Caleb said.

Jones smiled. "I know."

They boarded the lift and descended to Deck Twelve. From there, they took a winding path of corridors back toward the center of the ship, stopping in front of a heavy blast hatch with a control panel on the side.

"Everyone on the Deliverance will be injected with a chip into their wrist for easy personal identification. It'll also contain the security clearances for the individual. Normally it goes in the right arm but considering your wound we'll have to put yours in the left. In any case…"

He walked over to the panel beside the hatch and put his wrist to it. The door began to slide open.

A few seconds later, Caleb got his first look at Metro.

Chapter 12

The hatch opened up to what appeared to be a park. Trees lined the immediate area, surrounded by fresh green grass, bushes, and flowers. It was clean and beautiful and unblemished – a sight he hadn't seen in nearly two years.

Where everything outside felt gray and brown, burned and scorched and dead, his first impression here was of life and hope, and a real future for humankind. It overwhelmed him, bringing tears to his eyes almost instantly.

"And you've only seen the tail edge of the park," Lieutenant Jones said, noticing his reaction. "There's an identical one on the other side."

"It's amazing," Caleb said.

People were walking through the park. Men, women, and children. They wore civilian clothes, new and clean – unblemished by war and death. They looked over at him as though the open hatch behind them and their military uniforms were an affront to their peace. In a way, he supposed they were.

He tilted his head up to look at the ceiling, remembering what Sho had said about the atmospheric generators. He squinted at the brightness of the light shining down on him. Light wisps of white clouds lined the sky, moving in a realistic pattern, dimming the light when they passed in front of it. Caleb marveled because he felt like he was outside, even though he knew he wasn't.

"I assume the light moves from east to west?" he asked, forgetting in his amazement to add *sir* to the statement.

"Of course," Lieutenant Jones replied. "The generator also simulates the seasons and different weather. The floor has a porous surface, which allows rainwater to filter through and cycle back for reuse."

"What about the ceiling?"

"An ultra-high definition membrane screen. The light source is behind it, and there are heating and cooling vents that activate based on the intensity and angle of the sun and daily temperature. Metro is programmed to simulate an aggregation of weather patterns based on the Pacific Northwest, Southern California, and North Carolina. According to the scientists, those are the most favorable climates."

"Does it snow, too?"

"It can, but snow events are programmed to be very rare. Come on."

Lieutenant Jones led Caleb through the park. They walked along a meandering path between the foliage. There were residents having picnics on the grass, or sitting on the benches and reading.

"You can imagine how grateful these people are to be here," Jones said.

"How were they selected, sir?"

"Half of them were hand-picked by Command, based on occupation, experience level, age, gender, genetic screening, all of the good stuff. The other half were entered into a lottery. They had to pass the genetic screening too, but they're your artists, your chefs, your teachers, and the like."

"How many people?"

"Forty-thousand three hundred and twelve. The systems are designed to handle up to fifty-thousand, but we wanted to leave some room for growth."

Caleb could see past the trees now, to the edge of the city. Tall buildings rose in vertical columns ahead in blocks of tightly packed structures that reminded him of a circuit board. Each one was forty meters tall and apparently square.

"The layout is based on a best route algorithm," Lieutenant Jones said. "Artificial Intelligence optimized the placement of the blocks to maximize space efficiency. Every resident was assigned their apartment based on their occupation, age, and so on. There's an algorithm that will help shuffle living spaces around based on all of the appropriate factors."

"It's all pretty high tech," Caleb said. "How do you know so much about it?"

"I'm the Vice-governor. It's my job to know."

They reached the end of the park and crossed a wide street to the front line of apartments. The bases of the buildings were outfitted with different shops, just like a normal street.

"How are you going to manage inventory over two centuries?" Caleb asked, pointing at a clothing store.

"The clothes are all recyclable. There's an exchange further into the city where they'll take old threads and credit the family for them." Lieutenant Jones paused. "Oh. You probably don't know about the replicators."

"Replicators?"

"The next evolution in recycling. As long as you feed them raw materials, they can print pretty much anything you need. So you design a shirt on a computer, you put the recycled thread into the machine, and it makes it for you. It's a black box to me, but it's pretty amazing."

They kept walking down the street. Caleb pointed to another storefront which had a sign over it that read:

THE DANCING TRIFE

"A bar?" Caleb said.

"They'll be phased out over time, but we're trying to acclimate the civilians to living this way. According to the psychologists, too much change at once is likely to lead to malcontent and unrest, especially over time. It's easy to be happy when feeling safe is a new feeling again. What about ten years from now when you've been looking at the same people and places, and the trife are a distant memory?"

"I can't even imagine what that would be like."

Lieutenant Jones lifted his arm, checking his watch. "Caleb, I have a meeting with General Watkins on the bridge in twenty minutes. Here." He reached into a pocket and pulled out a scrap of paper, holding it out to him.

"What's that?" Caleb asked, taking it and looking at the writing.

Block Twenty-three, Cube 8-15

"It's Habib's apartment. Her husband should be there, waiting for her to come back."

Caleb stared at it. He hadn't even considered that Habib had already moved into Metro. Damn.

"Once you're done there, walk around a little and check the place out. And head over to the Law Office. It's that way. Sheriff Aveline is already on duty. She can show you around, and she can see you out when you're done."

"You're ditching me here, sir?"

Lieutenant Jones smiled and nodded. "If you decide you want to move into Metro, send me a message and I'll make it happen, just like I said."

Caleb stared at Jones. He couldn't say it wasn't tempting, especially knowing Jones would be one of the people in charge of the city.

"Yes, sir," he replied. "I'll definitely give it some thought."

"That's all I ask. Thank you, Sergeant."

"Thank you, sir."

Chapter 13

It didn't take too long for Caleb to locate Block Twenty-three. The blocks were all laid out the same, only the paths from one to the other were different, though most could be reached in a relatively straight line.

The inside of the apartment building was as fresh as everything else in the Deliverance. The glass facades were spotless, the interior smelled like fresh paint, and there were framed pictures on the walls and small tables with fake flowers on them down every corridor. The elevator was quick and silent, and the carpeting soft and plush.

Cube 8-15 translated to apartment fifteen on the eighth floor, about halfway up the building. There had been people in the lobby of the block, and judging by the way they greeted Caleb he assumed this complex was composed of military families.

Did they have any idea why he was here?

Caleb came out of the elevator on the eighth floor. He wasn't nervous about talking to Habib's husband. He would have preferred it if he were. But he had done this too many times already, and he had the small comfort of knowing this time would be the last. By tomorrow they would be rocketing through the atmosphere into space, and from space to a planet nearly a hundred light years away.

He approached apartment fifteen. He could hear the laughter of a child through the door. Habib's son. He reconsidered his nerves, a tightness forming in his chest. Just because he wasn't nervous didn't mean it was easy. He didn't know if he could live with himself if it were.

He knocked on the door, taking up a serious and somber posture in front of the door. He regretted not wearing his mess uniform for this. The simple utilities were too informal.

The door opened. Caleb had met Rohan Habib a few times before, and they recognized one another immediately. Caleb didn't need to say anything. Rohan stared at him in silence, his expression slowly fading from the joy he had been sharing with his son to the sadness of realization.

"Mr. Habib," Caleb said. "It's with my deepest regret and sympathy to inform you that your wife, Private Anaya Habib, was killed in the line of duty at oh six hundred this morning. As squad leader for the Vultures, it's a personally painful event. Your wife was an incredible Marine, and an even better human being. I'm very, very sorry for your loss."

Rohan stared at him, looking him in the eye. Caleb could see the tears forming there. He could feel the moisture forming on his own eyes. He glanced down when Habib's son, Rohan Junior, came to the door and put his arms around his father's leg.

"Daddy?" he said.

"Was it fast?" Rohan asked, still keeping eye contact.

Caleb nodded. "For whatever consolation it's worth,

she died a hero, and will be receiving a commendation for her actions."

"It isn't worth much, Sergeant."

"I understand. There are counselors available if you need to reach out to someone. I can also provide you with my personal contact ID if you want to talk to me directly. It's my job to keep my people alive, and I take full responsibility for my failure."

Rohan shook his head. "No, Sergeant. Anaya would never forgive me if I blamed you. She had so much respect for you, and so much pride in what you were doing. I know you did all that you could. I need some time to process this and to talk to my son. Thank you for coming here in person to deliver the news."

"If you need anything, you know where to find me."

"Of course, Sergeant."

"Again, I'm sorry, Mr. Habib."

"Thank you, Sergeant Card." Rohan looked down. "Come on, Rho. Let us sit and talk a little, okay?"

"Where's mommy?" Rohan Junior asked. He was looking at Caleb.

"Your mother is in a better place," Rohan said. "You'll see her again, but not for a while." Rohan glanced at Caleb and forced a smile as he gently closed the door, leaving Caleb standing alone in the hallway.

Caleb wiped the moisture from his eyes, turning away from the door. He heard Rohan Junior start crying a moment later.

Screw the xenotrife.

He left Block Twenty-three as quickly as he could, getting back out into the street and trying to calm his nerves. It was harder than he had expected, probably because Anaya had come so close to getting out of hell alive.

He remembered The Dancing Trife. He was tempted to head back there, to see what kind of alcohol they could provide. There wasn't any available in the barracks, and he could have used a stiff drink. It might be his one and only chance too. Yet he was drawn elsewhere, navigating to the Law Office, having to stop a couple of times to ask for directions.

The civilians on the ship were all friendly to him, happy to be of help and still in the afterglow of escaping the outside world. They guided him to the small three-story building near Block Eight, identifiable by the gold star hanging over the entrance.

He walked through a pair of sliding glass doors and into the front of the station. There was a central reception desk with four desks in the open space behind it, and then a short corridor that led back out of sight. There was no one in the front of the building, leaving him to wonder if anyone was there at all.

"Hello?" he said. "Anyone here?"

He waited for a second, and then started making his way toward the back. He couldn't imagine they would leave the door unlocked if the place was empty.

"Hello?" he repeated.

A woman moved out from the back of the corridor. She seemed pleasantly surprised when she saw him. "Oh, there is someone here." She smiled. The shape of her face and brightness of her eyes — the life in her — caused Caleb's general malaise to lift.

"Sheriff Aveline?" Caleb asked. He stared at her, thinking about Lieutenant Jones. Had the lieutenant sent him here to learn about being a sheriff or to set his eyes on this sheriff?

"That's me," she replied. "Formerly Captain Aveline of the United States Space Force. You're a Marine, right?"

Caleb nodded. He didn't know if he had a type, but this woman was his type. "Yes, ma'am." He almost came to attention, but she wasn't an officer anymore, right? She wasn't technically military at all. "Sergeant Caleb Card."

"Caleb Card?" She kept beaming. "Welcome to Metro Law, Sergeant Card. What can I do for you?" She kept coming forward until she was standing right in front of him. "We don't get too many, well, any Marines in here."

He couldn't stop his smile. Her demeanor was infectious. "Lieutenant Jones asked me to stop by. He's trying to convince me to join the department."

"Law? We still have a few spots open for deputies."

"As a sheriff," Caleb said.

She tilted her head slightly, squinting one of her eyes. "You must be something. All the other sheriffs are former officers. They pulled deputies from the enlisted."

"I'm not particularly special," Caleb said.

"Modest, huh? I like that. There's nothing worse than when a handsome man knows he's handsome and gets all arrogant about it."

Did she just call him handsome? He could feel his face heating up. "Uh. He thought you might show me around the office, and tell me a little bit about the job."

Somehow her smile had managed to get a little wider. She was enjoying his sudden discomfort.

"There's something about you, isn't there, Caleb Card?" she said. "You look like the kind of man who would climb a tree to save a kitten. Have you ever done that, Cal?"

He noticed she had a slight twang to her voice. It was subtle and cute.

"I don't think I've had the occasion to save a kitten from a tree," he said. "But I did save a dog that had been chained to a tree and abandoned."

"See? I knew it." She put her hand on his shoulder, her smile vanishing, her expression suddenly serious. "And you signed up to be a Guardian, didn't you?"

"It's like you can see right through me," he said.

"That's part of the job of being a sheriff," she replied. "Noticing the details. Observing. Figuring things out. There isn't going to be much cause for violence in here, which means most of what this department will be doing is saving cats from trees. It's kind of a one-eighty from being out there fighting the trife. Vice-Governor Jones wouldn't have sent you here if he wasn't trying to change your mind about staying outside. Maybe he even thought I would take a liking to you."

"Have you?"

Her expression changed again, and she started laughing. "I'm not telling," she said. "But yes." She winked at him. "What can I say, I've always been a sucker for soft-hearted men who aren't afraid to cry."

Caleb was impressed. "Observation. Is that it?"

"Yup. If I had to guess, I would say it's because you just told Private Habib's husband his wife is dead."

"You know who I am," Caleb said, only slightly surprised. Sheriff Aveline was sharp.

"I keep tabs on things, and I recognized the name. It's another part of my duties. I know the Habibs recently moved into Metro. I put two and two together."

"I have to be honest," he said. "Don't take this the wrong way, but you're coming on pretty strong."

"Am I?" She smiled mischievously. "The truth is, Sergeant, the old ways are done. Dead with the planet. We need to look at everything in a new light, including relationships. We're all in the same boat together. Literally. I see a man who's strong and sensitive and has a face I could stare at all night, and I'm not going to beat around the bush. It's too bad you're a Guardian. That's all I have to say."

Caleb's heart was racing, reacting to Sheriff Aveline. If he joined Metro, if his future could potentially include her, maybe there was something to surrendering his spot as a Guardian. There was nothing shameful about saving cats from trees.

"It's not my job to convince you," she continued. "But I think you should make an educated decision. Why don't I show you the rest of the station, and then give you a tour of the city? We can grab a bite at Oscar's, and then I'll give you a tour of my place."

"Your place?"

"Don't get any ideas. So you can see what the cubes are like for Sheriffs. We're considered high-value, which means we get nicer apartments. One of the perks of the job. As far as I'm concerned, if the Vice-Governor wants you to be a sheriff he has a good reason, and that's good enough for me. I've known Adam for a long time. He's one of the good ones. If he likes you so much, it's because you're special too."

"I appreciate that, Sheriff."

"Please Caleb Card, call me Lily."

"Okay, Lily. I can't think of a much better way to spend the afternoon than having you show me around Metro."

"Great minds think alike. Come on."

Chapter 14

Lieutenant Adam Jones made his way from the aft entrance to Metro, back to the lifts on Deck Seven and up to Deck Three, making the long walk toward the bow. The bridge was located on the third deck, about four hundred meters from the massive cargo hold that was home to the city, buried ten meters deep beneath the super-light alloy that composed the hull.

He had been there a few times before, and had returned more often as their days on Earth were coming to an end. As the commander of the Sixth Company, it had been his job to coordinate the search and rescue missions that had seen the Deliverance collect nearly one hundred target individuals who Command considered VIPs. It was a group made up of eighty-percent scientists and their families – people they had determined would be a real benefit to have on board. Not because they were expected to survive the two hundred year journey to the stars, but because they would bring their knowledge and intellect with them and pass it on to their expected descendants. They had a protocol for everything. A plan for any eventuality. Two years of trife occupation had given think-tanks plenty of time to prepare for the worst.

It was still hard to believe the worst had come to pass.

Adam didn't regret his part. He was already a Lieutenant when the trife arrived. He had watched his friends and family and fellow officers and Marines succumb to the virus. He had witnessed the combat deaths of hundreds of Marines ever since. He always hoped it would get easier to take. It hadn't. He'd never had a wife or children. He'd never even had a dog. He hadn't been kidding when he told Caleb he thought of him like a son. He thought of all the people serving under him as his children. He wished he could protect them all.

The ones who had made it though all the fighting were going to go up in the Deliverance with him, starting a journey very few of them would ever finish. He would never see the planet they were leaving Earth to settle. He would never witness its blue sky, its vast oceans, its abundant green landscapes. At least, that's what the scientists claimed it was like and what the artists had rendered. It would never be more than a dream for him. Never more than a computer-generated recreation.

He was okay with that, as long as humankind survived.

No one would have ever predicted or expected the trife. How could anyone prepare for what had happened? It was a one-in-a-million occurrence. A nearly impossible reality. But it was reality. The trife were Earth's new owners, and the Deliverance was being evicted.

Adam reached the door to the bridge. A Marine was standing at attention to the left of it, guarding the hatch. He stiffened a little more when Adam approached, and Adam nodded to him as the hatch slid open and he walked past.

The bridge of the Deliverance was deep and wide,

with a number of workstations positioned at the front, a large holotable located behind them, and a command station located behind that. There were no windows and no direct view of the world outside. Instead, high-resolution cameras were installed across the hull of the Deliverance, providing near-real quality feeds to a large, semi-circular display positioned in the very front of the bridge. From there, it wrapped all the way around to the back of the workstation. There was nothing on the screen right now because there wasn't much to see. Adam could hardly wait to get out of the cavernous hangar and into space to see how the view changed then.

A dozen men and women were positioned around the holo-table. Adam identified General Watkins at the head, his beard freshly shaven away and leaving him to look ten years younger. At seventy years old that didn't mean a whole lot, but he did appear more serious without the crumb-catcher.

He identified the other people in the assembly. Most were officers of the United States Space Force, the people he would be joining in Metro's new government. He had met most of them within the last few months, when the Sixth Company had been transferred to the at-the-time nearly completed starship and to the Space Force from the Marines.

Most of the people were fellow officers, but not all.

Riley Valentine was standing with the group, along with another of the scientists the Vultures had rescued earlier.

He tried not to moan audibly, pained to see the doctor had already gotten to General Watkins before he did. Still, she didn't appear angry. More like shocked.

What was going on?

He had thought his meeting with General Watkins was

private. He was expecting his superior to go over the transition procedures again, both for himself and for his Marines. One hundred of them would become Guardians. The rest were going back to civilian life, albeit a civilian life unlike any they had known.

"General, he's here," Major Jackson said to Watkins, noticing Adam's approach.

General Watkins didn't turn his head, but his eyes slid to the side to catch a glimpse. Adam stopped in front of the general, standing at attention.

"Lieutenant Adam Jones reporting, sir," he said.

"As you were," Watkins replied. "Adam, grab a spot around the table. Anywhere is fine."

Adam slid into place on the other end of the table, next to Doctor Valentine. She glanced over at him, keeping her emotions to herself. Good. He didn't need her glaring at him during the whole meeting.

"Let me cut right to the chase," Watkins said, reaching down to activate the holotable controls. An image was projected in the middle of the table. Earth. "My apologies to Lieutenant Jones, because I had originally intended for this to be a private meeting between us. Sorry, Adam. You know how things are."

"Of course, sir," Adam replied.

"As you know, the Deliverance is scheduled to launch tomorrow morning, oh eight-hundred. That leaves us less than twenty-four hours to finish our preparations, which I believe are well underway?"

"Sir, supply loading will be completed by sixteen-hundred today," a small woman with short dark hair said. Lieutenant Ng. "We're ahead of schedule."

"So, with less than twenty-four hours remaining before launch, Command decided to throw us a major curveball."

General Watkins moved his hand along the table's

control surface, and the Earth zoomed out until it was the size of a golf ball. Another planet appeared on the opposite side of the table, nearly identical to their homeworld. A line animated from Earth to the planet, showing a counter of years as it traveled across the galaxy.

"That's our original course," Watkins said. "We called the planet Earth-6 because its the sixth E-type planet our teams located. As you know, all of the ships were originally slated to be sent to different planets to maximize our chances of seeding and growing a successful colony."

Watkin's hand moved across the surface. A new planet appeared, smaller than Earth and nowhere near as lush.

"This is Proxima B, in the Proxima Centauri system forty light years away. We've received word from Command that all ships are to be reprogrammed to rendezvous at that location."

He tapped the surface and a new animated line appeared, showing the trip would only take twenty years. The group was respectfully silent, but Adam felt his own sense of worry and tension at the last-minute change, and he was sure the others felt it too.

"Sir," Lieutenant Ng said, unable to stay quiet. "Excuse my bluntness, but what?"

"Sir," Major Duvall said. "I think what the lieutenant means is, why the sudden alteration in course? What's changed to make Command suddenly think we're safer gathered on one planet versus two dozen?"

General Watkins put up his hand to settle them. "Command has come to believe the composition of the Proxima system may be more suitable for remaining hidden from the unknown hostile force that brought the trife to Earth."

"Sir, if a hostile force sent the trife," Major Jackson said without finishing as Doctor Valentine interrupted the Major.

"Proxima B is considered a harsh but habitable environment," she said. "There's a wealth of groundwater, and while the surface is barren and rocky, it is stable. The atmosphere is too thin to be breathable, which means we'll have to repurpose some of our materials to build habitable domes. It also means the trife can't breathe there, and there isn't much by way of resources for the enemy to be interested in claiming."

Adam looked sideways at her. "Did you have something to do with Command's updated decision, Doctor?"

"It wasn't a decision made in isolation," Valentine said. "We were in communication with all of the remaining governments who are sending ships. We formulated a new path forward by consensus."

"And assumptions," Lieutenant Ng said. "There's a theory the trife were meant to stop us from reaching the stars. Now you're suggesting they want our natural resources? So what, we leave the planet and then they show up and start enjoying our beaches?"

"Lieutenant," General Watkins cautioned quite sternly.

"Sir, the Lieutenant is right," Major Duvall said. "Less than twenty-four hours, and now we've decided to settle on a single theory about the trife? Last time I heard, it was fifty-fifty that they had been sent at all, and weren't some parasitic life form riding the rubble of their destroyed home planet across the universe."

"Understood, Major," Watkins said. "Allow Doctor Valentine to continue."

As the officers fell silent, Doctor Valentine took control of the table from her end, changing the view of space to one of a rocky surface with a river running across it. "We sent a probe to Proxima before the trife ever arrived. It was going to be one of the first places we delivered a human settlement due to its proximity to

Earth. A temporary testing ground, to prepare for a longer colonization cycle. Assuming we had gotten the funding." She smiled slightly, expecting her comment to gather a few chuckles. She continued when it didn't. "There are two issues at play here. One, we have theories of how and why the trife came to Earth, but that's all they are. Theories. We listed each one and tested them against Proxima. The planet can defend us against all but one."

"Which one, Doctor?" Adam asked.

"Direct attack. If another alien race delivered the trife, and that race has advanced combat potential, and they decide to hunt for us close to our home planet, there's nothing we can do. But that's just one scenario. Our original scenario of Earth-6 would allow four scenarios."

"What're the other scenarios?" Adam asked.

"First of all, we have no idea how the human psyche will hold up to an extended period on the Deliverance. If we set out for Earth-6, people are going to spend their entire lives on the ship, from birth to death without ever seeing the real sun or sky, without ever breathing non-recycled air, without – "

"The protocols for all that are in place," Major Jackson said, interrupting.

"We have no idea if the protocols will be successful. We're making educated guesses."

"Instead of last minute, rash assumptions."

"None of us want to die on the Deliverance," Lieutenant Ng said. "But we don't want to spend the rest of our existence living in a bubble either. How is that so much better than being in Metro?"

The statement got the rest of the officers to start talking again, making their comments about the situation. Adam remained silent. He had never been reactive. He liked to consider everything fully before he formed an opinion.

"Attention!" General Watkins barked, his voice booming over the multiple conversations. "You will reign yourselves in, immediately." The Marines fell silent, coming to attention. "Everyone here except Doctors Valentine and Omar are Marines. What do Marines do? They follow orders. Redirecting the Deliverance from Earth-6 to Proxima B is not a request. It's an order. It's the path Command has chosen for us. Not only United States Command, but the Russians, the Chinese, the Indians. Everybody. Four scenarios versus one scenario. We're unified on this. We get to Proxima, and then we start working on how to defend ourselves from a potential attack. Those are steps one and two. Do I make myself clear?"

"Yes, sir!" the officers barked.

"Sir, if I may?" Adam asked. Watkins nodded. Of course he had noticed Adam had stayed the most calm and asked the most reasonable questions. "Doctor Valentine, what kinds of procedures will be put into place considering the time differential between the trips? By that I mean, twenty years is a lot shorter than two-hundred. How do we plan to alter our approach to the civilians on board, and to Metro, considering everyone on the Deliverance should survive the journey and arrival?"

"We don't have time to alter procedure, Lieutenant," she replied. "We aren't planning on informing the rest of the population."

More than a few of the gathered officers blurted out their questioning of the statement in unison, drawing sharp glares from Watkins.

"We spent over a year putting the protocols in place. Changing them now would be disastrous."

"Isn't that the point the others are trying to make?" Adam asked. "Switching tactics last minute could have unintended negative consequences."

"When the Deliverance arrives ahead of schedule, the people of Metro will be overjoyed to have a new home in their lifetime. I know I will. Things will be hard in the beginning, but I believe in the strength of humankind to overcome. Don't you?"

Adam smiled. She had him there, and they both knew it. "Point made, Doctor."

"Each of you here was told because from a higher level of governance, it is going to mean a change in how we prepare for arrival," General Watkins said. "You're each going to have a role to play on Proxima, though it might be a slightly different role than you might think. The unification of global resources is going to affect everyone in ways we have yet to process completely, and as leaders it's your responsibility to manage those changes from the top down. Is that understood?"

"Yes, sir!" the assembly said.

"Sir, I have one more question," Lieutenant Ng said.

"Go ahead, Lieutenant," Watkins replied.

She turned to Doctor Valentine. "It is my understanding that you're a geneticist, Doctor Valentine?"

"That's right," she replied.

"What makes you qualified to have even been part of the conversation regarding the viability of Proxima B?"

Adam glanced at Watkins, waiting for him to stomp out the question and dismiss them all. Watkins surprised him by looking curiously at Doctor Valentine. It seemed he had the same question.

"Well," Valentine said, her face flushing. "I...I don't think I'm at liberty to say in this company. My directives came straight from Command, as a result of my ongoing research."

"What kind of research?" Ng pressed.

"I really – "

"What?" General Watkins said, cutting her off. All eyes turned to him. He had turned his head away, talking to someone through his comm. "You're sure? Now? Of all the damned luck. Get Eighth company up and ready asap. Pull three of the butchers from the hold and get them headed to the surface, and trigger the red alert."

Adam's heart jumped at the last few words. What the hell was going on?

"Sir?" he said.

Watkins turned to them, his face stone. "Get back to the barracks and assemble your troops. We're under attack."

Chapter 15

"There it is," Espinoza said, lowering his binoculars.

"Are you sure?" David asked. "All I see from here is the side of a mountain."

"The side of a mountain. Are you loco, kid? Here. Take a look for yourself."

Espinoza handed him the binoculars. He put them to his eyes and leaned over the rock they were hiding behind. He quickly scanned the mountainside, pausing when he reached the small building halfway up the hill. Worn tracks led into the rusted aluminum structure, but so what? They could be months old.

Not according to Espinoza. The scavengers' leader was insistent that the military had a base inside, an underground complex safe from the aliens that roamed the surface of the planet. He said he had seen more than one of the large ships they called hoppers cross over the landscape and come down nearby, though there was no sign of any vehicles from here, not even with the extra zoom.

And a hopper had passed over only a few hours ago. Big and loud, it had trailed out of sight within seconds, crossing over the terrain that the survivors had now spent the better part of a week covering on foot. There was no sign of it now, but for all David knew it was resting on the other side of the hill, along with all the evidence any of them could ever want that the military was operating in the area.

All they wanted was to get inside.

All they wanted was to be safe.

The trife were behind them. There was no question about that. The demons and the humans had already met a few times, leaving dozens dead on their side and hundreds dead on the other.

The scavengers had fought as courageously as they could.

It was nowhere near enough.

Espinoza whistled, waving to the larger group further down the small hill. Their group had swelled in recent weeks as scavengers in the area heard the former Marine was planning to rush a military base and force them to let him and his followers in. They were all American citizens. They all had a right to safety. Espinoza told David how the military was taking specific people in and offering them protection. Rich people, mostly. Politicians, celebrities. Why did they deserve to live when so many were still outside, doing everything they could to survive one more night?

He had been apprenticing as a mechanic when the trife came. He was great at fixing things. Wasn't that worth something? Didn't the military have choppers and drop-ships and all kinds of equipment that needed to be maintained? It wasn't his fault he had gotten sick a few times and turned down for enlistment. Should he pay for that with his life?

He had managed to stay alive on his own for nearly

two months before hooking up with Espinoza and his group. He had learned to avoid the trife, to rig traps and protection against them so he could sleep without fear. He had a gift for making something out of nothing, for taking raw materials and turning them into assets he could use. Wasn't that valuable?

He raised the binoculars again, scanning the area. He paused when he noticed something lying in the dirt near the building. What was that?

"David," Espinoza said, grabbing the binoculars before he could discern the item. "Believe me; it's there. I was a Marine. I know what I see ."

David turned to the man. Espinoza was short, with thick black hair and a dark complexion. His face was weathered and tired. He wore a pair of old army fatigues, his name sewn on the chest and carried an M-16 rifle over his shoulder.

"What do we do?" David asked.

"Look," Espinoza said, pointing behind the group of scavengers.

David could see the movement of the trife through a tree line in the distance. Normally, the demons didn't move all that much during the day, preferring to use the time to feed. But they had gotten a bead on the group, and the demons weren't about to let them get away.

"We don't have a lot of options here," Espinoza said, raising his voice so the rest of the group could hear. "We get inside that building, or we die. We get into the underground base, or we die."

The group rumbled in agreement. There were over five hundred people further below, mostly young men and women, with a few older people and children mixed in. Ninety percent of them were armed with firearms they had picked up from old sporting good stores, looted houses, stripped them from armed corpses they had found in the streets, and any number of other sources.

"What if they shoot at us?" David asked.

"Then we shoot back," Espinoza said. "I was one of them, remember? I know how things are in there. They push us out to die while they spend time and energy rescuing the people they think are important. Why do they get to decide? We all deserve to live."

"But they're our people."

"No, they aren't our people. They're willing to let us die. As far as I'm concerned, that makes them as much of an enemy as the trife." The scavengers behind him shouted their agreement. "If you want to stay here, be my guest." Espinoza turned to the crowd. "If any of you want to stay out here and take your chances with the trife, now's your chance. Otherwise, let's go!"

Espinoza pulled his M-16 from his shoulder, raising it into the air. Then he surged ahead, up to the top of the hill and over, charging down the other side.

The scavengers shouted behind him, moving forward as a solid mass, climbing the hill where David was perched, cresting it and running down.

David didn't move right away. He watched them, his heart pounding with fear. This wasn't a good idea. Espinoza said there probably weren't more than a hundred Marines inside, maybe less, but David didn't believe it. What could the military accomplish in a remote area like this with so few Marines? Unless it was a research facility? Yanez had claimed the military was trying to create monsters of their own to fight back against the trife. It was a terrifying thought.

His eyes shifted when he noticed movement near the

building. The doors had slid open, and now a squad of Marines were filing out. It wasn't the first time David had seen the Marines in their full combat armor. He could still remember hiding in a dumpster and peering into the darkness as a squad had moved through the streets of his hometown. They had killed a lot of trife that day, leaving their bloody and broken carcasses littering the streets. At the time, David had thought the Marines came to liberate the area from the trife.

He closed his eyes. He could still remember the scene like it had just happened, even though it had been more than a year. He could still see the girl running toward him, seeking the safety of the dumpster as three trife trailed behind her, giving chase. He could still hear her screams and feel her terror. He had started to stand, to lift the top of the dumpster and offer his hand to pull her in.

Then the Marines had appeared around the corner behind the trife. They started shooting, their bullets pinging off the dumpster when they weren't biting into the demons.

Or into the girl.

He had closed the lid and stayed there for hours after the shooting stopped. Then he had cautiously climbed out, approaching the girl. She was dead of course. Riddled with bullets. Killed by the Marines. It was a memory that had returned too many times since. It was the reason he had decided to join Espinoza's group. Safety in numbers, and a willingness to fight back against the Marines if the Marines made trouble for them.

Espinoza was right. They were the enemy, and they didn't care about people like him. He didn't fit into their twisted definition of a VIP.

David got to his feet, standing behind the rock. Espinoza was scaling the hill toward the building. The

Marines were standing in front of the door, waiting for him to arrive. Would they hold their fire or were they just waiting for more of them to get into range?

David heard rustling behind him and he spun around. The first of the trife were breaking out of the trees below, no more than a quarter-mile away. A long line of them trailed back, snaking through the trees in a slick that numbered in the thousands.

There was nowhere to go but forward.

David started down the hillside, his eyes on Espinoza, who had almost reached the Marines. He could tell by the way Espinoza was gesturing that he was trying to explain their situation. He motioned frantically toward the hill, likely giving warning of the trife and begging for protection.

David continued to run, reaching the base of the first hill in less than a minute. He could hear the stilted hisses behind him, growing into a single, solid buzz. He glanced back, finding the trife at the top of the hill where he had been standing less than a minute earlier. The demons were gaining in a hurry. Had he lingered too long?

The sharp report of gunfire sounded from ahead. More shots were ringing out by the time David got his eyes back on the scene. He watched the entire squad of Marines collapse, falling under the sudden outburst from the scavengers, who weren't going to let themselves be left for the trife again.

A bottomless pit formed in his stomach as his people swarmed over the Marines, grabbing their weapons on the way past and charging into the building. He heard more gunfire ring out, muffled by the closed space. A moment later he heard another rumble and watched as a pair of drones crested the far side of the hill.

What the hell had he gotten himself into?

He charged ahead as fast as his legs could carry him, the weakness of his prior illnesses causing him to tire too quickly. He looked back a second time, finding the trife rushing down the hill in his direction, the front line only a hundred meters to his rear. There was no way he was going to get all the way up the larger hill to the building and make it to the rest of the group before the demons ran him down.

He considered giving up and letting himself fall. The trife would be on him in seconds, and it would be over within seconds after that. He wasn't suited for this world, where it had truly become survival of the fittest. He had only survived because he was good at hiding. Good at staying out of sight. He survived because he adapted to his surroundings and his limitations. But there was nothing to adapt to out here, wedged between two hills, between two enemies, between two potential deaths. He had joined up with Espinoza because he didn't want to be alone anymore. He wanted a community, a place to belong with people who were fighting hard to stay alive.

Instead, he had followed them right to his death.

He slowed down. He didn't want to give up, but he could barely breathe. His lungs were weak, his legs weaker. He glanced back a third time. The trife were a sea of oily black monsters, the darkness broken only by the yellow-white of their teeth. They were almost close enough to pounce on him, and once they did, those claws would tear him in half before he could even cry out in pain.

He was looking backward. He didn't see the ground ahead. He didn't know the larger rock was there until his toe caught on it and got lodged there for a moment, throwing him off balance and sending him sprawling forward onto his stomach. He whimpered slightly as he hit the ground, reaching out and trying to scramble back to his feet, closing his eyes so he wouldn't see which demon was going to kill him.

Chapter 16

David first heard the sharp whine and then felt the heat as the missile exploded behind him, throwing dirt and trife body parts all over him before sending a broad swath of the demons flying through the air. He heard three more missiles strike a moment later, blasting hard into the front line of the creatures and creating a line of thick smoke smelling of cooked meat.

He lifted his head, looking back at the carnage. The trife were barely bothered by the initial assault, and he dropped his face to the dirt a moment later. Closing his eyes, he stayed as still as he could.

And listened.

He heard the creatures as they moved over him, hissing to one another while they charged past. Clawed feet touched down near his face, kicking dirt into his mouth. Sharp toes prodded at his back, stepping on it and over, the talons cutting through his old denim jacket to his flesh. More feet landed near his arms and legs, scraping him in multiple places. He clenched his teeth, desperate not to make a sound and reveal that he was still alive. The wounds hurt, but they weren't deep, and as long as he stayed silent maybe he would survive.

He heard a few more whines, and then another round of explosions sounded ahead of him, along with the screams of dying trife. He shifted his head slightly and opened his eyes, looking through dust and smoke to see large metal feet hit the ground a few meters in front of him. Gunfire followed, muzzle blasts spewing from the metal creation that had just fallen from the sky. It was taller than a human, wide and bulky, with thick arms and legs that hummed as they moved. Its rounded head was equipped with two glowing red eyes, and a large eagle and star logo was stamped to the front where its face should have been. It had a pair of machine-guns integrated into its forearms. The twin belt-feeds spat out rounds at a breakneck pace, chewing up everything in front of it. A stamp on its leg identified it. BUT/CH-3R.

Butcher?

As the robot waded into the thick of the battle, David heard the same rapid-fire sound a little further off, suggesting it wasn't alone.

The trife hissed and charged the machine, and they died by the handful, each bullet punching through the lead demon and the one behind it. Each round killed them by twos and threes while more trife feet drew closer to David.

It only took thirty seconds or so for the robot to run out of ammunition. Once it had, it started grabbing the trife by whatever body part it could reach, crushing limbs and necks alike, and then swinging the corpse into the demons behind it. It killed the demons almost as fast as more demons could join the fight.

David looked back for a third time, noticing the trife

were still there, the robot's attack barely making a dent in their overall numbers. Even so, the creatures had decided to take a wide path around the thing, leaving them both momentarily in the clear.

He stumbled to his feet. The robot shifted its head to look at him, taking an instant to identify him as human and then heading off at a run toward the nearest trife and leaving him alone in the middle of the battlefield.

David turned in a circle, trying to make sense of what was happening around him. He was still alive. He wasn't sure why or for how long. The trife had noticed the Butcher heading away and were beginning to redirect toward him once more.

He did the only thing he could think to do. He ran up the slope toward the aluminum structure.

The trife were all around him, bunched together in puddles of oily flesh and teeth everywhere he looked. He held his gun ready, knowing they would notice him at some point and attack. It was an old steel revolver with a six round cylinder and a wood grip. He had a dozen bullets shoved into his jacket pocket, plus six already loaded. He held it close to his chest, running as hard as he could to reach the building, his lungs already beginning to fail him again. Damn it.

He heard a trife hiss nearby, and he turned his head, dropping to the ground just in time to avoid the creature's pounce. It went over him, and he aimed his revolver at it and fired, catching it in the side. It spun and dropped.

Another trife came at him, hissing and slashing. David fell back as he fired three panicked rounds that managed to hit the demon in the chest. He fell for the second time, the dead trife tumbling on top of him.

David stayed there, trying to catch his breath again.

More trife passed him by, likely assuming he was dead. They rushed toward the structure, the entire slick beginning to condense as it approached the building. More of the creatures than David could ever count went past him, careful to step around the dead on their way. He tried to see past them, searching for the Butcher and managing to get a glimpse of it through their legs. It was on the ground and crawling in trife, still trying to fight them as its limbs were being cut from their joints, its head torn from its body. It had fallen to the horde too.

David stayed prone beneath the dead trife. The demon was light enough he could have thrown it off him, but what good would that do? He was safe here as terrifying as *here* was. He had to be better off than Espinoza or the other scavengers who had entered the structure and were no doubt caught in the crossfire between the Marines and the trife.

He flashed back to the girl, watching the Marines gun her down for what had to be the millionth time. It would be like that again. Espinoza had shot first, destroying any chance that any of the scavengers would survive. Not in this mess. David could almost picture the former grunt running toward the Marines, the trife right behind him. He could practically see the expression on Espinoza's face as he realized his miscalculation and the bullets started slamming into his flesh. David cringed at the thought, his bladder emptying of its own volition, warm and wet along the side of his leg and onto his thigh. He might have been embarrassed if there had been anyone around to notice.

The seconds passed, the sounds of fighting a miserable din around him. Drones fired down at the trife, cutting through entire swaths of the demons. He turned his head and saw Marines up on the hill above the building, shooting down into the mass. A large group of trife had broken from the main group to attack them, and the way they stood their ground told David that Espinoza had made a terrible, terrible mistake.

He had led the trife to the military base.

Now they were all going to die.

Chapter 17

"Are you ready for this, Caleb Card?" Sheriff Aveline asked.

"I don't know. It'll be hard for you to top the clothing exchange."

"Do I sense sarcasm in your tone of voice, Sergeant?"

Caleb smiled. "Maybe a little."

They both laughed.

He had spent the last thirty minutes with the sheriff, wandering through parts of Metro on the express tour. She had brought him into a few of the shops to get a feel for the businesses and the people who ran them, including The Dancing Trife and the exchange, where the Metro residents would be able to trade in old clothes for chits to purchase new ones. Everything in Metro was working on a faux economy, powered by both physical chits and digital cryptocurrency that were linked through the city's data network, which Lily called DAN, short for Deliverance Assistance Network.

They were hitting it off, talking about anything and everything, and laughing the entire time. Caleb couldn't remember the last time he had laughed so much. It was before the trife. He was sure of that much. There hadn't been much cause to be jovial since then, but maybe things were starting to change. By this time tomorrow, the Deliverance would be in deep space, preparing to fire up the ion thrusters that would bring them to half the speed of light within a couple of days.

And he would be on the other side of Metro's walls, destined to spend the next two hundred years cycling in and out of stasis when he could be inside the walls getting closer to Lily Aveline.

Lieutenant Jones had set him up, and like everything the man planned, he had done it very well indeed.

Lily put her wrist to the panel beside the door, and it clicked and swung open slightly. She smiled at Caleb as she brushed past him, reaching for the handle and pushing it open.

"Welcome to Cube Eighteen One," she said with a smile.

Caleb joined her in the apartment, his eyes quickly scanning the layout. The space wasn't large, but even his brief glimpse of Habib's cube told him it was almost twice the size of that one. Everything was painted a flat white, and there was little decoration. A small kitchen sat in the back of the room with a window above the counter offering a view of the next cube over. There was a tiny eating area ahead of it, and a small sofa, table, and terminal in front of that, arranged more like an office than an entertainment area. There was a single door on the right side, and two doors on the left.

"This has to be better than a barracks rack, doesn't it?" Lily asked.

"What kind of cooking are the people of Metro going to be doing?" Caleb asked.

"Admittedly, the food supply is all prepackaged and recyclable. But there are flavorings added to it to offer some variety. It'll all get cooked in the microwave, so no stove or anything, but there will be dishes to clean."

"Recyclable?"

"Two hundred years is a long time," Lily said. "All of the waste will be filtered, the nutrients captured and reconstituted."

"You're talking about piss and shit?"

"How very delicate you are. Yes. Have you read the protocols?"

"For the city? No. They didn't apply to me."

"Didn't?"

"I may be having second thoughts."

"Good. Am I responsible for that?"

"Maybe."

She laughed. "Good. Not only piss and shit," she said, lowering her voice to mimic him when she referenced the waste. "When a resident reaches a certain age, they'll be cut off from medical care. It's highly recommended they turn themselves in for end-of-life care, at which point they'll be painlessly put to rest. Their body will be processed similarly to the waste."

Caleb suddenly felt nauseous. "You're going to be eating the dead?"

"Technically, we're always eating the dead. Fertilizer goes into the ground providing nutrients to plants, which we either ingest directly or feed to animals to slaughter them and ingest. It's the natural cycle of life, with a technological twist to speed up the process."

"I never thought about it like that."

"Neither did I. Doctor Rathbone explained it to me the same way I just explained it to you."

"Doctor Rathbone?"

"She's the head of the hospital."

Lily walked to the kitchen and opened a cupboard, lifting out a square package the size of her fist. It was wrapped in foil and had a sticker on it. "Salmon with fettuccine," she said, holding it up. "I've tried it. It doesn't taste anything like what it says it is, but it isn't too bad."

She put it back and then opened the single door on the right. "Second bedroom, intended for any children I might have."

Caleb glanced into the room. It was small and empty and didn't have any windows. "How many kids can a family stuff in here?"

"Two bunk beds," she replied. "Up to four. That's the max family size they're allowing."

"In here?"

"So they say."

She closed the door and took him to the other side, opening the first one. "Standard head."

He glanced inside. It was a simple bathroom. He pointed to the last door. "Let me guess. Master bedroom?"

"You are sharp, aren't you Sergeant?"

"As a baseball. I miss baseball."

"What team?"

"Yankees."

"Ugh. And here I thought we were getting along."

"I grew up in Connecticut."

"So you should be a Red Sox fan."

"No."

They laughed for a few seconds.

"Is there a reason you're showing me the master bedroom last, Sheriff Aveline?" Caleb asked.

"Is there a reason you're asking me that question in that tone of voice?" she replied.

"What was it you said to me again?" Caleb said.

"About the old world being dead and new ways of thinking?"

She smiled. "Using my words against me?"

A loud tone sounded from the terminal at the front of the room. Both of their heads snapped to face it, reacting to the sudden noise.

"What is that?" Caleb asked. He could hear a similar noise from the apartment adjacent to hers.

"Emergency alert," she said. She was wearing a communicator badge on her shirt, and she tapped it. "This is Aveline, what's going on?"

"Sheriff, we've got orders from Space Force Command to help get the residents inside and locked down in preparation for launch."

"What?" Caleb said. They were still sixteen hours from launch.

Aveline looked at him, her face hardening, her expression deadly serious. A moment later, Lieutenant Jones' voice crackled through his comm.

"Sergeant Card," he said. "Sorry to do this, but your leave is over. Head to the ship's armory and gear up."

"What's happening, Lieutenant?" Caleb asked.

"The installation is under attack. A group of scavengers led a massive slick of trife to the base, and they're breaking through our defenses. We need to hold them at the hangar and keep them from getting on the ship. We're preparing for an emergency launch."

"Shit," Caleb said, forgetting himself.

"Shit is right, Cal. Get moving."

"Yes, sir. On my way."

Caleb looked at Lily. They both had a job to do. "It was a pleasure meeting you, Sheriff."

"You too, Sergeant," she replied.

"Maybe we can get together again once things are settled? We can share a salmon and fettuccine."

"Absolutely."

He nodded and rushed out the door, running down the hallway to the lift.

The fleeting hope of laughter and happiness quickly faded away.

Chapter 18

The realization that Espinoza had brought the trife to the military made David sick to his stomach. He lowered his head to the ground, looking up at the sky. There were still trife moving past him, and he watched the swing of their arms, the flex of the muscles in their legs, the pulsing veins in their necks and the saliva dripping from their teeth. He went into some kind of shock, prone and static beneath the dead demon, his mind pushing out the sounds around him so that all he heard was the thumping of his heart and all he felt was the struggle in his lungs to keep breathing.

He had always been too frail to survive in this world. He had been smart and lucky, but apparently that luck had run out. He should never have joined up with Espinoza. He should have realized how this was going to end. They had delivered the trife to the base like leading a starving man to a feast. How could they have been so dumb?

He sat there for what seemed like an eternity but it was really only a handful of seconds. The trife were swarming, but this was still a military base. It was still an underground facility. Would they really have designed it to be so easily overwhelmed by the trife?

David looked around again. The bulk of the horde was almost past, the stragglers the only ones still nearby. He shifted slowly beneath the dead creature, moving it off him. He carefully rolled onto his stomach and pushed himself to his knees, listening for the hisses of the demons to measure whether they saw him or not. He gripped his revolver in his left hand and took a few deep breaths, trying to draw in as much air as he could. This was going to burn his lungs as bad as anything, but it was his only chance to live.

He had to get into the base before they sealed it closed. Either he was going to make it, or he was going to die trying.

He glanced around one more time. There were two trife near him, and the rest were ahead. He could see them near the front of the building, nearly stopped in their tracks as they tried to all push in at once. There had to be thousands inside already, pouring down every corridor in search of people to kill. There was no way Espinoza was still alive. There was no way any of the scavengers were still alive.

He planted his foot and pushed off, rising in a dash, cutting to the right of the building. The Marines had come from somewhere. A hidden entrance the trife didn't know about. If he could find it, if he could make it there, he might be able to get inside.

The trife noticed him almost immediately, turning around and hissing. He aimed his gun and fired, one bullet for each of them – too close to miss. They fell in front of him and he ran past their dead bodies, sprinting as hard as he could.

The demons at the building saw him but ignored him,

maybe sensing better hunting inside. He found the Marines, their bodies prone near the top of the hill, bloody and shredded between the armored plates. One of them was holding a discarded rifle near his chest, and David decided he was going to take it.

Something caught his leg and he tripped, falling forward. He looked back and saw a trife had grabbed his ankle and was pulling itself up toward his face. He brought the revolver around and fired, just before the demon's teeth reached down to his neck. It collapsed on him, and he wiggled out, jumping back up and taking off again.

He made it to the Marine, grabbing the gun from his dead hand. He heard more trife coming and he turned and fell, squeezing the trigger on the weapon and watching as a dozen rounds tore through a pair of trife.

He gulped in air, trying to feed his starving lungs, jumping back up.

"Hey. Kid."

He was shocked by the voice, and he shook with fear, spinning around and aiming the rifle at the source.

One of the Marines was still alive, his helmet on the ground next to his head, his arm severed at the shoulder. He had put something on it to stop the bleeding, and he was lying still on the dirt, playing dead the way David had.

"Don't move," David said, feeling stupid right after he said it.

"Who are you?" the Marine asked.

"David. Who are you?"

"Corporal Carlyle, United States Space Force. What the hell are you doing out here?"

"Trying to escape the trife."

"Us too. Behind you."

David spun, firing the rifle as he did. His rounds cut an incoming trife in half.

"The warehouse is overrun," Carlyle said. "Look, I don't want to die out here. We're so close to escaping this bullshit. There's a bolt hole on the other side of the hill, that's where my squad came up."

"I thought there would be," David said. "You don't have many Marines in there, do you? Only one squad came out?"

Carlyle laughed. "We have plenty of Marines and plenty of gear, but we aren't going to waste it here. We're leaving."

"What do you mean you're leaving? How can you leave? Where are you going?"

"You'll see, kid. Sarge volunteered us to die out here to slow them down, and they did. I guess I'm the lucky one?" He lifted his remaining hand. "Help me up."

David took it and pulled Carlyle up. Then the Marine picked up his rifle and glanced at a small display on the side, tapping it. "Rounds remaining. How's yours?"

David turned the weapon. "Fifty-seven."

"Not bad. Take point, stay close. You see that rock down there?"

David found a large stone about two hundred meters down the slope. "Yeah."

"That's the bolt hole. We make it there; we get inside."

"And then what?"

"Hope we aren't too late."

David almost asked him what they would be too late for, but he decided to focus on making it to the hole alive instead. He started forward, running down the slope, slipping on some rocks and sliding. Carlyle started shooting behind him, and he heard the screams of dying trife.

"They spotted us," Carlyle said, navigating the rocky slope like he had done it a thousand times. The Marine started shooting again, killing more trife.

David looked over his shoulder. At least fifty of the demons were coming over the hill with renewed fervor, as though they understood the armored Marines were the real threat and were eager to take this one out.

"Help me thin them out," Carlyle said, his rifle going empty. David slid to a stop and turned around. The Marine had to swap magazines with one hand, and while he had gotten the empty one out, he had to cradle the rifle between his legs to put the fresh one in, slowing him immensely.

The trife were bearing down on him, and David brought his rifle up to shoot. He clenched his jaw, and then turned and started running again.

"Kid!" Carlyle shouted. "Kid! Wait!"

David was almost at the boulder when he heard the gunfire behind him. It only lasted for a second, and then Carlyle started screaming again.

David didn't look back. He raced to the stone, his lungs on fire, struggling to breathe. He was almost there, and Corporal Carlyle had said they were going to escape.

Not without him.

He reached the boulder, almost overshooting it as he fell onto his back to slide to a stop near it. He rolled over, looking back up the hill. The trife had finished with Carlyle, but they hadn't continued after him. They were headed back up the slope to the building. He was grateful for it, but he didn't understand why.

It didn't matter. He stood and moved behind the stone. A small plate was visible beneath a thin layer of dirt. David wiped the dust away, revealing a control panel. He tapped on it, sliding a bar from closed to open.

The boulder rotated away, revealing a long, narrow tube and a ladder that plunged down the hole into the darkness.

He tried to figure out how to carry the rifle in with him. He knew it attached to the Marine's body armor magnetically or something, so it didn't have a strap. He decided he couldn't take it, tossing it aside and quickly reloading his revolver before shoving it between the waist of his jeans at the small of his back. Then he threw his feet over the side, finding the rungs of the ladder. He climbed down a few steps, pausing at the control panel to close the hatch. Once it was sealed, a string of dim lights came on, lighting up the entirety of the shaft. David looked down, suddenly nauseated by the height. He couldn't believe how deep the cavern went.

He started to descend.

Chapter 19

The armory was above the hangar on Deck Twenty-nine of the Deliverance. It was part of the Marine Corps module that had been installed in the ship for use by the Guardians. Caleb made it there within seven minutes of Lieutenant Jones' call, having sprinted the entire way from Sheriff Aveline's apartment.

The space was almost empty when he arrived, save for the Master Sergeant who was in charge of the weapons and armor stored in the armory. With so much time before launch, most of the Marines were still in the external barracks rather than in here.

"Sergeant Caleb Card," Caleb said to the man, who was standing behind a desk. "I have orders from Lieutenant Jones to gear up and get into the fight."

"Confirmed," the Master Sergeant said, checking his tablet. "Hurry, Sergeant."

The hatch to the right of the desk slid open, and Caleb ran into the room. It was a standard armory, with multiple shelves of various weapons and racks of body armor in the back. He went straight to the armor, flipping through it to find something close to his size and then hastily stripping off his utilities to put it on. He grabbed a helmet from a shelf above the rack and pulled it over his head, expertly completing the ATCS connection between the two pieces of the SOS. Then he moved to the guns, grabbing a search and rescue standard carbine and sidearm and snapping them both to the armor, along with extra magazines for both. He connected the carbine to the ATCS as he ran out the door and past the Master Sergeant.

"Good hunting, Sergeant," the MS called out behind him.

With the ATCS online, Caleb was able to check the tactical, getting an overlay of a three-dimensional view of the hangar pieced together from the feeds of the Marines already participating in the fight. He was dismayed to see how much red was spread around the isometric view, with hundreds of the demons already finding their way to the bottom of the lift shafts and getting into the base.

"Display Washington," he said, asking the system to search for the big mute. "Display Sho. Display Rodriguez."

The ATCS pulled up the three Marines, putting their name and vitals across the top of his HUD. All three were online and in the fight.

"Link displayed," he said.

A line connected the three Marines, putting them in a subnetwork with him.

"Vultures, this is Sergeant Card," he said.

"Sarge!" Rodriguez cried out. "It's about time. We're in deep shit here."

"Mark displayed," Caleb said. The view of the battle adjusted, the green spots of the friendlies mingling with three yellow markers grouped near the industrial lift. "Sho, sitrep."

"Not good, Sergeant," Sho replied. "We're losing Marines faster than we're killing demons."

"Roger. I'm on my way to you."

"I hope you're bringing the cavalry, Sarge."

"Sorry, Vultures. It's just me."

"Sergeant Card," Lieutenant Jones said. "I've got you active on the grid."

"Yes, sir."

"We're packing in and prepping for launch. The hangar is lost. We're about to order a full retreat to the Deliverance. You're being moved to Eighth Company, Captain Lyle's command. He's running the ship defense."

"Roger, sir. What about the Vultures?"

"Sergeant Trask is picking them up. They'll be part of the retreat with everyone else."

"Roger. How the hell did this happen, sir?"

"I don't know. Bad luck? Jones out." The comm fell silent, but only for a moment.

"Sergeant Card, this is Captain Lyle. I've got you on my grid. Reverse course and head back to the lower hangar entrance. We got caught with our pants down, and the hangar blast doors are malfunctioning."

"Yes, sir," Caleb replied, pulling up and turning around. He was worried about his squad. His Vultures. There was nothing he could do. He had his orders, and he trusted the officers watching the battle unfold.

He ran back the way he had come, crossing within a hundred meters of the armory before hitting an emergency stairwell leading down to the hangar deck below. The sounds of the fighting faded in as he descended, and when he pushed the exit door open he was greeted by a scene of carnage.

There were pockets of Marines across the hangar deck, most of them behind the cover of the different vehicles loaded onto the Deliverance. They were concentrating their fire on the main entry to the deck, where a huge lift was locked into place but the blast doors that kept space out were jammed in a half-open position, leaving ten meters of space for the trife to climb in and up.

They congregated around the top and bottom and sides by the dozens, crawling along the surface of the Deliverance and dropping to the deck before charging into the gunfire. Most of them were heading straight for whichever fire team they caught sight of first, but Caleb noticed a group had broken off and was charging to the left of the blast doors. He tracked them, finding a team of engineers in bright orange jumpsuits working on the controls for the doors with two squads of Marines trying to keep the trife away.

"Sergeant Card, head over to the door controls to help out," Captain Lyle said.

"Roger, sir," Caleb replied, moving from the stairwell toward the group in the corner. He would have to cross the hangar to get there, threading his way through the incoming trife and friendly fire. Fortunately, the Marines' ATCS would freeze their weapons if they were in danger of accidentally shooting him.

He raised his rifle and fired as a trife rounded the side of one of the massive loading trucks that had helped bring the prefabricated apartment buildings to the ship. The round caught the demon in the chest, knocking it down. Four more immediately took his place, hissing and rushing him.

Caleb stayed calm, firing a single round into each of them and then dancing away, continuing toward the doors. He heard a hiss beside him and whirled to shoot, his eyes crossing the loader but finding nothing there. He hesitated a moment, aware Captain Lyle would be monitoring him on the tactical if not through his helmet feed. He didn't have orders to chase down all of the wayward creatures.

He saw an opening ahead and sprinted forward, ducking behind one of the half-dozen or so armored personnel carriers in the hangar. He stopped there, whirling out from the corner and finding a pair of targets that had tried to flank the engineers. He fired two quick rounds, taking both of the creatures out.

"Thanks for the save, Sergeant," Corporal Hafizi said over his comm.

"Anytime," Caleb replied.

He slid along the back side of the APC and broke from the corner, crossing fifty meters of open space toward the group. The trife assault intensified as the seconds passed, each wave making it deeper into the hangar. The metal floor was already covered in demon corpses, and it was only going to get worse.

A mass of them saw him crossing the open floor and broke away, redirecting their attention to Caleb. He saw them coming and shifted the carbine to his hip, using the connection to the ATCS and the reticle in his helmet to aim to the right while running straight. It took more rounds to knock down the trife − he had help from Corporal Hafizi and the other Marines near the engineers − but the creatures were killed before they caught up to him.

"Thanks for the save, Corporal," Caleb said.

"Anytime," Hafizi replied.

Caleb joined the group, watching the engineers for a moment. They had pulled a circuit board out of the wall and were busy running some kind of diagnostics on it. He turned away, looking out into the cavern.

There were trife everywhere. Hundreds of them, crawling along the floor of the cavern like an inky black spill, storming over everything they encountered. He could see the blast doors to the base from his position, and he noted that they were sealed. If anyone were still inside the base, they wouldn't be making the trip to the stars with the Deliverance.

"This is crazy," he heard one of the privates say behind him.

"Shut it, Gaines," Hafizi replied.

"Yes, Corporal. Sorry about interjecting my personal opinion."

Caleb aimed his rifle and fired, dropping the trife like flies. Five. Ten. Twenty. It didn't seem to matter how many he killed, how many his new team killed, they still kept coming. He risked a glance over at the techs, who had disconnected their diagnostic tablet and were in the process of soldering part of the board. They must have figured out what was wrong.

"Sergeant Card," Captain Lyle said. "The left flank is failing. I'm linking a squad to your command. Take them across the hangar and shore up the leak."

"Yes, sir," Caleb replied, watching the Vultures vanish from his HUD, replaced with five new Marines he barely knew, including Hafizi. Was he seeing things right? Had Rodriguez's monitor gone red? He hoped not. "Okay, echelon left, stay focused on the trife moving to the flank. Trust your fellow Marines."

" You got it, Sarge," one of the squad replied.

They started across the hangar, focusing their fire on the dozens of trife turning for the left flank. He could see how the defenses on that side of the hangar were failing, finding dead Marines on the ground near their cover, blood spilling from deep cuts and bites. The trife knew where their SOS was weak, and they went right for it.

"Sergeant, we can't afford to let them get deeper into

the ship," Captain Lyle said. "If we lose them inside the ship, we might never find them again."

Caleb swallowed hard. That was a terrifying thought. They all knew how one trife could quickly turn into hundreds given enough food, and the multiple reactors on board the Deliverance could probably fuel thousands.

"Fire at will," he said. "Focus on the flank."

His squad started firing, rounds cutting across the hangar and wiping out lines of trife from the side. The demons shifted direction in response to the assault, most turning directly toward Caleb while a few continued. It was like they were trying to infiltrate the defenses and sneak in.

"Take care of the group, I'm going after the break-aways," Caleb said. "Private Gaines, with me."

"I'm with you, Sarge."

Caleb and the private moved laterally to the incoming trife, sinking deeper into the hangar and chasing after the separated few. Caleb shot two of them in the back, but the third ducked beneath another loader to the other side.

"Shit, I lost one," Caleb said.

"We've got you covered, Sarge," Sho said. He heard the rifle fire, and the red mark he was chasing vanished from tactical.

Caleb's lips split into a wide grin. "Perfect timing, Private. Is Washington with you?"

"Affirmative, Sergeant."

"Captain Lyle, requesting privates – "

"Already done, Sergeant," Lyle replied, Sho and Washington's vitals returning to Caleb's HUD. "Now hold the damn line, or we're all going to have a very bad week."

Chapter 20

David's lungs were almost back to normal by the time he neared the end of the shaft, the climb down the ladder so much easier than running up and down the rocky terrain outside. The fact that he was free of the trife made it even easier, allowing him to calm his nerves somewhat while he descended.

Of course, unless he was planning on living in the small shaft, he would have to come out of it eventually. He was pretty confident of what he would find when he did. A scene of chaos and death and destruction that made what had happened outside look tame by comparison. According to Corporal Carlyle, the military wasn't all that interested in keeping the trife out, only in slowing them so they could get away.

Get away how?

That was the question that burned at him. The one he needed to answer. Even as he closed on the bottom of the shaft, even as the sounds of gunfire and shouting and hissing faded into earshot, he remained determined to make it to wherever the rest of the people were headed. If they were going to escape, he was going to escape with them.

He reached the bottom of the shaft, which emptied out into a small room, just large enough for two or three Marines in combat armor to stand in at one time. It was empty right now, a sealed blast door between David and whatever was happening in the spaces beyond the room.

Something was happening out there. Shouting and shooting, and all he had was a six-shot revolver. It was suicide to go out there. It was suicide to stay in here.

He walked over to the door. It didn't have a window, so if he opened it he was going out blind. Damn it. He should have helped Corporal Carlyle outside. The Marine would have known what to expect.

David reached for the control panel. He couldn't stay here, no matter what was going to happen. He tapped the panel to activate the door, and it slid aside, revealing the small cross-section of hallway.

A dead trife was on the floor across from him, along with a dead Marine. They were both torn and bloody, their plasma mingling on the corridor's metal surface. The Marine had a large knife still in his grip.

Opening the door let the full sound of the battle through to David's ears. It was horrifying and deafening, a constant barrage of gunfire echoing through the nearby hallways. He dove out of the room, sliding across the bloody floor on his knees and reaching for the Marine's knife. He pried it out of the man's still-warm hand, looking both ways down the corridor.

He was clear for the moment. But how long would the moment last?

He jumped up, unsure of which direction to go. His instinct was to run away from the fighting, but in this case he needed to go toward it. He turned left and ran to the end of the hallway, stopping and peering out at the adjacent passages. He saw a trife to the right writhe and fall, hit with a stream of bullets that seemed like a waste of ammunition. He looked left when he heard a sharp hiss and stumbled back as a trife lunged at him. He slashed the knife without thinking, landing a lucky blow that cut through the demon's neck and brought it to the floor beside him.

He needed to go to the right, without getting killed from behind.

He started in that direction, walking sideways and keeping his revolver pointed the other way. More trife started clearing the corner, one at first, and then four more. They spotted him and increased their pace.

He didn't shoot. He ran, charging toward the next intersection and hoping the Marines were sharp enough not to shoot him as soon as he appeared ahead of them. He tried to cut the corner when he reached it, managing only to trip over a dead demon and bouncing off the wall.

Bullets zipped past him for an instant before stopping. Someone had shot at him.

"Get down!" a Marine barked. David was already on his way down, and the bullets were a rhythmic cracking over his head, most of them hitting flesh instead of pinging against the wall. "Move! This way!"

David followed the order, rushing toward the Marine. He was one of a half-dozen positioned twenty meters away, ahead of a closed door. David reached the Marines and threw himself past them and onto the floor, at the same time they started shooting again. Trife screamed behind him – too close behind him. He dropped to his knees and looked back. The slick had reached the Marines.

They kept shooting, the demons pouring into them in an unstoppable flood of claws and teeth. David ran again, staying ahead of the creatures while the Marines died behind him. He raced for the closed door and what he hoped would be his freedom.

When he reached the door, he glanced back in time to see two trife coming straight for him. They had bypassed the Marines to chase after the weakest of the group.

He aimed the revolver and fired, his first three rounds missing completely. His next two hit the trife on the right, and his last grazed the trife on the left.

"Shit," he cursed, holding the knife in front of him and turning around, continuing to back toward the door.

The trife hissed at him, but then one of the others jumped on it, slashing it with its claws. The two demons fell together, fighting one another. David had seen them do this before when one was injured. They would always cull the weak from their midst.

His back hit the door; he leaned over and slammed his hand against the control panel. It lit up, and he slid the bar to the open position. The door slid out of his way, and he backed through, quickly activating the controls on the other side as the stronger trife finished off the weaker and started his way.

He hit the slider, the door coming down right in front of the demon's face, stopping it by inches.

"Too close," David said. He could hear more gunfire on this side of the door. A lot more gunfire, echoing all around him. Espinoza had started a full-scale war.

He spun around, to get a look at his new situation.

His heart both lifted and sank in rapid succession, cycling through the two emotions so quickly it made him dizzy.

He was standing in a massive cavern. Directly ahead of him, he could see a small metal building positioned beside a long, narrow bridge. On the other side of the bridge was the last thing he had ever expected to see.

A starship. It was a damn starship! And it was enormous.

Now he understood what Corporal Carlyle meant when he said they were going to escape. The Marines were leaving the planet. They were getting away from the trife the best way possible.

If only he could convince the hundreds of trife in this part of the cavern – all the way across the bridge to the sealed door on the other side – to let him through unharmed.

He stood in the shadow of the door, scanning the mass of trife, looking for some way to pass through them. There were at least four hundred of the creatures near the bridge, hissing and waiting for the ones at the front to continue scraping at the hatch of the closed airlock. Their claws were sharp, but there was no way they were going to get through the thick alloy.

A few of them had started climbing the outside of the starship, scaling the hull and searching for an alternate entry. Others were redirecting to an apparent lift shaft about twenty meters from where David was standing. He pressed himself into the corner to keep them from noticing him.

Unable to find a path to the vessel, he was getting increasingly desperate. Even if he got to the door, then what? He couldn't get inside.

He shook his head in frustration. He had come this far. There had to be some way to reach the ship. There had to be some way to get on board.

His eyes shifted to the small building near the bridge. The windows were broken, and he could see a bloody body through them, slumped over a row of controls. What did those controls operate? He shifted his gaze to the trife and back to the building. If he was quick, he could make it past them.

He tried to calm his nerves as he reloaded his revolver. He had spent the last two years avoiding the trife. Hiding from them, sneaking past them, doing everything he could not to be discovered. He could do this.

He broke from his cover, sprinting across the area between the door and the building, a twenty-meter break between him and the demons. He kept his eyes on them as he charged ahead, his revolver clutched tight in one hand, the knife in the other. His could swear at least one of them saw him, but it didn't give chase, remaining focused on the ship. Did the creatures know their quarry was trying to escape? Did they know they were looking at a starship?

David made it to the building. The door on the back side of it was hanging open, and there was a Marine on the floor, a deep cut in his neck. David felt nauseous at the sight, but he forced himself to go to the control panel. He pushed the corpse from it and then made a face as he wiped the blood off the panel with his sleeve.

He looked down at the controls. One was to operate the bridge, to disconnect it from the ship. Another was to remotely control the two lifts, which David could see more clearly from his new position. There was also a comm interface, currently disconnected. That was it.

David sighed in frustration, reaching for the comm interface and hitting the button to connect it. Immediately, dozens of voices started speaking over one another, adding to the din of gunfire.

"Right flank. They're headed for the thrusters."

"Keep them contained."

"Help! Man down! Man down!"

"Take that you son of a bitch!"

"Echo squad is offline."

"Already done, Sergeant. Now hold the damn line, or we're all going to have a very bad week."

David looked out to the trife. They heard the voices, and their heads started turning his way. He ducked behind the controls, reaching up and turning off the comm.

"Stupid," he whispered to himself. Still, he had no way to get from here to the ship, and certainly no way to get on it. "Think."

He closed his eyes for a second and then retreated from the building. The structure was on the edge of the platform, and he went to the corner and looked down. His heart found a new pace when he saw the chaos below, where hundreds of trife and dozens of Marines were still facing off. It only took him a few seconds to realize the demons were winning the fight and the ship would have to leave soon.

His thought coincided almost perfectly with a sudden change in the vessel. A soft hum reverberated through the cavern, and then a bright light appeared at the rear and bottom of the ship as multiple thrusters began to ignite.

Not yet. He wasn't inside yet.

He looked back to the bridge. The trife reacted to the pre-burn, hissing loudly. They started reversing course, moving away from the crossing to the lift shaft and vanishing inside. David watched them go, one after another, at the same time the light in the cavern increased and the thrusters gained more power.

It was time for him to go too.

He ducked back into the building, grabbing the downed Marine's rifle and putting his revolver away. Then he waited for what felt like an eternity until only a few trife were still near the bridge. He moved out from the building toward them at a run. They saw him and spread their claws, taking a more aggressive posture.

He lifted the rifle and squeezed the trigger, keeping it held down while bullets spat out of the weapon, chopping through the creatures. He released the trigger, jumping over their bodies and racing along the crossing. The hum of the ship was gaining in pitch, enough that the entire cavern felt like it was beginning to shake.

The platform hadn't looked that long from the side, but it felt to David like it took forever to cross. He was close to the end when a trife jumped down at him from above, and he barely got the rifle over his head in time to stop its claws from raking his scalp. The demon fell on him, and he rolled and pushed, throwing the creature over the side, plummeting to its death. He rolled over again and stood, getting to the airlock door. He stared at it for a moment and then started pounding the butt of the rifle against it.

"Help!" he shouted. "Help me!"

He had no idea if anyone was on the other side or if they could hear him or not. He continued to pound, the noise in the cavern increasing, the light increasing. He felt waves of heat rising from the ground, and when he looked back over the edge he could see the Marines were doing their best to retreat, the mass of trife in pursuit.

He continued pounding on the door. Was anyone there? He was too close not to make it. Come on!

The hatch hissed and slid aside. A pair of Marines with rifles pointed at him were standing in the doorway. One of them reached out and grabbed him, yanking him inside. The other reached for the panel to reseal the hatch.

A trife dropped in from above, claws slicing down and into the man's wrist, nearly severing his hand. The Marine screamed and fell back, the second Marine turning to shoot.

Four more trife came down from the side of the ship, taking them all by surprise. They must have been hiding close by, hoping the hatch would open again.

David aimed his rifle and squeezed the trigger. Nothing happened. The demon jumped at one of the Marines, its head darting in and biting between the helmet and the body armor. The Marine screamed, grabbing a knife from his hip and sinking it into the trife.

David didn't see what happened next. His gun was out of ammo, and he wasn't about to hang around to die. He dropped the weapon and ran, through the corridors and deeper into the ship, getting as far away from the trife as he could, as fast as he could.

He wasn't sure how far he went, but he paused at a hatch on the left side of the corridor, hitting the controls to open it. The door slid aside, revealing a storage room stocked with what appeared to be boxes of rations. Good enough. He threw himself inside, closing the door behind him. Then he fell to the ground, leaning back against the boxes.

He couldn't believe he had made it.

He couldn't believe he was about to go into space.

Chapter 21

"Pre-burn is go, General," said one of the privates manning the many control stations on the bridge of the Deliverance.

General Watkins smiled. "Here we go." He turned to the officers still present on the bridge, including Adam. "Major Jackson, sitrep."

"Sir," Major Jackson said, taking in the three-dimensional tactical map that had replaced Proxima B on the holotable. "All units are on the retreat, moving toward the lifts from the sled up into the ship. They're still taking heavy casualties, and it's only getting worse."

"I've lost ninety percent of my company, sir," Adam said, trying to hold back his emotion. So many Marines had come so close to escaping the hell that Earth had become. So damn close. "Everyone else was passed to Major Lyle for ship defense."

"I'm down ninety-five percent," Lieutenant Beak said. "What was left of my detail is with Major Lyle too."

"What about the hangar?" General Watkins asked.

"Techs are still working on it, sir," Major Jackson said.

"We're lucky our people have managed to keep the trife off them so they can do their job, but even for the ones who are still fighting, their ordnance load-outs are getting low."

Watkins' jaw flexed in frustration. "Have the bastards gotten into the ship?"

"We have a few rogues in the corridors. Once we clear the cavern, we can send units to track them down."

"Don't linger too long on that. We can't afford to have them starting a nest on the ship. We might never get them back out."

"Yes, sir. We'll be able to redirect our resources as soon as the Deliverance is clear of the hangar."

"What resources?" Doctor Valentine said. "How many Marines do you have left out there?"

Adam swallowed hard. He knew the current answer to the question. He didn't want to think about it.

"We've still got units making their way to the lifts," Major Jackson replied.

"How many units?" Valentine asked. Jackson didn't answer. She made a face. "General, are you sure you have enough Marines left to hunt down the trife?"

Watkins glared at her a moment. "We'll have enough people left."

Valentine didn't look convinced. "How the hell does this happen?" she hissed. "We're this close to getting out of here, and the trife just suddenly appear? Or some asshole group of scavengers figures out we're down here and leads the things right to us? For hell's sake!"

"We're all in this together, Doctor," Adam said, barely able to contain himself after her outburst. "And maybe I should remind you that we could have left yesterday if you weren't so damn insistent on packing up whatever it was you risked my Vultures' lives to deliver."

Valentine opened her mouth to speak.

"Enough!" Watkins snapped. "Lieutenant Jones, this isn't the time or place. "Doctor Valentine, you're welcome to go to your module whenever it suits you. Now might be a good time."

Valentine glared at the general for a moment, and then turned and stormed from the bridge, her assistant trailing behind her.

"Don't let the trife get you on the way down," Major Jackson called out after her.

"Major," Watkins said.

"That woman is like a tattoo."

"Tattoo?"

"She really gets under your skin."

"Agreed, Major. Let's focus on getting our people on board and getting the hell out of here."

"Yes, sir."

"Module, sir?" Adam asked. "Doc Valentine isn't staying in Metro?"

"No. Don't ask me how, but she has full operational authority over the USSF science teams, coming directly from Command. We had the research module installed weeks ago, and she didn't waste any time claiming it for her project."

"What project, sir?"

"Damned if I know. I haven't had time to ask much about it. Command sent the orders in."

Adam raised an eyebrow. General Watkins was the first step down from Space Force Command, a group of a dozen four and five-star generals and admirals pulled in from the old branches of the military when the mission shifted from fighting the trife to running from them. That he didn't know what Valentine had brought on board or why made his skin crawl like he was getting a tattoo.

"General," Major Ng said, her face pale. "We've got a

problem. Lift four is offline. A malfunction in the servos. We don't have time to fix it."

"Damn it," Watkins said. "What's the attrition rate?"

"Twenty to one right now," Major Jackson said.

"How many are down there?"

"Two thousand."

Adam did the math along with the General. Losing the lift was going to cost at least twenty Marines their lives.

"Pre-burn at eighty percent, General," the private announced.

"Sir, whoever isn't on board by the time we reach one hundred--" Adam started to say.

"I'm aware, Lieutenant. I hate losing them more than you do."

Adam wasn't sure that was true, but he could see the pain in Watkin's expression. Things had gone from bad to worse in no time flat. The rushed nature of the ship's construction was leading to malfunctions they weren't expecting, and it had already cost them more lives than they could count.

They could only hope the massive sled that was supposed to carry them through the atmosphere and into orbit didn't break down.

"Private Osborne, activate the cameras," General Watkins said. "Let's open our eyes."

"Yes, sir," the private replied.

A moment later, the dark displays around the bridge lit up. The light from the thrusters blinded most of them, but a few of the cameras revealed a view of the cavern from around the Deliverance. One of them was pressed against the side of a trife, exposing smooth black leathery flesh.

"Eighty-five percent," the other private, Delfina said.

"Are there any units still out in the open?" Watkins asked.

"Negative, sir," Major Jackson replied.

"Private Smith, prepare to trigger the charges."

"Yes, sir. Remote connection is active."

Watkins looked back at the officers. Adam knew the general was hesitant to bring the mountain down around them when there might still be people they could save. They didn't have a choice.

"Do it," Watkins said.

The bridge suddenly fell so silent Adam could hear Private Smith tap the control panel to activate the explosives. Everything seemed to hang frozen for a moment, peaceful and still and perfect.

Only for a moment. The first charges started detonating, muffled explosions closer to the surface of the mountainside. They were joined a few seconds later by the second layer of explosives, more powerful and closer to the Deliverance.

The ground started to shake, the rumble increasing in volume through the hull. The cameras showed the rock and debris begin to tumble down, the shaped charge pushing most of the dirt away from the Deliverance, but not all.

"Sir, lift two is offline," Major Ng said.

Something started beeping on the bridge, and Adam looked over to the station. A map of the ship was displayed there, with parts of it turning orange.

"Internal systems are malfunctioning," the private at the station said.

"We aren't holding up well to the shaking," Adam said.

"There's nothing we can do about it," General Watkins said. "We just passed the point of no return."

"Ninety percent," Private Delfina said.

"Private Junis, turn off power to the sled lifts," Major Jackson said.

"What?" Watkins said, glaring at him.

The Major's face was white. They all knew what the order meant.

Every ATCS outside the Deliverance was registering a flatline.

"Sled lifts disconnected, sir," Private Junis replied.

"Ninety-five percent."

"Junis, make sure all of the external hatches are sealed," Watkins said. "Run an emergency bypass to lock them down."

"Sir? What about the hangar?"

"The hangar too. It won't seal until the techs get it fixed."

"Yes, sir."

The rumbling continued, the Deliverance shaking, the cavern vanishing around it as the top of the mountain sank beside the massive vessel. Dirt had piled up on a number of the active cameras, hiding the world around them once more.

"One hundred percent burn, General," Private Delfina announced.

"Captain Rogers, release all mooring clamps and fire the sled thrusters, full power," General Watkins said.

"Yes, sir," Captain Rogers replied.

Adam couldn't see the ship's pilot from his position near the holotable, but he felt the change in inertia almost immediately. The sudden movement caused him to reach for the table, using it to balance himself. The ship's dampeners would only do so much, especially during liftoff.

"Three meters," Captain Rogers announced. "Six meters. Twelve meters. Thirty meters."

They were climbing.

Everyone on the bridge gave out a short cheer, muffled by the stark reality of their situation.

They were leaving Earth behind. The only home any of them had ever known. While they might all survive the trip to Proxima, the path that lay ahead was anything but smooth. The present was anything but smooth too.

They were leaving Earth behind.

And the trife were coming with them.

Chapter 22

Caleb turned slightly and fired, a burst of half a dozen rounds that cut down a group of incoming trife. Sho released a barrage of her own beside him, covering his flank and pulling down a few of the demons.

Washington stood close to them both, a large knife in his meaty hand. His rifle had gone dry a minute earlier, leaving him to settle for grabbing and stabbing anything that tried to get too close. The big man was fortunate his reach was longer than that of most demon's, making it easier for him to cut them before they could get to him.

The hangar was nearly overrun with trife, so many having broken through the stuck blast doors. It was a wonder any of the Marines defending it were still alive. They had mostly consolidated in the back of the space, using the massive loaders stored there as cover while they took potshots at the demons and did their best to keep them off the techs working on the doors. All of their ammo load-outs were getting low, and Washington wasn't the only combatant who had been forced to resort to close-in fighting.

Somehow, they had managed to hold the line.

Somehow, they had managed to keep the techs clear to finish their work.

But if something didn't change soon, Caleb wasn't sure it would last.

He rotated again, firing a single round into a trife that was trying to jump him from the wing of a drone. He shifted again, shooting a second that had ducked underneath the fuselage and tried to sneak up on him. Washington took care of a third, reaching out with his long arm and stabbing it in the chest as it tried to jump down at him.

Sho's rifle fired three more rounds and then fell silent.

"I'm empty," she announced, dropping the weapon to the floor and pulling her knife.

"We can't hold out like this," Corporal Hafizi said.

"We're almost there," Caleb replied. He could see the light from the sled's thrusters and feel the slight shivering of the Deliverance as it prepared to launch. "As soon as we clear the ground, we'll only have to clean up what's left of them."

"If there's anything left of us," Sho said.

Caleb's gut hurt from the comment. He had lost almost all of the Marines Major Lyle had given him, save for his two Vultures, Corporal Hafizi and Private Won. Of the nearly one hundred green marks that had been on the tactical a few minutes earlier, only a dozen or so remained.

The red marks still numbered in the hundreds.

The battle came to a pause a moment later, a sudden rumble sounding from somewhere above the Deliverance and taking both humans and trife by surprise. They all stopped fighting for a second as the ground started trembling, shaking the starship and prompting Caleb to reach out and grab the wing of the drone to steady himself. Sho fell to her knees, and a moment later tons of rubble began dropping past the half-open blast door. The deafening roar of the collapse drowned out everything else.

The trife recovered a split-second before the Marines. Caleb nearly lost his head as a demon bounded at him from the other side of one of the APVs, swinging a clawed hand at his throat. A knife sprouted from the creature's head, thrown with enough force to knock it sideways and away from him. Caleb looked back at Washington, who grinned in response. He flashed the big man a thumbs up and shot another trife coming his way.

The Deliverance continued to shake. One of the pipes along the hangar's ceiling burst and steam started spraying out from it, high enough over their heads that it didn't cause any immediate damage.

"Sergeant Card, we've got trife breaking through the line," Major Lyle said. "The right flank is broken, and the bastards are moving into the stairwell. Take your squad and get after them."

"Yes, sir," Caleb replied. "You heard the Major, once we get clear, we – "

A sudden mass of trife suddenly poured in through the open hangar door, pressing against one another, hissing and screaming in a chorus of fear. They were flowing like water, forced from the cavern into the hangar to escape the falling debris.

"Belay that order, Sergeant," Lyle said. "One thing at a time."

"Roger that, Major," Caleb replied. "Don't let them through."

Caleb aimed and fired, the trife gathered so densely in the entrance to the hangar that one round dropped two of them. He fired again and again, killing another and then another before killing two more. The other Marines in the hangar did the same, taking measured shots one round at a time, the number of trife making it impossible to miss.

The creatures didn't stand near the open door for long. They started moving, splitting and spreading away from the center and rushing the remaining humans, including Caleb and his squad.

Caleb remained calm. Aim and shoot. Aim and shoot. Aim and shoot. Trife dropped in front of him like bowling pins, but more replaced them right away, closing the gap in a hurry. Caleb fired his last round, dropping the rifle and switching to his sidearm to continue the defense.

The Deliverance continued to rumble, and a moment later he felt the sudden pressure on his body, inertia pulling him back and down. He shifted his feet to stay upright, watching the trife stumbled before regaining their balance. He glanced at the blast door and could see the world moving outside.

They were starting to rise.

"Got it!" he heard someone shout over the deafening cacophony.

The blast doors finally started to move.

"Great timing," Sho said. "That might've helped five minutes ago."

Caleb didn't reply. He moved his gun hand, firing a round into a closing trife, finding another target and shooting again. The pressure was increasing, the Deliverance continuing to accelerate. They were in the process of leaving Earth behind. It should have been an experience to savor and remember, regardless of what came next.

Except the hangar was still overrun with trife, and they didn't stop their attack just because the Deliverance was lifting off. If anything they were fighting harder, ever more desperate to kill their sworn enemy. Caleb heard the screams nearby as another Marine was overcome and torn apart by the horde. He aimed and fired, again and again until his pistol was empty. He tossed it aside, pulling his knife and glancing back at his squad.

"We need to block off the stairwell," he said, pointing to the right side of the hangar. He could see trife there, moving through the doorway. The demons were pushing further into the Deliverance, gathering where the defenses were weak and breaking through the line.

Caleb knew it was too little, too late.

The Deliverance was airborne and headed for space, but they weren't even close to leaving their problems behind.

Chapter 23

"Thrusters are at maximum output, sir," Captain Rogers announced. "Vector and velocity are within range. We're at ten thousand meters and climbing steadily. Time to orbit, three minutes forty-seven seconds."

"Thank you, Captain," General Watkins said. "Private Junis, damage report."

"Sir, most of the damage to the Deliverance is minor," Junis said. "There were a few coolant line ruptures and power surges that knocked out all but the emergency lighting in some parts of the ship. Some of the sensors are also offline. We've contacted engineering for an update on estimated repair times."

"Once we've finished with the trife," Major Jackson said. "Reports from the hangar aren't good, sir."

"Define not good, Major," Watkins said.

"ATCS is estimating three hundred sixteen trife and fourteen Marines."

"Fourteen?" Watkins said, his face flushing. "My Lord. What else do we have to back them up?"

"We've enlisted the loading crews, General. Sergeant

Pratt and his team are in the armory right now. We also have half a dozen sheriffs and a dozen remaining deputies we can call on to help bolster the ranks. They're all former military."

"Negative," Watkins said. "I'm not sending law enforcement out there. Metro is going to need them, now more than ever. Are the routes into Metro sealed?"

"Yes, sir."

"Make sure they stay that way. Shut down ID chip access to anyone who isn't on the bridge except Major Lyle."

"Yes, sir," Private Junis replied.

"Having the trife on the Deliverance is bad enough. If they get into Metro, it'll be a damned nightmare."

Adam stared at the holotable and the battle playing out in the ship's hangar directly beneath them. He knew Caleb and the Vultures were part of that fight. They were the only members of his original company that had survived the liftoff. How much longer could they survive down there?

How much longer could any of them survive?

He glanced up at the primary display hanging over the bridge. The blue sky of Earth was getting darker as they continued to claw their way through the atmosphere, the massive sled mounted to the bottom of the ship ferrying them ever upward. Once they reached sixty kilometers, the sled would run out of fuel and disconnect, and then the ship's main thrusters would fire, taking them the rest of the way into space, through orbit and in the general direction of the Proxima system.

He barely had time to think about reaching a destination in twenty years instead of two hundred. A new thought interrupted that one, and he hurried over to Private Junis' workstation.

"Private, you said some of the sensors are offline?"

"Yes, sir."

"Which ones?"

She used the control surface in front of her to adjust the map of the Deliverance, shifting to a three-dimensional, isometric view.

"Failed circuits here, here, and here, sir," she said, pointing to different sections of the ship. "The main corridor lights are also offline here and here." She moved her hand across the map. "Sensors include heat, flood, and life, which is a combination of motion and thermographic imaging."

"Life sign detectors are out?"

"Yes, sir."

"There?" He pointed to a section of the ship.

"Yes, sir."

Adam traced the outage, following the orange marks on the screen across the ship toward the center. Directly to the bridge.

"General Watkins, we have a problem," Adam said, getting the general's attention.

"What is it, Jones?" Watkins asked.

"Sensors are out leading to the bridge. The trife can head right up here and we'd never know they're coming."

"Is that right, Private?" Watkins said.

"Yes, sir," Junis replied.

"Seal the bridge. It's not a problem if they can't get in."

"Sir, the door seals are electromagnetic. Without proper power balancing, we can't lock down the bridge."

"Damn this bucket of bolts," Watkins said. "Jackson, contact Lyle. We need a security detail near the bridge ASAP."

"Sir, what about the hangar?"

"We don't have enough Marines left to be everywhere the trife could be," Watkins said. "We need to pick our battles, and right now one of those battles may be headed up here."

"Yes, sir."

Major Jackson lowered his voice to speak through his comm, ordering Sergeant Pratt and his team to redirect their way.

"Do we have an estimate on the number of trife who got out of the hangar?" Watkins asked.

"No, sir. They split up once they made it into the stairwell. They could be spreading anywhere on the ship."

"Wonderful." General Watkins rubbed at his forehead with concern. "Captain Rogers, how long before we can activate the automated systems and set this thing to autopilot?"

"About three minutes once we reach orbit, General," Rogers replied.

"Coordinates to Proxima are set?"

"Yes, sir. I started entering them as soon as they were handed off."

"Good work, Captain."

General Watkins fell silent, continuing to rub at his forehead while he decided what they should do.

"Sir," Major Jackson said. "Sergeant Pratt's team has encountered resistance near the central lift banks. They're going to be delayed."

"Have them reroute through the port stairwell," Watkins said. "It'll take a little longer but we don't need to defend the lifts, we need to defend the bridge. Junis, any chance we can get engineering here to fix the circuits?"

"With the trife out there, sir?" Adam said.

"Good point, Lieutenant." General Watkins raised his

voice. "If you have a sidearm on your person, make it known."

Private Delfina put up a hand. "I do, sir."

"Me too," Captain Rogers said.

That was followed by silence.

"Only two of you?" Watkins said.

"We didn't think we'd need them once we left Earth," Major Ng said.

"We shouldn't have needed them," General Watkins agreed. "Lieutenant Jones, Major Ng, you were both enlisted before you went to officer training, and you have direct combat experience. Jones, take Captain Rogers' sidearm. Ng, Private Delfina's."

"Yes, sir," Adam said. He walked across the bridge toward the pilot station, raising his eyes to the large display again. The blue sky was gone, the world around the forward cameras turning red and blue and white as the Deliverance began to cross into the thermosphere.

"Ejecting the launch sled," Captain Rogers announced as Adam rounded her station. She had a vectoring stick in her left hand, her right hand resting on a flat control surface. She tapped the surface to bring up a secondary menu and then tapped a button to disengage the sled.

There was little indication the sled had detached outside of a slight shudder and a small shift in inertia as the Deliverance lost velocity, the thrusters pushing it upward shutting down and falling away. Captain Rogers kept her hands steady, sending power to the ship's main thrusters. If they malfunctioned in any way, the Deliverance would fall back to Earth hard and fast.

"My pistol is strapped to my thigh," Captain Rogers said, motioning with her head. The pressure of their ascent began to return, and Adam could see the numbers changing on her display, showing the main thrusters successfully taking over the duties of pushing them ever higher

"Yes, ma'am," Adam replied, looking down at her leg. The gun was somewhere between it and the seat, meaning he would have to reach under her rear to find it.

"Don't be shy, Lieutenant," Rogers said. "The trife don't care if you grope my ass or not."

"Yes, ma'am," Adam said, slightly embarrassed by his hesitation. His rank was lower than Rogers' but he was still ten years her senior. He leaned over, reaching under and finding the handle of the sidearm, pulling the weapon from under her backside.

She shifted in her seat. "That's actually more comfortable," she said without taking her eyes from her display. "Time to orbit, forty-eight seconds."

Adam carried Rogers' sidearm back toward the entrance to the bridge, joining Major Ng there. He wasn't particularly nervous about the idea of the trife trying to get into the room. He had served six years as infantry, including a tour during the second Korean War. He knew how to use a gun, and he knew how to stay calm when the fighting started.

He glanced over a Major Ng. The older man's weathered face was hard and tight, the pistol resting gently in his left-handed grip. He met Adam's gaze for a moment, nodding slightly.

"Orbit in five. Four. Three. Two. One." Captain Rogers finished the countdown by reducing the power to the thrusters, allowing Earth's gravity to pull them into position to continue the journey.

"Initiate the autopilot sequence as soon as possible," General Watkins said.

"Yes, sir," Captain Rogers replied.

Something hit the door.

"They're heeeerrreee," Major Jackson said, though he had no real proof the banging was from trife.

They hit the door a second time, and then a third. There was no way the creatures could know the bridge was behind the door, and yet they had made almost a straight line to it from the hangar. Could they sense how many people were inside? If so, it was a damn good thing they were able to lock down the entrances to Metro.

Adam raised the pistol, aiming it at the door. The trife weren't smart enough to hit the control panel on purpose, but their constant scraping and banging could potentially activate it by accident. The system's designers hadn't accounted for the creatures getting onto the ship.

His heart was thumping steadily, his muscles looser than he would have expected. The Deliverance had made it into space. That part seemed a bigger challenge to him than the creatures on board. Of course, they were ruining his ability to savor the moment and to be amazed by the view of their planet from beyond its atmosphere. It was his last chance to see Earth and it was his once in a lifetime opportunity to see it from space.

Screw the xenotrife.

They continued hitting the door, the banging reverberating through the room in a rhythmic pattern. General Watkins retreated, backing up toward the front of the bridge. Major Jackson stayed in place, continuing to monitor the hangar. A quick glance told Adam the battle was still going poorly.

Bang! Bang! Bang! The sound of their collisions echoing in the space. Still, the hatch remained sealed – the enemy outside the gates. Adam began to relax, starting to believe the demons wouldn't get in.

Except there was something about the way they kept hitting the door that was bothering him. Something he couldn't quite place. The cadence was so regular. Too regular. It was as if they were trying to create the noise.

It was as if they were trying to distract the people inside.

Adam looked around the room, suddenly concerned the trife were smarter than they had given them credit for. His eyes landed on an air vent a few meters above one of the large displays.

"Does anyone know where that vent goes?" he asked.

Major Ng looked at him, eyebrows slowly raising as he slowly shook his head.

"You don't think?"

He was cut off when the grate covering the vent exploded from it. A trife pulled itself from the opening, leaping down from its perch toward Private Delfina, the person closest to it.

Adam aimed and fired, catching the demon in the head. Not before it had gotten its claws on the private, tearing into her neck. She screamed and slumped in her chair.

Another trife leaped from the vent, followed by another, and another. Ng joined Adam in shooting at them, while General Watkins started angling for the other side of the room.

Adam turned around, looking up. A symmetrical vent was on that side.

"General!" he shouted.

Watkins looked up as that vent cover fell away, hitting him in the face. He collapsed beneath it, shouting as a trife fell from the new opening and landed right on top him. Adam fired his pistol again and again, knocking the creature away from Watkins.

"Captain, how long to autopilot?" Adam shouted.

"Two minutes," she replied.

They had to hold the bridge for two minutes.

"Ng, cover the right side. I'll hold the left." There was no reply. "Ng!" Adam spun around again. Ng was on the ground, three trife over him. Adam shot them in turn, but it was too late to save the major. "Jackson, grab Ng's gun. We have to keep the bridge."

"Roger," Jackson said.

Adam activated his comm. "Sergeant Card, are you still out there?"

"God only knows how, sir," Caleb replied.

"If you can get to the bridge, you need to get here now!" Adam shouted, his voice desperate. " We've got trife on the bridge."

"The bridge is under attack? We're on our way, sir."

Adam rushed over to General Watkins. His nose was bloodied, but he was up and alert, using the metal grate to keep a pair of trife away from him.

He shot one of them point-blank in the head, and punched the other in the face, hard enough to knock it aside. General Watkins swung the grate into it, breaking its jaw and knocking out teeth.

One of the other trife saw it and jumped on the injured demon, finishing it off. As soon as it did, Adam shot it.

More screams sounded from the other side of the bridge, as Private Osborne was cut down. Adam saw a pair of trife heading for Captain Rogers. He had to keep them away from her, at least until she could set their course and let the ship's computer take over.

He hurried to her side, standing his ground.

The door to the bridge slid open, letting the rest of the demons in.

Chapter 24

"You heard the Lieutenant," Caleb said through his comm to Sho, Washington, and Hafizi. They were all that was left of the Marines under his command, the rest long dead. "We need to get to the bridge."

He checked his HUD, glancing at the tactical grid. Fourteen Marines were still in the hangar, including himself. Fourteen. Out of how many? He shuddered to guess. What should have been their liberation had turned into a damned nightmare.

"Roger that, Sarge," Sho said, speaking for herself and Washington. The big man was holding the rear, a knife in each hand, his SOS covered in dark trife blood. He didn't dare take his eyes off the demons for a second.

"Sir, what are we going to do?" Corporal Hafizi asked. "We don't have any guns, and there have to be a hundred trife between here and the bridge."

"We're going to do the best we can," Caleb replied. "That's how the Vultures work. We head for the stairwell and we start climbing, step-by-step."

"Yes, sir," Hafizi said, though he didn't sound too comfortable with the idea.

They were already fairly close to the stairs, having made their way across the hangar behind one of the loaders to catch a group of trife by surprise. Fortunately, the hangar was nearly clear of the demons, and few enough remained that the ten Marines still fighting could handle it.

Unfortunately, it was nearly clear because so many of the trife had moved further into the vessel.

"Sergeant Card, where are you headed?" Major Lyle said, noticing the movement of the Vultures.

"Sir, direct orders from General Watkins," Caleb lied. He figured he could get away with the fib since the general was on the bridge, and Lieutenant Jones had called him for help. "The bridge is under attack."

"Shit," Lyle said. "Confirmed. Good hunting, Sergeant."

"Thank you, sir."

The Vultures pushed onto the stairwell, running up as quickly as they could. Caleb checked the tactical, noticing Sergeant Pratt's ATCS was active near the central lifts. A blob of red surrounded him and the two remaining members of his team.

"Sergeant," he said. "What's your situation?"

"Pinned down," Pratt replied. "The lift we fought our way to is malfunctioning, and we're stuck inside. We're supposed to be on the bridge, damn it."

"We're on our way," Caleb said. "We get you loose. You share your guns."

Pratt laughed. "Roger that."

They scaled three flights of steps, running right into the backside of a smaller group of trife. Caleb and Sho sliced into them with their knives, stabbing them as they tried to turn to fight and pushing the first few back for Washington and Hafizi to finish off. The quartet punched through the demons in no time, breaking out of the stairwell on deck twenty-seven.

"Sixteen trife in three corridors," Caleb said, taking in the situation. "Marking connecting passages here and here. Washington, you head down Alpha, Sho and Hafizi take Beta. I'm heading straight in."

"Straight in?" Sho said. "Sarge, that's too dangerous."

"Not if you get there at the same time I do. Run faster."

"You got it."

They reached the intersection, and the Vultures split up. Caleb watched them all on his HUD, timing their circuitous route with his arrival in the central hub, where a larger group of trife currently covered the lift banks. Sergeant Pratt and his team could probably have gotten clear of the creatures if they were aggressive, but he was playing it safe to keep the rest of his people alive. Caleb understood the motivation, even if he didn't agree with the decision.

"Vultures, I'm coming up on the central hub. I'll get their attention; you save my ass."

"Copy that, Sarge," Sho said.

"Pratt, you copy on that?" Caleb asked.

"Affirmative," Pratt replied.

"Here we go. Don't let me die."

Caleb drew in a deep breath as he turned the corner and burst into the central hub. There were multiple corridors all leading into the hub and a bank of four lifts in the center. The trife were gathered around them, hissing and clawing at one of the doors.

"Hey, uglies!" Caleb shouted as loud as he could, brandishing his knife. "Come get some."

The trife hissed and turned, surprised by the sudden attack from the crazy human. One of them charged right away, and Caleb barely got the knife up in time to stop a large claw from slashing his neck.

Sho, Hafizi, and Washington charged out of two of the corridors behind the creatures, knives slashing and cutting into the demons' backs. At the same time, the door to the lift slid open, and Pratt and his men started shooting.

Caleb dropped to his stomach to avoid being hit, the bullets and blades slamming the trife and quickly tearing them apart.

It was over in seconds. Caleb looked up when the shooting stopped, finding Sergeant Pratt standing above him, holding out his hand. Caleb took it and let the other man pull him to his feet.

"Thanks for the help, Cal," Pratt said.

"Thank me later. We still need to get to the bridge. Do any of the lifts work?"

"Probably the one I didn't try to use," Pratt said. "Damn it. I lost half my squad trying to cut through the bastards instead of going around like Jackson suggested. It's a good thing you came along."

"Sarge, I'm carrying," Sho said, coming up beside him holding a rifle. She must have taken it off one of Pratt's dead Marines.

Washington and Hafizi joined him. Washington had picked up a rifle too.

Pratt grabbed the pistol from his hip and held it out to Caleb. "A deals a deal."

Caleb took it and smiled. "You have seniority. This is your lead, Sean."

"Screw that, Cal," Pratt replied. "You have more combat experience in your pinkie than I have in my whole body."

Caleb nodded, and he quickly pulled Pratt and the two members of his squad – Gurshaw, and Ning – into his direct subnet.

"The lift goes up to the central hub on Deck Six. It's one hundred meters from there to the bridge. We don't have time to mess around. Washington, you have point. Sean, cover our six."

"Will do," Pratt said.

Caleb went into the lift next to the broken one and tapped the controls. The panel didn't show any damage. He waved the others in and then directed the cab to deck six.

They started to rise.

"Lieutenant," Caleb said, trying the comm link to the bridge. "What's your status?"

There was no response.

"Lieutenant, are you there, sir?" he repeated.

Nothing.

"Shit. We may be too late. All out sprint; don't slow for anything."

"We're good to go, Sarge," Sho said. Washington flashed him a thumbs-up.

The lift reached Deck Six. Caleb was out the door before it finished opening. He nearly ran headlong into the back of a trife.

He stuck Pratt's pistol against the back of its head and pulled the trigger, blowing its brains out without hesitation and without slowing down. Another trife ahead spun to confront him, and he put a bullet in that one too. His ATCS started filling in the data from his camera and sensors, passing it to the Marines behind him as he ran point, a faster runner than Washington could ever be.

He entered the corridor leading to the bridge. There were trife here too, but he didn't slow as he charged past them, blowing by before they could react. He heard the gunfire and saw the red marks vanish from tactical, his Vultures so close on his heals he could almost feel Washington's hot breath on his neck.

He kept running, following a slightly curved passageway toward the bridge. It took him twenty seconds to reach the door to the bridge, finding it already open. The lights inside were flickering, and he could see the shapes of trife directly ahead of him.

He started shooting, cutting the first two down. The demons hissed and whirled around, recognizing the new threat. Caleb came to a sudden stop. There were so damn many of them. Thirty at least. His eyes tracked to Major Jackson, bloody on the floor in front of the holotable. Then they shifted to Major Ng, also dead.

Was anyone still alive in there?

The trife rushed him, too many for him to kill at once. Fortunately, he wasn't alone. Washington and Sho were still close enough to assist, and they opened fire on the demons as they started pouring from the bridge, cutting the creatures down one after another. Caleb jumped back, firing his sidearm into the ones who got too close.

Pratt, Gurshaw, Ning, and Hafizi followed after, joining the assault. What had been a massacre a moment before became a sudden rout, the demons dying in a hurry.

"Lieutenant Jones!" Caleb shouted. "Lieutenant!"

He entered the bridge. A trife jumped at him from the shadows, and a gunshot rang out, catching it in the temple and knocking it down.

Caleb traced the muzzle flash to a dark hand, and from the hand to the bloody face of Lieutenant Jones.

"Sir!" he said. The others trailed into the room, sweeping the area.

"It's done, Lieutenant," a woman said from the other

side of the station where Lieutenant Jones was standing. "We're on autopilot."

The lieutenant smiled. "Hell, Sergeant. You couldn't have cut that any closer. Have your Marines secure the bridge. We have another complication."

Chapter 25

Washington guarded the closed hatch to the bridge, keeping his rifle trained on it in case it slid open again. Sho took the vent on the port side, Hafizi the starboard vent. Caleb, Lieutenant Jones, and Captain Rogers gathered around the holotable. Pratt and his two squad mates were guarding the bridge from outside.

The room was a mess. There were dead trife every-where Caleb looked – slumped over the consoles, curled up on the floor. There was even one hanging from a coolant pipe on the ceiling. Everyone who wasn't standing at the table or guarding the room was dead, including General Watkins. Lieutenant Jones told Caleb that he and Rogers would have joined them as corpses if the Vultures hadn't shown when they did, distracting the trife and saving their lives long enough for the captain to activate the autopilot.

The ship's computer would manage the rest of the journey from their current position just outside of Earth's orbit all the way to their destination, leaving the surviving humans free to figure out how to salvage the disaster.

"What's the complication, sir?" Caleb asked, as soon as

they were all settled.

"Let's start with the basics," Lieutenant Jones said. "General Watkins is dead." He motioned to the corner where Caleb assumed the general had fallen, though he couldn't see the body in the dimness of the failing lights. "Major Jackson, Major Ng, both dead."

"Doctor Valentine, sir?" Sho asked, smirking.

"I don't know. She was on the bridge right before the attack. There's a research module installed closer to Metro, here." Lieutenant Jones brought up the partial map of the Deliverance on the holotable and pointed to an area between Metro and the hangar. "I'm not that familiar with the ship's systems, but since we don't have a dark spot there like we do here," he pointed to the empty holes in the projection, "I'm guessing they still have full power and were able to seal themselves off."

"Wishful thinking," Sho said.

"The modules all have their own control systems," Captain Rogers said. "Subnet worked into the main ship's computer. They have limited access to the main systems, but you wouldn't be able to fly the Deliverance from down there. Anyway, now that we're in space it doesn't matter. The computer can handle the job from here to Proxima."

"Proxima, ma'am?" Caleb said. "Is that what they're calling Earth-6 now?"

"No," Jones replied. "That's why Valentine was on the bridge. Command decided to redirect us to the Proxima system, four light years away."

"Four light years? That's twenty years travel time, right sir?"

"Approximately."

Caleb smiled. "So we're good. I mean, we don't have to go to sleep, sir."

"We'll get to that," Captain Rogers said, glancing at

Lieutenant Jones.

"Yes, ma'am."

"Back to the basics," Lieutenant Jones said. "Major Lyle is the highest ranking officer on the ship." The lieutenant tapped on the control surface of the holotable, activating the comm. "Major, are you still with us?"

"I am, Adam."

"Ultimately, the fate of the Deliverance is yours, sir," Jones said.

"Not completely mine," Lyle replied. "Military chain-of-command is well and good, but the situation we're in now, we need to break down some of the protocols and focus on survival. If you have ideas, Lieutenant, I want to hear them."

"Captain Rogers is second," Lieutenant Jones continued. "And then me."

"But, sir?" Caleb said, recognizing the tone of the man's voice.

"I'm getting to it, Sergeant. Looking at the sensor grid, we've still got a minimum of four hundred trife loose in the ship, not counting what's hidden in the dark spots. The largest group looks like it's headed aft, which makes sense since there's a ton of energy flowing through the reactors to the main thrusters. They'll be looking to feed and recover."

"And start a new colony," Doctor Valentine said over the comm, interrupting them.

"Doctor Valentine?" Major Lyle said.

"Did you patch her in?" Captain Rogers whispered to Lieutenant Jones. He shook his head.

"I've been watching events unfolding," Valentine said. "I had Harry hack into the bridge comm system controls from Research because I wanted to help. I wasn't expecting you Space Force Marines to be moving ahead without us."

"Why wouldn't we?" Captain Rogers said. "You're a civilian, and this is a military ship."

"No, Samantha, this isn't a military ship. Check the protocols. The moment the Deliverance left Earth's orbit, it was to be converted to a peacetime vessel. A civilian vessel. The military was to be disbanded save for the Guardians, who were to fall under a special status as law enforcement agents."

"Doctor, I don't think the protocols apply in this situation," Major Lyle said.

"Of course you don't. You're a Marine. Marines never want to give up their control."

"With all due respect, Doctor. I think you can agree that there is still a sound reason to maintain what's left of the military presence on the Deliverance? We have at least two hundred trife loose on the ship."

"I understand that, Major. But wouldn't you then assume it would be wise to include the science team that has spent the last two years trying to understand the xenotrife and formulate a means to combat them effectively in the damned conversation?"

Caleb winced at the harshness of Doctor Valentine's tone. So did the others. She did have a point, though.

"Haven't you caused enough trouble already?" Sho said. "Your delay is the whole reason we're in this – "

"Private, be quiet," Major Lyle said.

Sho's mouth snapped shut.

"Okay, Doctor. You're in anyway. Let's forget the past and focus on what we need to do now. We've got trife spreading across the Deliverance."

"As I was saying, they're going to try to start a nest. Maybe multiple nests."

"Don't they need a Queen for that?" Lieutenant Jones asked.

"Interesting thing about the trife, Lieutenant. When they don't have a Queen but want to make a nest, they'll elect one, and the community, no matter how small, will both generate and transmit the genetic material to make that happen."

"You're saying they can turn one of themselves into a Queen?" Major Lyle said.

"Exactly."

"Shit."

"Exactly."

"We need to get after these bastards as soon as possible," Lyle said. "Lieutenant Jones, take Sergeant Card and — "

"Hold on, Major," Lieutenant Jones said. "You're forgetting the complication." He tapped his finger on the second largest group of trife. "These uglies look like they're headed for Metro. What do you think, Doctor?"

"Agreed, Lieutenant," Valentine said. "They can sense the people inside. They'll want to get at them."

"Isn't Metro sealed, sir?" Caleb asked.

"Mostly," Lieutenant Jones replied. "They won't be able to get through unless someone tries to go in or out."

"I'm already inside," Major Lyle said. "Who else is out there that has access?"

"Me, sir," Jones said. "I think that's it. But that isn't my point."

"What is your point, Lieutenant?" Valentine asked.

"Back to basics," Jones said. "We have a number of trife loose on the ship. We have a total of twenty Marines if we all pull together. I recommend trying to regroup in the Marine module as soon as we're done here."

"I'll send the orders out to the remaining units now," Major Lyle said.

Caleb heard the Major's message in his helmet comm a

moment later, calling the Marines back to the module. So few were left to respond. How the hell were they going to do this?

"I hope we can get the trife off the Deliverance," Jones continued. "But we have to have a contingency in case we can't."

"A contingency, sir?" Caleb said.

"I think I know where you're going with this, Lieutenant," Captain Rogers said. "I'm not sure I'm on board with that idea."

"We can't wait until we fail. It might be too late by then."

"Too late for what, sir?" Sho asked.

"He wants to close off Metro," Caleb said, his heart beginning to sink. "Permanently."

"What?"

"That's part of it, Sergeant," Jones confirmed. "But only one small part. Doctor, how long can the trife survive in an environment like this?"

"With access to an energy source?" Valentine replied. "It's hard to say. We only have a two-year history with the creatures. We know they can reproduce quite quickly. We haven't determined a potential lifespan of a single trife, let alone a nest."

"Based on what you know about them, what would be your educated guess?"

Valentine was silent for a long moment. Caleb wondered if it was the longest time she had spent in silence in her life. "A little over a hundred years. But that's still a guess."

"Lieutenant," Major Lyle said. "I don't know if this is the right move."

"Sir, like I said earlier, it's your call, but you wanted to hear my thoughts."

"I do."

"It isn't his call," Valentine said. "Not in isolation. Not now. The Deliverance is a civilian vessel. That's spelled out quite clearly in the protocols. Having trife on board doesn't change that."

"What are you suggesting then, Doctor?" Lyle snapped.

"A vote."

"We don't have time to have everyone on this ship vote every decision."

"Not everyone on this ship. Everyone on the comm channel. Including my team."

Caleb looked over at Lieutenant Jones. The lieutenant's jaw was tight, his anger evident.

"Can we focus on killing the damn trife, instead of nitpicking protocol?" he said.

"I'm sorry, Lieutenant," Valentine said. "But the actions we take now will shape the actions we take in the future. I'm not willing to give up my seat at the table because of the trife, and neither is my team."

"Could somebody tell me what it is we're planning to do?" Sho asked. "I seem to be the only one who hasn't already worked it out."

"Step one; we reprogram the ship's computer such that it will remain at a fixed distance from Proxima as long as there are trife detected on board. We don't want the computer landing us and letting the creatures run rampant on our new homeworld. Step two, we lock down Metro. I mean sealed. No one goes in or out once we're set. Only one identification chip should have access. Step three, we take volunteers from the remaining Marines. I only want volunteers. Our new Guardians. They'll try to cleanse the trife from the ship. If they succeed, they follow the proto-cols as originally designed, at reduced strength. If they fail, when we reach Proxima we contact the ships that arrived ahead of us and make them aware of our situation. There's a chance we'll be able to work out a plan to either get the trife off the Deliverance or at the very least get the people of Metro out."

"If we can rely on the rest of the fleet to help us with the trife, why not have everyone enter Metro?" Captain Rogers asked.

"There are two to three hundred of them right now," Jones replied. "In twenty years, there could be three thousand. Or thirty-thousand."

"Enough of them to make hitting the Deliverance with a few nukes a more viable option," Caleb said. "Let's see the bastards survive space."

"Let's hope it doesn't come to that."

"Yes, sir."

"I don't like it," Major Lyle said. "We're going to lock ourselves in the city, surrounded by the enemy? We have forty-thousand souls inside Metro. Why not arm them and have them help kill the trife?"

"That's a terrible idea," Valentine said.

"Why?"

"Sir, with all due respect," Caleb said. "I've been in the field almost since the beginning. I think you'd agree me and my team have a lot of experience against the xenotrife. If you give civilians guns and put them face-to-face with a trife, ninety percent of them will freeze in fear."

"And when they freeze, they die," Sho said.

"Beyond that, the Deliverance is a closed system. The passages are too tight for more than a few people to get into a clear line of fire at one time. I don't believe adding more bodies will make fighting them any more efficient. In fact, I'd argue in the opposite."

"I have to agree with the jarhead on this one," Valentine said.

Caleb's jaw tightened. Did she have to be such a bitch all the time?

"I agree with Sergeant Card as well," Lieutenant Jones said, giving Caleb a long-suffering look.

"If we pull everyone into Metro..." Captain Rogers said. "...if we tuck in like a snail in a shell like you suggested, Lieutenant, when we get to Proxima we'll have not only the United States fleet but the entire global output of generation ships to help solve the equation. I would think a nuke would be the last option considering the number of lives at stake."

"That may be true ma'am," Lieutenant Jones said. "I hope it would be true. But that's why I want volunteers. Nobody out here who doesn't want to be out here. There's a chance they can clean the trife off the ship. That would make things so much easier."

Captain Rogers nodded. "Okay. I can't argue that. If people want to try, they have a right to try."

"Unless someone has a better idea?" Lieutenant Jones said. "Doctor Valentine, what about you?"

"I'm on board with your plan, Lieutenant," she replied. "But me and my team will be staying outside Metro in the Research module."

"That's not what we were just discussing."

"That's not up for debate. We have important work that we're continuing. If things go well, we might even be able to form another option to get rid of the trife. The Research module is self-sufficient. We have food, water, and stasis pods. I've got six people down here with me. What I will need are two or three of your volunteers to assist in locking down the module, helping to make the ventilation trife-proof and ensure the demons can't get in."

"I don't know if we'll be able to spare two or three

people. I don't know how many we're going to get."

"Or my team can vote with Major Lyle to send the civilians out to fight."

Caleb met Lieutenant Jones' angry gaze. Was Doctor Valentine for real? Was she willing to use the civilians in Metro as a bargaining chip to get her way?

"Major Lyle, you can't seriously be thinking about accepting that outcome?" Jones said.

"I am thinking about it," Major Lyle said. "I respect Sergeant Card's opinion. I do. But I also feel confident that we can clean the trife off the ship and take less than fifty percent casualties."

"Fifty percent?" Caleb said. "That's twenty-thousand people."

"I can do the math, Sergeant," Lyle said. "That's also less than all of us dying."

Caleb started shaking his head almost subconsciously. He could barely believe what he was hearing. Had the trife put so much fear into people they were willing to sacrifice any signs of morality to save their own asses, or get their own way?

He already knew the answer to that. He had seen it plenty of times on the ground. Mothers leaving their children behind, even though the trife didn't attack children. People killing one another to escape the demons. Looting, murder, and worse. The trife hadn't just started a war. They had turned large swaths of humankind into worse monsters than they were.

Those monsters had joined them here too.

"We're wasting time arguing," Captain Rogers said. "While the trife are moving freely around the ship."

"What do you say, Lieutenant?" Valentine asked.

"I'll get you two Marines to help out."

"Then you have my support."

"Major Lyle?" Jones asked.

"Fine, Lieutenant. I said I would be open to your opinion and I meant it."

"Thank you, sir. Doctor Valentine, can Harry make the adjustments to the control systems to tie the navigation into the life sign detectors?"

"He says he can."

"Sir," Caleb said. "What about the dark spots?"

"Private Delfina said there was a broken conduit. Doctor Valentine, do you have any electrical engineers on your team?"

"As a matter of fact, I do."

"I thought she was a geneticist?" Sho whispered to Caleb. "Why does she have a computer hacker and an electrical engineer on her team?"

"I don't know," Caleb replied.

"Okay," Jones said. "Let's put this plan in action. Everyone on the bridge will head down to the Marine module to regroup. Major, Doctor, I'll contact you from there once we're organized."

"Agreed," Valentine said.

"Confirmed," Major Lyle said. "But seeing how General Watkins is dead, the ship is technically a civilian vessel, and I'm now inside Metro instead of acting as a Guardian, I suppose it's logical that I should take on his position as Governor of the city."

"It makes sense," Captain Rogers agreed.

"No argument from me, sir," Lieutenant Jones said.

"Good. I'll be waiting for your next communication, Lieutenant."

"Will do, Governor. Sergeant Card."

"Yes, sir?"

"Get us to the Marine module in one piece."

"Yes, sir."

Chapter 26

Caleb got everyone from the bridge to the module alive, the resistance from the trife limited in the direction they were headed. As Lieutenant Jones had noted, most of the creatures were spreading out in groups, heading for different parts of the ship, and likely planning to create new nests.

It gave them a small break in the action, a small space in time to regroup, but they had to be quick, before Doctor Valentine could tell them to get a move on, before the trife would solidify their foothold. They all knew how quickly the trife could establish a nest and multiply..

The remaining Marines were already present when Caleb and the rest of the group entered the barracks section of the module. The Marines were covered in sweat and blood, obviously tired and downtrodden. More than a few were injured, and at least two were in no condition to continue the fight, having lost a limb and quickly slapped a patch over the wound to keep from bleeding out. He had never seen a group of warriors look so defeated.

Not that he blamed them. They were supposed to be

safe. Free from the trife. It was supposed to be the smallest of victories, but a victory all the same. Instead, they had gotten their asses handed to them. Again. They had lost more of their friends and comrades and were thinking about the Deliverance suffering the same fate as Earth.

"A-TEHN-SHUN! Officers on deck," he barked as he entered ahead of Captain Rogers and Lieutenant Jones. Maybe Doctor Valentine thought the ship was civilian now and they should treat it as such despite the situation. He was holding on to the one thing that made sense to him. He would always be a Marine first.

The rest of the Marines came to their feet, some more readily than others. Their attention was sloppy and disheveled, but he knew the lieutenant wouldn't allow it to last.

"Straighten up," Lieutenant Jones snapped as he entered the space and saw them. "You're Space Force Marines, damn it, not some football team that just lost the damned Super Bowl."

"I miss the Super Bowl," someone said.

"We all miss the Super Bowl," Jones said. "But it isn't coming back. None of what you knew before the trife is coming back. We're Marines, and it's our job, our duty, to be an example to everyone."

"Like who?" another Marine said. "There's no one left."

"Bullshit. There are forty-thousand civilians on board. Do you want them to see you like this? Do you want them to see you defeated? Broken? Feeling sorry for yourselves like little babies? Marine up and come to attention properly!"

The Marines made an audible snapping sound as they stood up straight and proud, joining Caleb and the Vultures at attention.

"That's better," Lieutenant Jones said. He paused a moment, walking to the center of the room with Captain Rogers, making eye contact with each of the Marines. "Most of you know me, even if we haven't served together. I'm Lieutenant Adam Jones. This is Captain Samantha Rogers. I hate to say it, but we're the ranking officers on this boat."

A soft murmur went through the group. They knew what the statement meant.

"What happened to Major Lyle, sir?" one of them asked. "He just sent us a comm message a few minutes ago."

"He's in Metro," Captain Rogers said. "As the acting Governor."

"Lucky bastard," someone said.

"We have to face the situation head-on," Lieutenant Jones said. "The trife are on board. We did our best to hold them at the hangar, but we weren't able to do it. That isn't the fault of any one of us. We did the best we could. We have to accept that we lost this round, and we have to come back stronger. That's what Marines do. Isn't it?"

"Sir, yes, sir!" the group shouted, less enthusiastically than the lieutenant wanted.

"I said, isn't it?"

"Sir, yes, sir!" they said again, gaining some strength.

"Damn it, how the hell are we going to get the trife off our ship if we don't believe we can get the trife off our ship? Are you ready to go blast some more trife ass?"

"Sir, yes, sir!" they all shouted, loud and firm.

Lieutenant Jones smiled. "You're damn right. Captain Rogers and I haven't been sitting on our asses while you've been out there dying. We have a path forward."

"Everybody dies?" someone joked.

"No."

"We're going to lock down Metro," Captain Rogers said. "Seal it off from the trife and keep the civilians safe."

"The civilians? What about us?"

"Anyone who wants to join the civilians in Metro is free to do so." Lieutenant Jones pointed to the two Marines who had lost parts of their arms. "You two are joining the population."

"Sir, I can still fight," one of them said. "Give me a replacement, and I'll be good to go."

"We don't have any replacements on board," the Lieutenant replied. "We weren't expecting to need them."

"I'm supposed to live the rest of my life without an arm?"

"There are replicators in Metro. They can produce a prosthetic, but not as quickly as we need you."

"Understood, sir. Still, I want to help."

"I appreciate that Corporal," Jones said. "We'll find other ways for you to help."

"Yes, sir."

"We're looking for volunteers to stay outside the city. Your first mission will be to eliminate the trife from the ship. Your second mission will be to take over as Guardians for the remainder of the journey. If you want to stay and fight, join me here in the center of the room."

Caleb's mind flashed to Sheriff Aveline. He could see her face, picture her smile and her laugh. The sparkle in her eyes. They had hit it off so well in such a short amount of time. Less than an hour with her had given him pause in his decision to be a Guardian. He had never been that concerned with women. His duty was his passion, especially after the trife came.

Now he had to choose.

It was still an easy choice.

"I'm in, Lieutenant," he said, stepping forward.

Lieutenant Jones bit his lip and nodded. His expression was an apology that it had come to this.

"I'm in too," Sho said, joining Caleb.

"Sho," Caleb said. "What about – "

"Save it, Sergeant. I wasn't allowed to be a Guardian before." She looked at Jones. "You can't afford to leave us women out now, can you, Lieutenant? You'll lose a third of your pool of volunteers."

"No, I can't," Jones agreed. "If you want in, you're in."

Hafizi and Washington stepped in with Caleb. So did Pratt. Ten more Marines followed them.

"What about you, Captain Rogers?" Sho asked.

"I'm sorry," she said. "I'm a pilot, not a Marine." She moved away from the group near Lieutenant Jones, adding herself to the small group on the sidelines.

Of those staying behind, only the two Marines who had lost their arms didn't look guilty about the decision. They wanted it enough they were making it regardless of what their conscience was telling him. Caleb understood. He could never put anyone else over his duty – not when there were lives at risk – but that didn't mean it wasn't tempting.

"Okay," Lieutenant Jones said. "You have five minutes to relieve yourselves of your gear in the armory and meet me back here. Sergeant Card, Private Sho, Private Washington, you'll help me escort the civilians to Metro."

"Civilians?" one of the Marines said.

"That's right," Jones replied. "As soon as you step through the hatch into Metro, you become a Metro citizen. There's no military inside. No Space Force. No Marines. You can talk to Law to see if they'll take you on as a deputy. Otherwise, Governor Lyle will find work for you."

"Yes, sir," the Marine said. He sounded disappointed. It still didn't change his mind. He joined the other Marines in retreating from the barracks toward the armory to return their gear.

"Sergeant Pratt, you're in charge down here until we get back. Get these Marines ready to fight again. The trife are looking to establish nests deeper in the ship. We need to make sure that doesn't happen."

"Yes, sir," Pratt said.

"Sergeant Card, come with me. The rest of you, take a breather. You have five minutes of downtime."

"Yes, sir," the other volunteers said.

"Oh, and welcome to the Guardians."

"Yes, sir!"

Caleb followed Lieutenant Jones out of the barracks, through a short corridor to the module's central control room, where the Master Sergeant was waiting.

"Sir," the Master Sergeant said, coming to attention.

"As you were," Lieutenant Jones said. "Master Sergeant Gold, can you link me in with the Research module?"

"Yes, sir," Gold replied, moving to the nearest terminal. He slid his hands over the control panel and then pointed at the lieutenant to indicate they were connected.

"Doctor Valentine," Lieutenant Jones said. "I have fourteen volunteers."

"Congratulations, Lieutenant," she replied. Caleb couldn't tell if she was being snarky or sincere.

"I'll be sending Sergeant Pratt and Private Ning to assist you with your preparations as soon as I finish delivering the new Metro citizens to the city. Figure about twenty minutes."

"That will do nicely, thank you Lieutenant."

"How is your man coming on the networking hack?"

"It's only been ten minutes, Lieutenant. He'll get it done. Don't worry."

"Right. Jones out."

He slid his finger across his throat to signal Gold to cut the comm and then turned to Caleb.

"Cal, I'm really sorry about bringing you into Metro to meet Lily. I figured you two might gel and you would change your mind about the city. Win-win for both of us."

"You don't need to apologize, sir. I get it. And yeah, we did gel. But my place is here for as long as the Deliverance is under threat."

"I knew you would be pragmatic about it. But I wanted you to know that I recognize what I did and the way it was resolved."

"Thank you, sir. That's why you'll always have my deepest respect."

"I don't know that I will, Sergeant. There's another reason I pulled you aside, beyond an apology."

Caleb watched Jones' face. The lieutenant's expression shifted to match the Marines who had decided to lock themselves in Metro.

"Sir?" he said, shocked and saddened before anything more was said.

"The only thing that's kept me going is knowing I would be getting out of this," Jones said.

"We'll get out of this," Caleb replied. "We'll kill the wayward trife, and you can go to Metro inside of a week."

"We hope," Lieutenant Jones said. "You're a strong Marine, Cal, but there are no guarantees. I want to stand with you. I want to keep fighting. But there's a big part of me telling me I can't. Not after all I've been through. Not after everything I've seen. I had a wife. A family. The trife took that from me. I know that isn't unique, but I want to have that again before I die. And I can in Metro."

Caleb stared at the lieutenant. This man had been his mentor, his role model for over a year. He couldn't believe he was going to give it up when the Guardians needed him the most.

"Is that the real reason you wanted volunteers, sir?" Caleb asked.

"Don't call me sir, Sergeant," Jones replied. "Call me Adam. I'm a civilian too." He reached up to his uniform, taking hold of the name patch on his jacket and tearing it off. His jaw was tight, his eyes pained. "I'm sorry, Cal."

"You set us up to die out here," Caleb hissed. "How could you do this to me, Adam? How the hell can you do this to them?" His voice rose as he spoke until he was screaming.

"I deserve whatever you want to give me," Adam said. "But you aren't going to die. You're going to take this group of Space Force Marines, and you're going to make everyone in Metro proud. That's what you do, Sergeant Card. That's what you are."

"You do realize once you go, that makes Master Sergeant Gold the ranking enlisted?" Caleb said, unable to think of anything else to say. "No offense to him, but he's been behind a desk since before the trife came to Earth."

"The situation is changing faster than we can make rules to keep pace," Adam said. "You were slated as a lead for your Guardianship cycle. I think you're the only lead in the program who's still alive. Since we're moving to Guardian Protocol, that makes you the CO. Guardian Alpha, in the new parlance."

"This isn't what I wanted," Caleb said.

"It's not what I wanted either, Alpha," Adam said. "But this is how it has to be. I'm sorry."

Caleb nodded, still internally furious. "Fine. I'll get you to the city safely, Mr. Jones, or Vice-Governor Jones, or whatever the hell you're called now. Leave the trife to me. I wish we were still going to Earth-6 so I would be assured I would never have to look at your miserable face again."

Caleb turned and stormed away from Adam, headed back to the barracks. He didn't have any more time to worry about what the other man did or didn't do.

He had a mission to accomplish.

Chapter 27

Caleb led the civilians, including the former Lieutenant Jones, up from the Marine module on Deck Twenty-nine, through empty corridors to the lift to Deck Sixteen, and from Deck Sixteen toward the bow in the direction of Metro's south entrance. He was in the lead of the small unit, with Sho beside him and Washington and Hafizi in the rear. He had already informed them of the former lieutenant's decision, and they had taken it in stride, keeping their comments to themselves, at least until they had delivered the group to safety.

Doctor Valentine stayed in contact with them, monitoring their exodus from the Research module's sub-network terminal, watching the sensors for signs of trife, both their current location and suspected paths. The goal for the moment was to avoid confrontation, to get the civilians into the city and make it back to Deck Twenty-nine in one piece. Once that was done, Caleb would start worrying about coming up with a plan to get the trife off the Deliverance.

There was only one group of trife that threatened

them on the way, a small segment of five demons who were wandering across their path, likely in search of any wayward survivors. Caleb kept the group well away from them, circling the area and back to the entrance to Metro.

The second group of trife had taken root there, hanging out near the hatch in case it opened, somehow aware of all the people on the other side. Caleb and Washington moved in on them first, coming hard around the corner of an adjacent corridor and gunning them down before they had much of a chance to react.

"Valentine, any reaction from the others?" Caleb asked. His ATCS showed the area was clear, but he couldn't see anything the sensors on his or his unit's SOS couldn't see.

"Negative, Alpha," Valentine replied. She seemed to have gained a new respect for him after Lieutenant Jones informed her of the change in command. Caleb supposed some respect was better than none. "If they heard you, they aren't interested."

"Roger that," Caleb replied. "Adam, you have the key." It still felt strange to call the lieutenant by his first name, but there was no way he wasn't going to do it.

Adam approached the security panel, putting his wrist to it and letting it scan his ID chip. The door thunked and began sliding open.

"Alpha, we have movement," Valentine said as soon as the hatch started to rise. "Hurry them in; you've got three groups rushing your way that we can see, nearly a hundred in total."

"Shit," Caleb muttered. "No time for goodbyes. Get in and close the hatch."

The hatch was large and heavy and hadn't been designed to open and close in a hurry. It rose at a snail's pace, revealing a few pairs of feet on the other side.

"Vultures, cover the rear, full line defense fire. Hawks, we need you at the Metro entrance."

He had organized the Guardians in three teams of four, sticking with the names of birds of prey as callsigns for the units. The Hawks were headed by Corporal Johansen, a muscular woman with blonde hair and hard eyes.

"Roger, Alpha," Johansen said. "We're on our way."

"Alpha, here they come," Valentine warned.

"Already?" Hafizi said.

The trife had covered the distance in seconds. They had to be moving at a full sprint.

Caleb glanced back. The hatch was almost halfway open, and the civilians were beginning to drop and crawl through the space. Adam waved them on, staying behind to keep them organized.

Caleb shouldered his carbine and moved to the corner. His ATCS registered the incoming trife as a red blob on his right.

"Right flank," he announced to the other Vultures. "Skirmishers."

The squad organized quickly, getting in position as the trife suddenly stopped, still out of visual.

"They stopped," he said. "Valentine?"

"I don't know," she replied. "All of them just stopped."

"Watch the vents," Adam warned behind him.

Caleb scanned the corridor. There were vents on either side. How many shafts were there across the ship?

"Vultures, wedge formation," he said, switching their focus to all-around defense. There was a still in the air he didn't like. The calm before the storm. "Valentine, are their ventilation shafts inside the main hold? Inside Metro?"

"There are, but they have a locking mechanism to seal

them off in case of a hull breach. The city is airtight. Alpha, it looks like the size of the groups are shrinking."

"Roger." Caleb wasn't sure what that meant. Were they finding a path through the ventilation?

He looked back to the hatch. It had nearly finished opening, and the rest of the civilians had gone through. A small party had waited for them on the other side, including Governor Lyle and not all that surprisingly, Sheriff Aveline.

They made short eye contact, offering one another a nod and a smile. He could sense her support in her expression, confirming that he was doing the right thing. He started turning back, to watch the corridors.

Something fell from the ceiling beside him, nearly hitting him in the shoulder. He jerked aside as the large piece of grating clattered onto the floor, and a trife dropped out of it, claws already slashing at him.

It happened so fast. He heard a pair of gunshots, and the trife was thrown back and into the wall beside him with two large holes in its chest. He jumped back as two more came out, landing right in front of him. He shot one, and the other was hit from somewhere behind him.

He spared a half-second to look back at the hatch. Aveline had her sidearm, a large silver revolver, in hand. Smoke was leaking from the end of it.

"Good luck, Caleb Card," she shouted as the hatch began to close again.

"Good hunting, Alpha," Adam said, the last to duck through.

Then it was back to the fight. The trife at the intersection were moving in with sudden ferocity, charging the Vultures in an effort to get through them, through the hatch, and into the city. The others were already shooting, the corridors suddenly so thick with oily black flesh and teeth it was impossible not to hit them.

Another demon fell from the overhead shaft, dropping in the middle of the Vultures. It didn't go after Caleb, instead pivoting and jumping on Sho, tackling her and knocking her to the ground. It raised a claw to strike, and Caleb hit it with the carbine, putting three rounds into its back. It hissed and fell over.

Sho was only down for a few seconds, but the loss of her firepower gave the trife the extra push they needed. They poured in on the group like an oil spill, threatening to drown them.

"Fall back!" Caleb shouted.

There wasn't much room to move, but at least they could concentrate their firepower. The Vultures pulled back, moving toward the closing hatch.

"Spread out!" he heard Sheriff Aveline say. They did, and he glanced back and saw her and another sheriff lying prone behind the hatch. The sheriffs helped fire into the demons as the creatures came at them, the short corridor ahead of the blast door forcing them into a bottleneck.

"This is Hawk One," Corporal Johansen said. "Swooping in to save your asses Vultures."

The trife ahead of them collapsed, taking sudden fire from the left flank. The Hawks appeared a moment later, the passages cleared.

"Nice work, Hawks," Caleb said, taking the opportunity to let himself breathe again. "Perfect timing. Valentine, what's the status?"

"They're drawing back, Alpha," she replied. "I think they realized they couldn't get through you."

"Roger. Smart bastards, setting us up like that."

"They almost seem smarter without a queen," she

replied. "It's interesting. We haven't had much of a chance to study them in this kind of environment before."

"I don't want to study them. I want to kill them."

"You will. But I'll be taking notes. I'm sure Command will find them useful in the years ahead."

"Whatever makes you happy, Doctor."

"I see we agree on something for once, Alpha."

Caleb shook his head. The woman was impossible. He turned back to the hatch. It was only a foot or so above the floor. He leaned down to look in one last time.

"See you on the other side, Sergeant," Sheriff Aveline said, reaching her hand through the gap.

He took it and squeezed. "Are we keeping that date?"

"Absolutely."

He let go of her hand. She pulled it back. A few seconds later, the hatch sealed.

Caleb leaned back against it, closing his eyes and resting for a second. Even with the assisted strength of the SOS, he was exhausted.

He opened his eyes when he sensed Private Washington standing over him. The big man held out his hand, and Caleb let himself be pulled easily to his feet.

"How are you feeling, Wash?" he asked.

Washington gave him a thumbs-up.

"Good. Valentine, how quickly do we need to hit the group headed for the thrusters before the queening?"

"Six to ten hours at best, Alpha. Why?"

"My Guardians are exhausted. Hell, I'm exhausted. A few hours to regroup would do us a world of good."

"Understood. Keep in mind that every minute we aren't putting pressure on the trife is a minute they're preparing to put more pressure on us."

Caleb sighed. He had to balance the enemy's comfort with his team's. "Roger that. We're headed back to the mod to plan our next steps." He checked his ATCS. "I see Pratt and Ning made it to you okay."

"They did. I've already got them welding vents."

"How long before I can have them back?"

"Four hours or so."

"What about the changes to the ship's computer?"

"Harry's nearly done with the updates."

"It's fortunate you have a guy like Harry on your team, Doctor."

"Are you trying to imply something, Alpha?"

Caleb smiled. Of course he was. Like Sho had mentioned, there was something about Valentine and her team that didn't quite fit, and now that he had a short break from fighting demons, he had something else to occupy his thoughts. "I don't know, am I?"

Valentine fell silent. She wasn't going to answer his unspoken question.

At least he had shut her up.

Chapter 28

The Guardians – everyone except Pratt and Ning – gathered in the Marine module's CIC. Caleb had taken the few minutes needed to get out of his SOS, while Washington remained suited up, guarding the entrance to the module. Caleb had already set his third unit, the Raptors, to welding the vents in their module similarly to how Valentine and her team were getting it done, creating a mostly safe haven for the Marines to work from.

He stood in the back of the room, near the main command terminal. Like the Research module, it was sub-networked into the ship's primary computer and had access to some of the functions, most importantly the sensor readings. Not that it meant all that much since the trife had quickly discovered how to avoid the sensors. Valentine had informed him that Harry would be working on getting a map of the ventilation system delivered as soon as he was done with the programming updates, so they would at least have an idea where the demons might try to hit them.

He pulled the map of the Deliverance up anyway,

showing the locations where the trife had spread. There were still three main groups that had gone in opposite directions, the largest to the aft and two smaller groups toward the bow. He didn't know why those two groups had split off or what their overall intent was. The link between the reactor and the thrusters was the best place to absorb the energy the demons used as food, so it didn't make a lot of overall sense.

He was sure they had a logic to it. The creature's actions on the ship had already proven they were smarter than he ever imagined. And if it wasn't intelligence, then their instincts were more evolved than he had thought. Nobody had ever considered locking trife in a maze to see what they would do. Now he wished they had. With all his experience in the field against the aliens, this was completely uncharted territory.

"We'll get a more detailed plan together to go after the larger group once Valentine's team provides the layout of the potential access points the trife might use. I gathered you here in the meantime so we can organize smaller reconnaissance of the groups in the bow, and so we can discuss strategies and capabilities. I know none of us were planning on spending our time on the Deliverance this way. Even as Guardians, I was expecting to be walking the ship and making calls to Metro for engineers every once in a while, and otherwise watching a lot of streams and playing a lot of poker."

The Guardians laughed at that.

"Bastards are keeping us from having any fun," Sho said.

"We can have all the fun you want," one of the Marines replied. "Come on over here."

Caleb whirled to face him. A younger man, in good

shape, dark hair and a chiseled face. "Stand up, Private," he snapped.

The man stood, his face already flushing.

"What's your name?" Caleb asked.

"Shiro, Alpha," the man replied.

Caleb pointed at Sho. "Private Shiro, when you look at this Marine, what do you see?"

"Uh. I. Uh."

"What do you see, Private?" Caleb said.

"Sarge, you don't need to – " Sho started to say.

"I do," Caleb said. "Here and now, to get this over with." Caleb walked over to the man, getting in his face. "What do you see?" he repeated sharply.

"A fellow Marine."

"A fellow Marine, what?"

"A fellow Marine, Alpha!"

"Are you sure?"

"Yes, Alpha!"

"So you would make the same comment to any of your other fellow Marines?" Caleb asked. "What about to him?" He pointed at Washington.

"I. Uh. No, Alpha."

"Why not?" Caleb said.

"Alpha, I'm not gay."

"And therein lies the problem, Private. Drop and give me push-ups. You don't stop until I tell you that you can stop."

Shiro went to the floor and started doing the push-ups. He was already tired from the fighting, and the added reps weren't doing him any favors. Caleb didn't care. He couldn't afford any one of the Guardians any leeway.

"And by problem, I don't mean you should all be gay or not gay. I don't really care either way. That's none of my damn business. What I do care about is how effective we are as a platoon. We're all this ship has by way of defense. Forty-thousand people are counting on us to protect them. Give that a second to sink in." He paused and waited a few seconds. "There are no men here. There are no women here. There are only Space Force Marines. Guardians. Is it going to be lonely for you out here? Maybe. But any distractions from the mission, from our duty, will be met with swift punishment that's a lot worse than a few push-ups, I promise you that. Is that understood?"

"Yes, Alpha!" the Marines barked in reply.

"Good. Master Sergeant Gold."

"Yes, Alpha?" Gold replied, stepping forward.

"We have a lot of ordnance in the armory. I grabbed the carbine because that's what I'm used to, but I'm open to suggestions. If there's more effective equipment on board, we should be using it."

"Yes, you should," Gold said, smiling. "We've got a dozen P-50 plasma rifles. They were fresh out of R&D when we received them. It's the most modern gun we'll ever see. The cells hold enough fuel for a hundred bolt rounds each, but they also have two firing modes. Single round bolts and a secondary stream mode that acts more like a flamethrower, only its tossing out superheated gas instead."

"Sounds nasty," Caleb said. "What's the downside?"

"The ship's surfaces can only take so much of the heat before they start to melt. So you might be able to stream for a few seconds and burn an entire corridor of trife, but too long and you might melt something critical."

"Good to know."

"We've also got MK-12 assault rifles. They're an upgrade from the carbine you're carrying because they have a larger magazine and are higher caliber. They also have a secondary trigger that fires twenty-millimeter high-density explosive rounds. Again, you have to be more careful with them on board, but if you're in a pinch?" He shrugged. "We have a handful of laser pistols too, again the newest tech out of R&D, but I haven't had a chance to play with them yet. I'd imagine too long a shot would burn a pinhole through the hull and start venting oxygen. We don't want that to happen."

"No, we don't," Caleb agreed. "What about drones? Do we have anything that can help us scout ahead?"

"We have a bunch of Dragonflies," Gold said. "They were originally designed for diagnostic scanning of the ship's conduits since they can fit in small spaces. They have cameras with full infrared, so I think they could come in handy for peeking into the vents."

"Until the trife eat them at least," Sho said.

"There is that."

"Do we need to do anything with them to make them viable in the shafts?"

"No. Set them loose in one and they'll follow it. Unfortunately, they're AI driven, no external control, so if they reach an intersection we can't make them follow the one we want. But otherwise they're plug and play."

"I'll take what I can get," Caleb said. "Hawks."

"Yes, Alpha," Corporal Johansen said, stepping forward.

"I want you to make the first recon." He looked at the map of the ship and pointed at the smallest group of trife. "Head toward this group here, but don't engage unless they come after you. I want to see how close you can get before they notice you. If you make it to here." He pointed at a spot a few hundred meters from the group. "Stick a Dragonfly in the vent and send it on its way. Use another one to try to reach the demons and see if they react to it."

"Roger that."

"Stay on the comm. We'll keep you informed on trife activity from here. Also, designate someone as your main gunner. Gold, get the Hawks two Dragonflies and a P-50."

"On it, Alpha," Master Sergeant Gold said, leaving the room.

"Sho, Hafizi, you'll assist the Raptors in completing the modifications to the module. Washington, stay on guard until that work is done and we can lock up tight. Then you're all to hit the rack and get as much rest as you can until I need you."

"Yes, Alpha," they replied.

Caleb turned his attention to Private Shiro, whose push-ups had gotten labored while he was talking. He knelt down beside the man. "I trust you've gotten the message, Private?"

"Yes, Alpha," he replied breathlessly.

"Get up and help the others."

Shiro hopped to his feet and joined his squad. Caleb stood up. "Let's go, Guardians. We have a lot of work to do."

Chapter 29

"Approaching corridor nine," Corporal Johansen said, her voice crisp in Caleb's ear.

"I've got you, Hawk One," he replied, splitting his attention between the sensor grid on the display ahead of him and the camera feed running from her helmet to his ATCS.

He hadn't been all that eager to put the SOS on again so soon, especially to stand around the CIC, but it was the best and most effective way to keep an eye on the squad, at least until they fell out of range.

Which they were threatening to do. The network signal on his HUD was down to a single bar, suggesting he would be dropping from their network any moment now. He was thankful to at least have the sensor grid and the more powerful comm link through the ship's network, which would allow him to stay in communication with the Hawks as they approached the first group of trife.

He had ordered them not to engage the demons, but now that they were closing in it was tempting to change those orders. The group was the smallest of the three, and couldn't be composed of more than twenty or thirty trife. It sounded like a lot, but against four well-trained Marines? It was nothing.

Still, he had planned the recon to test the trife's reactions and to sample the data the Dragonflies could provide. To change the parameters now would be risky, and he didn't want to lose any more Marines.

He didn't really want to be in charge, either. Not like this, anyway. He wanted to be out in the field, standing alongside Corporal Johansen and the others. Sticking his neck out, not hiding in the safety of the module.

"Alpha, I'm going to activate one of the Dragonflies in the port side vent," Johansen said.

"Confirmed," he replied. He glanced at Master Sergeant Gold, who tapped on the main terminal's control surface and brought up six individual feeds across the top of the primary display.

He watched Johansen's feed as two of her Marines kneeled next to the vent cover and quickly removed it. Then Johansen reached forward, a tiny robot with delicate wings cupped on the palm of her hand. She spread her fingers and gently tapped the top of the machine. Its eyes immediately started to glow in yellow light, and its tiny, gossamer wings began to flap too fast to be more than a blur.

It slipped out of Johansen's hand and dove into the vent. A moment later the feed from its camera activated in one of the black boxes on the main display, revealing a grayscale view of the shaft's innards.

There wasn't much to see, but a lot of dark metal with solder lines where one piece joined another. Caleb could hear the Dragonfly's wings humming through its audio feed as it skirted a straight line down the tunnel.

"Alpha, we're moving ahead," Johansen announced.

Caleb shifted his attention back to her feed, watching as she led the Hawks down the passageway. He glanced over at the sensor display every few seconds, monitoring the squad's proximity to the trife.

"No movement yet," he said. "Stay on course, take it slow."

"Roger."

Caleb leaned over the terminal, attention flickering from one data source to the next, trying to stay in sync across the views. His job got easier a moment later as the ATCS link went out of range.

"Hawk One, you're off tactical," he said.

"Roger, Alpha," Johansen replied. "Not much to see down here anyway. All the damn corridors look the same."

"She was made to get us from Point A to Point B, not be pretty," Caleb said.

Johansen chuckled. "Copy that."

The new Point B was only twenty years away. He hadn't told anyone else that truth yet. Like Lieutenant Jones, he didn't want to get anyone's hopes up, especially with no guarantee any of them would survive. Would Sheriff Aveline wait that long for their dinner together? He doubted it, but it was fun to think she might.

Caleb glanced over at the Dragonfly's feed. The small robot had shifted itself to the upper left corner of the shaft. It was an odd maneuver, and he couldn't help but wonder why. It had also fallen behind Johansen and her team, its small size unable to carry it very quickly along the route.

"Hawk One, slow down a little. The drone is having trouble keeping up."

"Roger."

"Master Sergeant Gold," Caleb said, calling the older man over and pointing at the feed. "Why do you think it's doing that?"

"I'm not all that familiar with the drones," Gold replied. "They came in late in the preparations, almost as an afterthought. I think they just made them and figured they would pawn them off on us." He smiled. "I can check the diagnostics though, if you'll excuse me."

Caleb moved aside, and Gold used the control surface to open a new screen beneath the Dragonfly's feed. It showed some different graphs and numbers, but they didn't mean anything to him.

"There," Master Sergeant Gold said. "It looks like its picking something up on one of its audio sensors."

"What kind of something?"

"I don't know. It must be coming from the corner of the vent."

"Inside the wall?"

Gold shrugged. "I guess so."

Caleb stared at the drone's view of the shaft for a moment and then switched the terminal's comm channel.

"Valentine, are you there?" he asked.

"Guardian Alpha," a male voice replied. "I'm Doctor Byrnes. Doctor Valentine is busy right now. She asked me to stay at the terminal in case you needed something."

"Can you see if you can find out if there's anything behind the ventilation shafts on Deck Twenty-two near the bow. You can get the position from the sensor grid."

"Standby, Alpha."

Caleb kept his eyes shifting between the grid and the Dragonfly's feed. They stopped moving when he saw a light up ahead in the shaft, coming from the left side.

"Byrnes, scratch that request. I think I've got it."

"Sure thing, Alpha," Byrnes replied. "Let me know if you need anything else."

The Dragonfly moved toward the light. It appeared to be another vent, with thin slits feeding out into some other open space. The drone rotated toward the space, its vision obscured by the metal dividers. It went ahead, ducking beneath the strips and flitting forward and into the room.

It turned again, rotating back the way it had come.

Caleb's breath caught in his throat. His heart started pounding.

Three trife were standing in what appeared to be an access corridor, tall but narrow. They were taking turns slashing at something on the wall.

The Dragonfly was AI-powered, and it hummed its way toward the demons without concern, trying to get a closer look at the area and what they were doing. The trife ignored it until it was right on top of them and Caleb could see what it was they were attacking.

One of four thick conduits running along the passage there.

It was nearly worn away.

The rear trife's head snapped toward the Dragonfly, suddenly realizing the drone was there. The last thing Caleb saw was a set of claws whipping toward the machine, and then its feed went dark.

A moment later the entire module went dark with it.

Chapter 30

"Shit," Caleb said. It took a moment for the night vision sensors in his helmet to register the sudden darkness, and by the time they did the lights in the module were already coming back on. He blinked his eyes rapidly, the flash nearly blinding him. "What the hell was that?"

"My guess would be a power interruption," Master Sergeant Gold said. "Based on what those bugs were doing."

"Why would it affect the module here from all the way up there?"

"I don't know. Maybe they've got some subsystems linked that shouldn't be? The Deliverance was a rush job. Hell, all the generation ships were rush jobs."

Which is why so many parts of it were breaking, and at the worst times. The display was coming back to life, and while the terminal hadn't shut down completely, it had gone into a hibernation state and was only now becoming active again. Caleb reached down and switched the comm channel.

"Hawk One, do you copy?" he said. There was no

response. "Hawk One, this is Guardian Alpha. Do you copy?" Still nothing. "Damn it." He moved around the terminal, grabbing his carbine from its resting place against the front side of the station. "Washington, we're going out there."

Washington flashed his thumb.

"Alpha, I don't think that's the best idea," Master Sergeant Gold said. "We don't know what the trife are doing out there. The sensor grid in that area hasn't come back online."

'Understood. I need to get back into ATCS range so I can at least see what's going on down there. I'll make a decision once I do."

Then he and Washington were through the module hatch and out into the passageway at a run, racing toward the bow of the starship. The area nearby was supposed to be clear, and he wasn't all that concerned about running into any of the demons. Besides, he had Washington.

They made their way forward and then took a stairwell from Deck Six to Deck Twelve, putting less metal between them and the Hawks. The ATCS operated on multiple frequencies and would keep trying them all until it gained a connection. It beeped a moment later, Caleb's HUD showing it was networked with Hawk Four. Private Flores.

"Hawk Four, this is Guardian Alpha," he said. "What's your status?"

"Alpha," Flores said. "Hawk One sent me back to bridge the link after the power went out. The trife attacked us when it did. Hawk Two is down."

Caleb watched his HUD as the rest of the Hawks connected, the mesh network hopping from the squad to Flores to Caleb and back.

The tactical showed the area immediately surrounding the team. It was clear.

"Hawk One, sitrep," Caleb said, coming to a stop.

"Alpha, the trife jumped us when the power went off. About a dozen. We took them out, but not before they snuck up on Corporal Seth. He's dead. It happened so fast."

Caleb could see the red mark on the Corporal's monitor in his HUD. Hawk Three was orange, the SOS indicating a wound to the shoulder.

"Do you think they planned it, Alpha?" Johansen asked. "To turn the power off like that and hit us while our LLVS was adjusting?"

"They aren't that smart," Caleb replied. "I think they went for the conduit to feed, and it just happened to knock out the sensors. And even if they did go for the sensors, they couldn't have known about your helmet's low light vision system. I think part of it was a coincidence."

But only part. And which part? The thought of the trife springing a trap was a scary one. That wasn't how the demons were supposed to fight. Were they adjusting tactics because they didn't have a queen? Or because their numbers were so much fewer than normal? Some people believed the trife had been sent to Earth, delivered by a more intelligent and malevolent alien race. Had the creatures been programmed to act differently in situations like this?

Had they been used on starships before?

Caleb could imagine alien ships being assaulted by trife. Maybe it was like the old days when pirates roamed Earth's seas. Come broadside, gain a hold of the target vessel, and then board and overwhelm the defenses.

Two years ago, he would have thought the idea of space aliens warring with one another was reserved for the science-fiction novels he liked to read and the movies he liked to watch.

This shit wasn't supposed to be real.

"Hawk One, get your team back to base. I intended for your mission to be recon only. We'll regroup and send out a larger hunting party later."

"Roger that."

At least he knew where the damaged conduit was. Would he be able to get Valentine's engineer out there to fix it?

"Alpha," Master Sergeant Gold said, cutting through his comm from the module's link. "Do you copy?"

"I hear you, Sergeant," Caleb replied.

"Keep your eyes peeled. You wandered into a dead zone. I can't cover you from here."

Caleb hadn't realized they had gone into one of the dark spots on the ship. He raised his carbine and scanned the corridor around him, quickly locating the vents.

"Washington, we're in a dead zone," he relayed to the big man.

Washington exaggerated his nod so Caleb would see it. Then he brought his carbine up and turned slowly, scanning the opposite side of the corridor.

"We're clear for now," Caleb said. "Let's get ourselves back under coverage. Gold, what's the shortest route?"

"Take the stairwell," Gold replied. "It looks like the sensors there are on a different conduit. I've got eyes on the whole thing from top to bottom."

"Roger that."

Caleb and Washington started for the stairs. They were only a hundred meters away, with a single intersection between it and them. It was as straight a shot as they came.

They jogged down the corridor toward the stairs. They had gone twenty meters when a mark appeared behind them, caught by the sensors on Caleb's ATCS. He and Washington spun to face it in unison.

A blurry shape crossed the corridor ahead of them, too small and too pale to be a trife.

"Was that a person?" Caleb said, glancing at Washington.

The other Marine spread his hand in question. He wasn't sure either.

The ATCS became active with two more marks, and a pair of dark shapes crossed the corridor a moment later, chasing after the first.

"I don't believe this," Caleb said. "We have to help him. Or her. Come on." Washington joined him, reversing course and running down the corridor. "Master Sergeant Gold, we have visual on what may be a lost civilian. We're in pursuit. Wake Raptor One and have him assemble his team in case we need backup."

"Confirmed, Alpha," Gold replied.

They reached the intersection, turning right. Caleb had visual on the tailing trife, but the person had already turned the next corner.

A sharp crack echoed in the corridor from beside him. One of the trife stumbled and fell, its head snapping forward. A second crack sounded less than a second later, and the other one collapsed.

"Nice shooting, Wash," Caleb said. "We're--"

Something hit him from behind, knocking him forward. He felt heat at the base of his neck, followed by wetness. He landed on his knees, the weight vanishing from his body as he eyed his HUD. There were more trife behind them. They had come out of nowhere. Or at least, that's how it seemed.

Washington's carbine fired a third time, followed by a spray of rounds that left discarded shells clinking on the floor beside Caleb. They seemed to move so slowly, and he watched how they struck the metal floor and bounced up, turning over in the air and catching the light.

He reached back, putting a gloved hand to the hot spot on his neck. When he pulled his hand away, it was covered in blood.

He felt sick. Was this how it was going to end? Caught off-guard by a trife, just like that? After two years of hell?

He was getting dizzy as Washington's hand wrapped around him, scooping him up in a fireman's carry. He was vaguely aware of the big Marine's feet pumping below him, the echo of the boots on the floor, and the rocking motion as he was carried back to the stairs.

Then the world faded away.

Chapter 31

David flinched at the sound of the gunshots, turning his head back to see the two trife behind him slide across the floor of the corridor into the corner, spilling their dark blood. He pulled to a stop, looking at them for a moment and trying to decide if he should go back. Someone had shot the creatures. He couldn't imagine they would shoot him. When the trife were involved, every human was on the same side.

He started walking back, toward the dead trife.

More gunshots rang out, and he flinched a second time. More bullets meant more trife. He turned a second time and continued running.

He should have never left the safety of the storage closet he had found. He had ridden it from Earth to space, safe from the trife that had gotten onto the starship behind him before the airlock had automatically sealed. They would never have found him in there.

But then he had heard the fighting. The gunfire and the hissing of the creatures in the distance. He was afraid of having Marines find him hiding out alone in the middle of the ship. He was worried they would blame him for the trife getting in. They would have been right to blame him. It was his fault. He had left the airlock open. He had let them sneak through. The starship had left Earth, but the demons had come with it.

Were they all going to die?

He didn't know what he was doing now. He had left the storage area to get away from the fighting. To find another place to hide that wasn't so active. He had wandered the halls, climbed the stairwells and searched for somewhere to go.

But the trife were everywhere. No matter what deck he came out on, no matter where he tried to go. They seemed to be ever-present. He didn't think he had let that many in. A hundred maybe. The ship was so big, how come they were all grouping in the same area where he was?

He wanted to find a place where the trife weren't. There had to be one. Not enough of them had come through to overrun a ship this size completely. But once he found somewhere, then what? He had traded an entire planet where he could hide for a much smaller space. He hadn't improved his situation. He had made it worse. And not just for himself. He didn't know how many people were on the ship, but every one of them who died would be his fault. His cross to bear.

"So stupid," he said to himself. He was still clutching the revolver in one hand and a knife in the other. He hadn't needed either so far, though the last pair of trife had gotten almost too close for comfort. He was lucky the Marines had taken them out. He was lucky he had escaped.

To where?

He didn't know where he was going or where he would end up. Joining Espinoza was the worst decision he had ever made. A part of him had known that getting involved with a group of survivors was a mistake, that he was better off on his own. Staying alone was hard. Humans were social animals, and isolation didn't work well for him.

So of course, now he was isolated again. Cut off from home. Trapped in a metal maze with the demons he was trying to escape. Running from the only people who might be able to help him.

The whole thing was a nightmare.

He slowed as he neared the end of the corridor. A door on his right had a label next to it. "Crew Mess." He tapped the control panel, and the hatch slid open, revealing a large room with metal tables and chairs spread around it, all of them bolted into fixed positions on the floor. At the back of the room was a long steel counter with cutouts for food.

Mess. That's what the military called cafeterias. He had forgotten. This one was big enough to seat a hundred people at a time. It was strange. He didn't think there were even a hundred people on the ship. Had the trife killed them all before they had gotten on board?

But someone had launched the starship. Someone had gotten them into space. At least, he assumed they were in space. He had felt the shuddering. He thought he had heard the roar of thrusters. But there were no windows on the ship. There was no way to see outside. For all he knew, they were still on the ground.

Was that why the ship was so quiet? Had they evacuated the starship when they discovered the trife had gotten in?

He should have gone back to the airlock to try to open it, to confirm they weren't still on the ground. At least there weren't any trife in there.

The hatch slid closed behind him. He passed the tables to the counter and then went past the counter to a swinging door in the rear. He pushed it open, revealing another storage space, filled with more boxes of MREs. There were so many. It was as if they had been planning to feed an army for a long, long time.

How long was the starship supposed to take to get wherever it was going, anyway?

And where exactly were they going?

David opened one of the boxes, looking at the labels on the MREs. He picked one out. Thanksgiving Dinner. He tore it open, looking down at the brown block. He brought it to his nose and sniffed. It did remind him of Thanksgiving. He could smell the cranberries, the turkey, the gravy and the pumpkin pie. He was reminded of how his mother used to spend the whole day cooking for their family. He remembered his sister. His father. His grandma and grandpa.

His eyes welled with tears.

Gone. They were all gone. Killed by the virus, the trife, the damned military. It didn't matter how they died, only that they were all dead.

Except for him.

Caleb took a bite of the MRE. It was dry, and it didn't taste anywhere near as much like Thanksgiving as it smelled. He forced the bite down and threw the rest on the floor.

He slumped down beside it and began to cry.

Chapter 32

The first thing Caleb noticed was how much his head hurt. He felt it before he even opened his eyes. The throbbing in his temple and at the base of his spine. Normally, he might have felt the pain and lamented it.

In this case, pain meant he was still alive.

He was glad to be alive.

His eyes slid open slowly, his vision already sharp. The Marine module had a small sick bay in it. Four racks aligned in a circle around a central monitoring station. Hawk Three, Private Yasuka, was on the rack beside him, sitting up, a patch on his shoulder.

"Alpha," Yasuka said, noticing he was awake. He smiled. "How do you feel?"

Caleb shifted his tongue in his mouth, trying to clear the dryness. He didn't know which of the Guardians was the medic. He didn't even know if they had a medic. Considering he had survived a trife claw to his neck, he assumed they did.

"Head's pounding," he replied softly. He wiggled his

fingers and toes, testing them. They both worked. "I can move."

"You were lucky," Sho said, standing up in the center of the monitoring station. "One centimeter deeper and you would be paraplegic. Three centimeters and you would be dead." She circled the desk to stand beside him. "You're also lucky you had Washington with you. He killed four more of the bastards getting you back here, and he carried you fast enough you didn't bleed out on the way. Oh, and you're lucky Private Shiro decided not to hold a grudge at the chewing out you gave him, because he happens to be our medic."

"I can barely keep up with everything you just said," Caleb said. His eyes were working fine, but his brain still felt a little sluggish.

"That's the painkillers."

"Painkillers? They aren't working for the pain."

The hatch to the sickbay opened, and Private Shiro walked in. "I didn't want to give you too much, Alpha," he said. "I knew you wouldn't want to sleep too long."

"How long was I out?"

"Six hours."

"Six?" Caleb tried to sit up. A wave of dizziness forced him back down. "Damn it. We don't have time to waste."

"Relax, Sarge," Sho said. "Pratt finished up his work for the Research team and took over for you here. We already knew the plan, so it was no big deal. I went out with the Raptors, back to the first pocket of trife. We killed about thirty of them, and Valentine's guy got the sensors back online over there."

"All that in six hours?"

"Damn right, Sarge. You aren't the only one who knows how to get stuff done around here."

Caleb smiled. "What about the other conduit? The one that knocked out the area around the bridge, and where I was hit?"

"Still offline. According to Craft, its a general malfunction of the breaker, and it'll take hours to pull the board and replace it with a new one, plus we'd have to bring the whole sensor grid offline to do it."

"I assume Craft is Valentine's tech?"

Sho nodded. "You assume correctly. Smart son of a bitch. And cute too." She smiled.

"But," Caleb prompted.

"Like you were already thinking, Sarge. There's more than meets the eye with those scientists."

"Including Valentine?"

"Especially Valentine. Pratt said whatever they're working on in Research, they seemed to be doing their best to keep him from getting even a whiff of it while he was down there. The whole module was clean, as in there was still plastic wrap on the expensive science equipment. And he said they were really specific about which vents they wanted help with."

"Their little project is classified," Caleb said. "Nothing we can do about that."

"Except this isn't a military vessel anymore, right? So technically there's no such thing as classified."

"Do you think we should storm down there and demand to know what they're working on?"

"Valentine claims it might help with the trife. It would be nice to know."

"Private Shiro, how long until my head calms down enough I can get out of this bed?"

Shiro walked over to the monitoring station. He tapped on the control surface. "Tell me if this feels better."

Caleb felt something cold race into his veins through his IV. A moment later, his headache was gone.

"What did you just give me?"

"A different painkiller. It'll weaken your muscles, though. No combat activities for you for at least another six hours." Shiro glanced at the display. "The patch is healing the wound nicely."

"You'd think R&D could have come up with a stormtrooper suit that had better neck protection," Caleb said.

"They probably could, but you wouldn't be able to turn your head," Sho replied. "It would have been nice if they could have produced more of the Butchers too, but there was only so much capacity to go around."

Caleb pushed himself to a seated position. "Private Yasuka, how is your wound?"

"I'll live, Alpha," Yasuka replied. "The tendon was severed. Shiro put it back together, but it's going to take a few more hours for the patch to finish me up."

"I don't want him using it for days," Shiro said. "But I know that probably isn't an option."

"No, it isn't," Yasuka said. "I want to get back out there and kill me some bugs."

"They're not bugs," Sho said.

Yasuka laughed.

"Private Shiro, you should have told me before that you're a medic. What if I had sent you into the field?"

"That's why I didn't tell you, Alpha. I want to be in the field. I did two years of medic training before the trife showed up, and then I transferred to infantry."

Caleb was annoyed by the answer, but he swallowed it. "You're here until either the trife are all dead, or we're really desperate."

"Understood. Also, I recognize I should have spoken up sooner. I can do more pushups if you'd like."

"Forget it. Taking responsibility is enough for now. We have bigger problems to solve." He slid off the rack to his feet, only then realizing he was naked. "Can someone get me some clothes?"

"I was waiting to see how long it would take you to realize," Sho said. "It would have been amusing to watch you traipse out into the CIC in your birthday suit."

"It's nothing anyone in here hasn't seen before."

"In the shower maybe, not in the CIC."

Shiro picked up a black t-shirt, underwear, and dark cargo pants and tossed them on the bed next to Caleb. "Here you go, Alpha."

"Thank you," Caleb said, grabbing the clothes and quickly putting them on. He tried to do it quickly, anyway. He could feel the weakness in his muscles as he tried to move.

"Would you like some help with that, Sarge?" Sho asked.

"I've got it," he replied. He sat back on the bed and managed to maneuver the underwear and pants onto his legs, getting them halfway up and then standing again to pull them the rest of the distance. The activity made him frustratingly tired. "I'll take a little help now," he said, reaching out and putting his hand on Sho's shoulder before he collapsed.

She caught him, helping him stay upright. "I've got you, Sarge. Where are we headed?"

"To Wash, I want to thank him for saving my ass. Then to the CIC. I want the trife off our ship."

"Roger that."

"Private Shiro, thank you for putting me back together."

209

"It's my duty and my pleasure, Alpha."

Caleb started for the exit, with Sho helping to keep him from falling. They went through the hatch together, turning left toward the small barracks.

"I'm glad you didn't die, Sarge," Sho said.

"Me too."

Chapter 33

Washington wasn't sleeping. He was sitting on his rack, a tablet in hand and a big smile on his face. The smile got even larger when Caleb entered the room. The big Marine put down the table and came to attention.

"As you were," Caleb said.

Washington approached Caleb and Sho, holding his arms out wide and wrapping both of them in a tight hug. Then he let go and motioned to the back of his neck.

"It was close," Caleb said. "Three centimeters from death, one centimeter from paralyzation."

Washington made a hissing sound, the best he could do to emulate a whistle. He held his thumb and forefinger close together.

"That's right. That close. I'm okay now. Getting better. Shiro gave me some meds for a headache, and it made my muscles feel like jelly. Anyway, I wanted to come by to thank you for getting me out of there."

Washington flipped his thumb up.

"What were you up to, Wash?" Sho asked.

Washington went back to his rack and grabbed the tablet. He rotated it so they could see.

It was the beginning of a picture the big man was drawing on the touch display. A portrait of a woman. It was only half-finished, but Caleb already recognized her from a photo Washington used to have.

"Your wife?" he said.

Washington nodded, tapped his head and shook it.

"You don't want to forget her?"

He nodded again.

"Like you ever could?"

He smiled.

"She was beautiful Wash," Sho said.

"He used to have a photograph," Caleb explained. "It got burned during a mission, probably fifteen months ago. A few months before you joined the Vultures."

Washington made a face indicating he was still upset at the loss.

"What happened to her?" Sho asked. "Virus?"

Washington shook his head.

"Trife?"

He shook it again. His eyes began to moisten at the memory. He didn't like to talk about Charlene. As far as Caleb knew, he was the only one who knew Washington ever had a wife in the first place.

"Looters," Caleb said. "Of all things. We should have been taking care of one another, but some people just didn't get it. They thought because the world was burning, they should grab what they could."

Sho's face paled. "I'm sorry, Wash. You never told me."

He shrugged. She put her arms around him, and he put a large hand on her back to hold her close for a second.

"It's a great drawing," Caleb repeated. "I didn't know you were an artist."

Washington nodded. He turned the tablet around, tapped a few screens, and then his fingers started moving. He flipped it back.

I prefer pencil and paper, but we don't have that here. I miss her.

"I know you do," Caleb said. "She'd be proud of you. You're helping a lot of people."

He nodded and pointed at Caleb.

"I'm headed to the CIC to check in with Sergeant Pratt. I heard we cleared one of the groups of trife. Two more and we can all relax for the rest of the trip."

Washington thumbs-upped again, and then signaled that he was coming with him.

Sho slid under Caleb's arm again, helping him keep his balance while he headed out of the barracks and back down the short corridor to the CIC.

The command center was quiet but active. Master Sergeant Gold and Sergeant Pratt were positioned near the main terminal, the large display providing sensor data that quickly showed Caleb that the Hawks were closing on the second forward group of xenotrife. A pair of smaller windows in the corner showed the camera feeds from a couple of the Dragonfly drones, one in what appeared to be a ventilation shaft and the other in a secondary access passage.

"Hawk One, no sign of trife outside the main passageways," Sergeant Pratt said. He was wearing a full SOS to run the sortie.

"Roger that, Sergeant," Johansen replied. "We're continuing ahead, fifty meters to contact."

Pratt's ATCS must have registered the people behind

him, because he glanced back over his shoulder, turning all the way around when he saw Caleb.

"Guardian Alpha," he said. "I see you're back on your feet."

"I am, Sergeant," Caleb said, his eyes narrowing slightly at Pratt's tone. He didn't sound happy to see him. "You sent the Hawks after the second group?"

"We did," Master Sergeant Gold said. "We couldn't wait for you to come to, Alpha."

"I'm not complaining. I'm glad we're making progress."

"Quick progress," Pratt said, turning back to the display. "The first group went down easy with my guidance. I even got Craft out there to fix the damage to the conduit and restore the sensors. No problem."

Caleb continued staring at Pratt's back. "I heard. It's great work. The trife haven't caused any other damage?"

"Not so far, and we've got the Dragonflies in the walls watching the service areas. They won't be able to surprise us like that again. I don't want to speak too soon, but I think we're going to win this one."

"Don't jinx it," Sho said. "We've thought that before. Remember New Zealand?"

They had been close to getting the trife off the island. Some counts had put them at less than ten thousand. The military was confident they would have their area cleared within a week.

A year later, the trife were still there and most if not all of the humans were gone. The takeaway was never to assume anything.

"It wouldn't have happened if I had been in charge," Pratt replied. "Hawk One, ATCS just picked up the targets."

"We aren't out of ATCS range?" Caleb asked.

"Nope," Gold said, looking pleased with himself. "A little human ingenuity. The Hawks brought extra armor out with them, powered up and placed along their route to pass the network signal."

"It was my idea," Pratt said. "I've got full tactical and visual. We're looking clean so far. The trife haven't even noticed our squad is there."

Caleb's eyes drifted back to the sensor grid. Only one group of marks was moving. The Hawks. The other was static, as though the trife were asleep. He wished the armor's HUD could be transmitted to the terminal so he could see what Pratt saw. He was tempted to head to the armory to grab an SOS of his own, but he didn't want to miss the excitement or the hopeful lack of it.

"What the hell are they doing?" Pratt said.

"What do you see, Sergeant?" Caleb asked.

"I'm not sure. Looks like the things are all bundled up together, rubbing against one another and covered in some kind of sticky white crap."

"Like semen?" Sho asked.

"Ugh. I wasn't thinking of it that way until you said it, but yeah, sort of. They're just slip-sliding away if you know what I mean, probably thirty of them all rubbing each other up. It's disgusting is what it is."

"Master Sergeant Gold, can you switch the comm over to Research? Let's ask Doctor Valentine what they're doing."

"One second, Alpha," Gold said. "Done."

"Doctor Valentine," Caleb said.

"Guardian Alpha Card," Doctor Byrnes replied instead. "What can I do for you?"

"I was hoping to get a word with Riley," Caleb said.

"I'm sorry, Alpha, she's not available right now. She's tied up with her research."

"It's been six hours."

"She's very dedicated, as I'm sure you already know. I heard you were injured. How are you feeling?"

"Well enough," Caleb said. "We've got a team near the remaining trife in the bow of the Deliverance."

"I have them on sensors," Byrnes said.

"They've got the trife on visual. They look like they're all pressed together, and spreading some kind of ichor across one another."

"We call it serumen. They use it to transfer new genetic information. It sounds like they're queening. How much have they secreted?"

"A lot," Pratt replied. "They're all coated in it."

"They've almost completed the process," Byrnes said, his ton concerned. "You need to stop it, Alpha. Right now."

"You heard him, Sergeant," Caleb said.

"Hawk Three, move into position and set your weapon to stream," Pratt said. "Burn those bugs to ash."

Caleb watched the sensor display. Every mark ahead of the Hawks vanished within a few seconds.

"The quarterback is toast," Pratt said, smiling. "Grid is clear. ATCS is clear. That P-50 is something else."

"Nice work," Caleb said. "Do me a favor and keep the Dragonflies running their scans, just in case, and have the Hawks do a sweep of the area."

"The zone is clear," Pratt snapped. "You can see it yourself."

"I can, but I don't want to take any chances. Maybe it's just me, but didn't that seem a little too easy?"

"You were in sickbay when we hit the first group," Master Sergeant Gold said. "They went down the same way. The trife don't handle the plasma well. I bet if we had these things when the war started we wouldn't even need to be out here now."

"I wouldn't go that far. The plasma stream may work well within the confines of the ship, but most of Earth isn't so easily contained. Just do a quick sweep of the area."

"Confirmed, Alpha," Pratt grumbled. "Hawk One, Guardian Alpha requests a sweep on the area for wayward trife. Keep the Dragonflies active in the vents and service passages. Huh? Yeah, he's fine. Well enough to question our success. I'll tell him you said that." Pratt turned to Caleb. "Johansen said she's glad you're feeling better, and she's happy to do an extra sweep for you. You want to take bets that she doesn't find anything?"

"I heard we have a map of the vents and service tunnels from Research?" Caleb said in response. He still didn't like Pratt's tone. Something was going on with the Sergeant.

"That's right."

"Is it complete?"

"Not one hundred percent. The problem is the schematics have changed a bit since the original prints were made. They built the Deliverance so fast, they had to make some changes on the fly, and they aren't reflected."

"But you're confident the Hawks aren't going to find anything?"

"As confident as you are that they will."

Caleb smiled. "It's a bet. Loser gets a service tattoo. Winner gives it to him."

Pratt's laugh was humorless. "Oh, I'm going to love it when you lose."

"Wait a second," Sho said. "This is hardly fair. Alpha is on meds."

"He's well enough to tell the Hawks what to do."

"Sergeant Pratt," Master Sergeant Gold said. "Alpha. We have… something happening. I'm not sure what to make of it."

Caleb and Pratt both turned to the grid. The marks at the stern were disappearing one at a time.

"Check the map Research provided," Caleb said. "Are there any passages in that area?"

"Hang on," Gold said.

"Pratt, call the Hawks back."

"I guess I win the bet."

"No. The bet is canceled. I like what those trife are doing less than my gut feeling about the bow."

"I'm calling it a win, Alpha. I'll let you slide on the tattoo."

"Whatever makes you happy. Joke time is over. Sho, help me sit. Washington, can you get me an SOS?"

Washington flashed his thumb and left the CIC. Sho helped Caleb over to the central command station behind the primary terminal. Pratt moved aside to let him sit.

"Hawk One, belay the previous order and return to base," Pratt said. "Double time it, we've got vanishing trife moving from the stern." He looked at Caleb. "They're on their way."

"What do you think the trife are doing, Sarge?" Sho asked.

Caleb was still watching the grid. They were moving into an unmonitored passage, that much was clear. Where did it lead? Did the demons even know? They were still vanishing one-by-one, nearly half the larger group already off the map.

"Byrnes, are you there?" Caleb said.

"I'm here, Alpha," Doctor Byrnes replied. "And yes, I see what you see. And no, I don't know the purpose either. You're the Marine."

"I was going to ask you if you think the larger group might have finished queening yet."

"Oh. It's entirely possible, Alpha. You can't put a time-stamp on something like that."

"Damn," Pratt said. "We should have gone after the larger group first."

"Without knowing how they would react or what their potential is in a confined space like this?" Caleb said. "This way was safer."

"Then we shouldn't have played it safe."

Caleb's eyes narrowed, and he pushed himself to his feet. He could feel his legs burning as he did, but he refused to stumble or look weak. "I don't like your attitude Sergeant," he hissed. "You're barking back at every damn thing I say."

Pratt's eyebrows sank, and he faced Caleb, his stance aggressive. "My problem is that we burned too much time bouncing off the damn bugs and not enough time extermi-nating them. I just took out two of the three groups of trife in six hours. You spent the first two running so-called recons against them, lost a Marine, and got another one hurt, not to mention your own injury. The P-50s can wipe the bastards out like this." He snapped his fingers. "We should load up the troops and rush their position. We can take out their queen before she can start making babies. If you were still in sickbay where you belong, that's exactly what I would do."

Caleb's instinct was to roar back. He held the anger in, forcing himself to stay even. He didn't know where any of this was coming from. He and Pratt had been in the same battalion for over a year, and Sean had always been collected.

"Maybe you haven't spent enough time in the field, Sergeant," Caleb said. "The trife seem stupid on the surface, but they aren't. They adapt to their environment, which means the rules are different here. If you rushed them, you would get everyone who went out there with you killed."

"Like you got Habib killed?" Pratt said.

Caleb couldn't do it. He lunged at Pratt, who stepped back and out of the way, moving aside to let Caleb tumble to the ground, his legs unable to keep him upright.

"You son of a bitch," Caleb said. "You're way out of line."

"I should be Alpha here, Card. Not you. I have seniority. I was in the service when you were still in diapers."

"When was the last time you were in the field against the trife? Before today, when was the last time you saw combat?"

"It doesn't matter," Pratt said. "I know how to lead men. I'm doing a better job than you are."

"You're doing a bang up job earning our respect," Sho said, coming to Caleb's defense.

"I think everybody here knows where you stand, Yen. You're like Cal's little love-sick puppy."

Washington picked the right time to return to the room. He had a SOS cradled in his arms, along with three of the P-50 rifles. He noticed Caleb on the floor, and he dropped the whole bundle, hurrying over to him.

"Washington," Caleb said. "Take Pratt to his rack. I think he's getting a little cracked."

"Cracked?" Pratt growled. "I'll show you cracked."

He started for the door toward the barracks, shouldering past Sho and Washington. He paused when he reached the rifles Washington had dropped, bending over and grabbing one.

"Pratt, what the hell are you doing?" Master Sergeant Gold said.

Pratt aimed the rifle at them, switching the control to stream. "I could burn all of you to a pile of goo," he said. "You want to hide in here, take it slow, let them start multiplying, you be my guest. I'm going to kill those bastards. Every last one of them."

He stormed toward the exit. The hatch slid open at the same time he reached it, the Hawks returning from the bow. "Don't try to stop me," he shouted, pointing his rifle at them. Once he was past, he took off down the corridor at a run.

"What the hell was that?" Sho said.

"I don't know," Caleb replied. "But that wasn't the Sean Pratt I've known for the last year." He lowered his voice so only Sho and Washington would hear him. "Something is going on, and I think it has to do with Valentine. Sho, find Private Ning and bring him to the CIC."

"Roger that, Sarge," she replied, heading away.

Washington extended his hand, and Caleb took it, pulling himself to his feet. "Help me with the SOS, will you? It'll help me stay on my feet." Washington nodded. "Byrnes, are you still there?"

"I'm still here, Alpha."

"I want to talk to Doctor Valentine. Now."

"I'm afraid that won't be possible, Alpha. She's very--"

"Now!" Caleb snapped. "Or you'll find a few very angry Marines breaking through the door into your module."

"You have no authority to – "

"I don't need authority, I've got all the guns. And I want some damn answers."

"Let's not overreact, Alpha."

"Now!" Caleb repeated.

"Standby," Byrnes said.

Caleb glanced at Washington. "I have no clue what the hell is happening on this ship," he said.

Washington nodded emphatically as if to say me neither.

Chapter 34

"What can I help you with, Alpha?" Doctor Valentine said sharply. She sounded pissed off and tired.

Caleb didn't care. She had left him waiting for nearly five minutes, wasting time to show him how he couldn't just tell her what to do, even when there was at least one life at stake. Just because Pratt had lost his mind, it didn't mean Caleb didn't want to get him back to safety.

He had spent the time getting loaded into a fresh SOS with a lot of help from Washington. Sho had returned with Ning in tow, after having found the Private in his rack, sweating profusely.

"What the hell did you do to my Marines?" Caleb asked.

"What do you mean?"

"Don't give me that bullshit. I loaned you two men to help you fortify the Research module. One of them is sick, and the other ran off to take on the trife all by himself."

Caleb looked at the sensor grid. Master Sergeant Gold had highlighted Pratt on it, leaving him as an orange spot headed toward the rear of the ship. He was taking a haggard path, cutting down random corridors and doubling back over areas he had already covered. It wasn't even close to normal.

"Does the word coincidence mean anything to you?" Valentine said.

"Does the word bullshit mean anything to you? I'm done with the secrets, Riley. Your team and my team are the only humans out here, and we should be working together, but if I have to bring my squad down to beat the truth out of you, I'm almost ready to do that."

"How macho," Valentine said. "It won't get you very far. We aren't defenseless down here."

"That's kind of my point. Who the hell are you, Doctor Valentine?"

"I'm a scientist, Caleb. A genetic researcher. Anything else you think I might be is coming from your imagination. From your mistrust. Have I given you a reason not to trust me?"

"Two Marines went to help you with the module. Both of those Marines are exhibiting individual signs of illness, yet you claim you had nothing to do with it. That's one reason why I don't trust you. Whatever the thing you had wrapped up under the tarp, that's another. The way you conveniently got off the bridge before the trife attacked, that's a potential third. And the fact that your genetics team contains a network specialist and an electrical engineer? Strike four."

Doctor Valentine laughed, long and hard enough Caleb knew she was mocking him. "Please, Alpha. A combination of coincidences and easily explained circumstance. You're boxing shadows. Haven't you heard? When humans are fighting trife, there are only two sides. Us and them."

"Then why did Pratt storm out of the module to chase the trife alone?"

"Marines break," Valentine replied. "I'm sure you've seen it before."

He had. He was sure all of the Guardians had. But that wasn't what happened to Pratt, no matter how she tried to spin it. Sean had been a Marine for nearly fifteen years. If two years of fighting the trife on Earth hadn't broken him, this situation wasn't going to.

He realized Valentine wasn't going to give him anything, no matter how hard he pushed. If he wanted it, he was going to have to take it. Despite his threats, he didn't have the time or Marines to do that.

"And what about Ning? I've got him here with me, but I'm close to sending him to sickbay. He's burning up."

"He could have gotten sick before we ever left Earth. It could be as simple as the flu. I'm sure you'll figure it out. How is your head, by the way? I heard you had a close call."

"It's fine," Caleb said. "Since I have you direct on the comm, maybe you can tell me what you think the xenotrife in the stern are doing. Ninety percent of them moved somewhere off the grid."

"Byrnes informed me," she said. "I honestly don't know."

"Give me your best guess, Doctor. I know you have experience with the trife."

"Not in this environment, I don't. Best guess? They finished the queening and went to build a nest."

"Off the grid?"

"They're going to put it as close to the thrusters as they can. The energy exchange between the reactors and the ionic generators provide an excellent nutrient source for them. It also acts as a shield against most electronic communications, including the sensors."

"You mean we're blind down there."

"Worse than blind. If you aren't careful with your weapon fire, you're liable to blow the entire ship into a billion tiny little pieces."

Caleb closed his eyes. He should have guessed.

"So we need to try to draw them out?"

"That would be best."

"No rest for the wicked," Sho said.

"Confirmed," Caleb replied. "Well, don't let me interrupt your busy schedule any more than I already – "

A loud bang drowned out the rest of the statement. Caleb's head whipped toward the hatch leading from the corridor into the Marine module. A second bang followed, and then a third. His eyes shifted to the grid. Dozens of trife were materializing like ghosts right outside the door.

What the hell?

He heard a crash, followed by a scream.

From inside the module.

Chapter 35

"Gold, sound the alert," Caleb said, grabbing his plasma rifle and getting to his feet. His knees were weak, but the assistive musculature of the SOS kept him from falling, helping him stay upright and walk from the primary station toward the source of the scream.

The alert tone shrilled an instant later, a wail that echoed off the walls and would wake any of the Marines who were still at rest. The Hawks had headed for the shower and a nap after their mission. Were they still in the head?

"Wait here, Sarge," Sho said. "I'll check it out."

"No," Caleb said. "You aren't armored. Cover the door. They shouldn't be able to get through, but then they shouldn't be in here either. Washington, take Ning and get to the armory. When you're done, replace Sho so she can get her gear."

Washington acknowledged the order.

"Are you sure you can walk?" Sho asked.

"I don't have a choice. I'll be fine."

"Holler if you need us, Sarge."

"Will do."

Caleb moved from the CIC, out into the short corridor. He heard another scream. It was definitely coming from the barracks. He increased his pace, breaking into an unsteady run as other Marines moved into view, headed for the armory.

"Alpha, what's going on?" Private Shiro asked.

"I don't know. Get dressed. All of you. Get dressed."

They ran past him, joining Washington and Ning as they headed for the armory. He continued in the other direction, still able to hear the demons pounding at the door behind him. Why would they bother? They couldn't open it.

He moved into the barracks, glancing in each of the rooms as he passed them by. All of the Guardians were up and out, but he hadn't seen Johansen or Goth.

The hatch to the head slid open. A dark, oily shape stood in the frame, blood dripping from its teeth and its claws.

It hissed at him as he raised the plasma rifle and fired. The bolt caught the trife in the chest, burning a hole straight through. The demon lunged at him despite the wound. He fired again, putting a hole in its brain that dropped it to the ground.

"Johansen," Caleb said. He stepped over the trife toward the showers.

Another demon came around the side of the door and reached for him. Caleb fired point-blank, the smell of cooked flesh raising from the instant kill. He stepped into the bathroom. A third trife came at him from the other side, bowling into him and knocking him off his unsteady legs. He fell into the door to one of the toilet stalls and bounced off, swinging the rifle like a club and catching the trife in the side of the head. Its neck cracked wetly, and it fell to the floor.

Caleb looked past the toilets to the open shower stall. One of them was still running, still spilling water into a too-large hole in the floor. Johansen was against the wall behind the hole, right next to Goth. They were both dead.

A trife appeared in the hole, climbing out of it. Caleb didn't understand. He didn't have time to understand. He shot the demon, rushing to the scar in the floor and looking down.

Damn it, why hadn't he realized? The floor of the shower was like the floor of Metro, a porous surface that allowed the water to pass through to be recycled. It dripped down into a basin which fed out into a drain pipe.

The pipe looked too small for the creatures, but their bones were light and flexible, and they could squeeze into small spaces whenever they needed to do so. They had come up through it, taking them by surprise. Johansen and Goth hadn't stood a chance. If any of the other Marines had been in the shower with them, they would have died too.

Caleb heard motion behind him. He looked back as Shiro entered the room, fully SOSed and ready.

"Alpha?" Shiro said.

"We need to seal off the larger drain pipes. Cut and solder them." It was a perfect job for Pratt if he hadn't gone insane. Or whatever it was that had happened to him.

"I thought those things hate water?"

"I guess they don't mind that much if it's the only way they can reach us. Stand guard here while I get Master Sergeant Gold."

"Roger that, Alpha."

Caleb hurried from the barracks, stopping Privates Flores and Wagner from the Hawks on the way and redirecting them to the CIC with him. The other Marines had nearly all finished assembling there, including the injured Yasuka and the sick Ning.

He immediately noticed the banging from the door had stopped.

"They came in from one of the drainage pipes," Caleb said. "Into the showers. Johansen and Goth are dead."

He could feel the sudden tension in the Marines at the news.

"How did they get through the floor without Johansen or Goth hearing them coming?" Sho asked.

"Joe and Goth had a thing," Wagner said. "They were probably preoccupied."

"Damn it," Caleb said. "If someone had told me I would have separated them. This isn't the time for that kind of distraction."

"I don't know, Alpha," Wagner replied. "Lost in space, surrounded by killer aliens, locked in a shower together? If you had someone, you might want one last chance too."

Caleb wasn't going to argue. He had bigger problems. "Master Sergeant Gold, we need to close up the pipe. Make it smaller so they can't fit through. Can you make it happen?"

"Confirmed, Alpha. I'll need help."

"Wagner, go with him."

"Yes, sir."

The two Marines left the CIC. Caleb went to the primary terminal and checked the comm.

"Research, come in."

"Guardian Alpha, this is Craft."

"Taking over for Byrnes?"

"Just be thankful we're listening at all, Alpha. I personally don't appreciate the attitude you've taken with Doctor Valentine."

"It's not personal, Craft. I'm trying to keep my people alive." And failing. Had Pratt been right? Was he doing everything wrong?

"What do you need from us now?"

"Nothing. I wanted to warn you. The trife used the drainage for the shower to bypass module security and kill two of my Marines. Regardless of our differences, I don't want the same thing to happen to you."

"Roger, Alpha," Craft said, suddenly stiff and serious. "Thank you for the warning. If you'll excuse me."

Caleb closed the link, and then looked over the Marines who were left.

Sho, Washington, Hafizi, Yasuka, Ning, and Flores. Gold, Wagner, and Shiro were out of the room. Ten Marines in all. Out of nearly a thousand who had been stationed with the Deliverance.

How many trife were still out there?

And even if they managed to stop the queen somehow, how the hell would they ever know they had gotten them all with enough certainty to let the people in Metro come back out.

He wasn't sure they could.

"Pratt was right about one thing," he said, glancing at Sho. "We can't afford to waste any more time. I hope I did the right thing. If I didn't, I'm sorry. To all of you, I'm sorry."

"I think I can speak for all of us when we say we don't envy the position you're in, Alpha," Flores said. He smiled. "Hell, I don't envy the position I'm in, and I have the easy job. I just have to go where you tell me to go when you tell me to go there and shoot what you tell me to shoot."

"Thanks, Flores," Caleb replied.

"We all volunteered, Alpha," Hafizi said. "We could

have gone to Metro with Lieutenant Jones. We wanted to be out here. We wanted to fight. We trust you."

"We aren't giving up, Sarge," Sho said. "Let's finish the job or die trying."

"Finish the job or die trying," Caleb repeated. He cupped his chin in his hand, rubbing it against the stubble there and thinking. "All right, Guardians. I tried doing this the easy way, but the trife don't seem to like the easy way. So you know how we're going to do it?"

"The hard way, Alpha!" the Marines replied.

"That's right. The hard way. Gold and Wagner are busy patching the pipes to keep the trife out. We can't afford to wait for them. I'm reorganizing the squads based on what we have left. Hawks will merge with Raptors to form one fire team. Vultures stay with me. We have enough plasma rifles for everyone, so everyone will carry one. They can be dangerous in such close quarters, so each team will designate a primary gunner. If your primary gunner is incapacitated or if you have a confident and clear line of fire, take the shot. Just be careful. A bolt doesn't need to hit your squadmate to burn. If I assign you an MK-12, you don't touch the grenade launcher unless I give the order. Is that clear?"

"Yes, Alpha!"

"I need one person from each squad to be in charge of the Dragonflies."

"I've got it for Raptors," Flores said quickly.

"Vultures," Hafizi said.

"Good. Okay. According to Valentine, the trife are probably done crowning their new queen, and she's leading them back toward the engines to build a new nest. She suggested the area where they're settling is a bad place to get into a firefight, so we'll need to figure out how to get them to come after us. We've been successful getting them to chase on Earth by sending in pairs and leading them back into ambushes. I have a feeling that isn't going to work as well here. Our experience so far suggests they'll use the tactic against us, and while we're trying to bring them in, they'll be flanking us for an ambush of their own. It seems ridiculous, but it's almost like they know the Deliverance better than we do."

"Scent, Alpha," Hafizi said.

"What's that, Corporal?"

"They can smell us. Or feel us. Or something. They know there are lots of people in Metro. They knew there were lots of people on the bridge, and in here. Probably in Research too."

"Do you think Valentine would say anything if the trife attacked them?" Sho asked. "She probably took some of them prisoner to experiment with."

"I don't know if we should reach that far," Caleb replied. "You saw the way the scientists defended themselves on the way back to the hopper."

"I didn't see everything, Sarge. The trip out was chaotic, to say the least."

"Half of them died."

"And half didn't. A suspicious half."

"Valentine thinks we're boxing shadows. And she may be right. I can't believe she isn't on our side. I just can't. Not against the trife. We have to go forward assuming she's with us, whatever the truth about her team may or may not be. We need them to help us run the gauntlet. We don't have a spare man to act as an operator and keep an eye on the sensor grid for us."

"You're going to ask them to help us?"

"Yes."

"I'm not sure that's a great idea, Sarge."

"I can't go there. And you shouldn't either."

"Roger."

"It isn't just scent," Caleb continued. "I know they react to sound and I'm sure they can hear us in the corridors." He paused, an idea coming to him. It was risky as hell, but it might be worth it. "I think we can use that to our advantage. I have an idea. Actually, I have two ideas."

Washington stepped forward, raising his hand to get Caleb's attention.

"What is it, Wash?" Caleb asked.

The big Marine mimicked running with his fingers, using one hand and then both.

"Running?" Caleb said, frowning.

Washington nodded and repeated the gesture, and then pointed at Caleb and himself.

"Us?"

Thumbs-up. Running motion again.

"Running?"

Thumbs-up again. A motion to the back of the neck, like claws.

"My injury?"

Nod.

"It's getting better. Don't worry about me. I'll be well enough to fight."

"Me too, Alpha," Ning said.

"Me too," Yasuka said. "I'm good to go."

Washington shook his head and repeated the whole sequence. Caleb watched it carefully, stumped for the next two rounds. Then it dawned on him.

"Shit. I totally forgot."

"Forgot what, Sarge?" Sho asked.

"Before I was hit. Wash and I were chasing somebody. A human."

"What?" Flores said. "There's a civilian running around outside Metro? How the hell did he get out here?"

"Good question. The trife were chasing him. We killed those trife and then I got sideswiped."

"We should find him, right Alpha?" Hafizi said.

"How? He's been running around the dead zone since we launched. He might as well be a ghost." Caleb shook his head. "No. He's not our priority right now. One life for forty-thousand? It works great in movies. Not so much in real life."

"So what's the plan then, Alpha?" Sho asked.

"Stop the trife, save the city. What do you think, Guardians?"

"Yes, Alpha!"

Chapter 36

David's eyes snapped open. His heart pounded, and he pushed himself backward instinctively, slamming into the boxes of MREs. He looked around, confused. Where was he? How had he gotten here?

He remembered a moment later. He was on a starship. A United States Space Force starship. Espinoza was dead.

He wasn't.

He opened his mouth to take deeper breaths, trying to calm himself. The ship was silent around him, save for an occasional slight vibration along the floor. He had fallen asleep. For how long?

He stood up, his body sore and stiff from all the running. He was used to being outside with the trife, but he preferred to hide. He couldn't outrun them anyway. He knew it was a miracle he was still alive.

Now he had to decide what to do with that life.

He turned and looked through the boxes, searching for another flavor. The Thanksgiving MRE he'd had earlier had made him feel sick. He found one labeled Chocolate Cake. He tried to remember the last time he had tasted anything baked. His diet for the last two years had consisted of small urban game like rats and squirrels, fortified by whatever he could scavenge from apartments and stores. A lot of canned foods, since they didn't spoil easily. He had scored a Hostess chocolate something a few months back, but he wasn't sure that counted.

It probably counted more than the block of brown nutrition he unwrapped from the packaging. He wrinkled his nose as he took the first bite. It was chalky and not that chocolatey, but it was way better than the Thanksgiving MRE.

He ate it quickly and then found himself wishing he had some water to wash it all down. There had to be some around here. The ship was supposed to have people on it. He wondered if he dared leave the area. He had been sleeping safely for some time. Obviously the trife weren't interested in MREs. He definitely understood why.

He grabbed his revolver from where it had fallen to the floor, holding it as he made his way out of the storage room and into the mess. His eyes went right to the hatch at the front.

It was still closed.

He was still alone.

There was another door on the other side of the room. He crossed to it and pushed it open, entering a small kitchen. It was little more than a sink and some plastic dishes. Plates, cups, trays, forks, and knives. Not that you needed forks and knives to eat the MREs. Maybe they figured the crew would prefer to act at least like they had a real meal. He grabbed a cup and went to the sink, turning it on. He drank quickly, refilling the cup four times. By the time he had finished drinking, he realized he had to pee.

He looked around. He was sure there were rooms on the ship. Apartments or even just simple bunks. There had to be toilets too. Somewhere. But he didn't want to rush out into the ship with the trife just to relieve himself. He looked back at the sink. It was at hip level, too high to go into directly.

He climbed the counter, kneeling beside the sink, his head nearly touching the metal support beams above. He unbuttoned his jeans, pulling the front down with his underwear and making sure his aim was good. He was nervous at first, feeling odd about the situation. He had to relax. Just for a minute. He had been in here for hours and nothing had come after him. He was safe.

He started to go, the urine making a tinkling sound against the aluminum as it hit the bottom of the sink and went down the drain.

He finished, zipping up and climbing down from the counter. His basic needs were taken care of. Now he could think about something else.

He went through the door, back out to the mess. He had just cleared the frame when someone put the end of a gun to his head.

"Drop the gun," the man ordered. His voice was gruff. Angry.

David opened his hand, letting the revolver thunk on the floor.

"Who the hell are you?" the man said.

"I'm David," David replied. "David Nash." The man didn't answer right away. David tried to get a look at him from the corner of his eye. A Marine. Someone had found him. "I can't tell you how happy I am to see you. I thought I was going to die out here."

"You came from Metro?"

"Metro? No. I'm originally from Detroit. But I was going to school in Atlanta, and--"

"Shut up," the Marine snapped.

David did.

"How did you wind up on the Deliverance? Why are you out here?"

"I'm unarmed now. Can you backup a few steps?"

The Marine shifted, hooking the revolver with his foot and pushing it across the floor, under one of the tables. Only then did he take a few steps back, giving David a little space.

David turned slowly to face him. He couldn't see the man's face through his helmet. The gun he was carrying wasn't like anything he had seen before. "What kind of gun is that?" he asked. He didn't see anywhere to put a magazine, and the muzzle was an odd shape.

"I asked you a question, string bean," the Marine said. "Two questions actually. Answer them."

David's heart raced. He wanted to feel safe with the Marine. Everyone knew that when it came to humans and trife there were only two sides. Still, there was something about this guy that was making him uneasy.

"Espinoza," he said. "He was the leader of our group. We're scavengers. Well, we were scavengers. He noticed one of the military hoppers fly over once and he got hell-bent on tracking it back to its base. We followed him because he was smart. He knew how to stay alive, and keep other people alive."

"I didn't ask for your damn life story, stringer."

"Right. Well, we found your base, but we maybe attracted a nest of trife on our way to it. We managed to stay ahead of them for a while but you know, sometimes they'll just follow and let you wear yourself out. Sometimes they'll hurry and get ahead of you and set an ambush. Sometimes they'll just go full Conan the Barbarian on your ass."

"And sometimes they'll let you lead them to a bigger prize," the Marine said, clearly unhappy.

"Um. Yeah. I guess so. I didn't know about that. We were just trying to get to safety. With you or through you. I guess the trife kind of messed the whole thing up."

"What you're saying is that your people helped the trife get into the hangar and onto the ship?"

David's face flushed. He felt hot. If he hadn't just peed, he might have wet himself. "It wasn't me. I was just a follower. Espinoza had the idea. He started the fight. I really didn't mean for this to happen. I'm awful sorry."

"Any of your friends make it on board?"

"Not that I know of. I don't think so."

"How'd you get through the trife?"

"Just lucky, I guess."

"Bullshit. Do they attack you?"

"Some of them. A lot of them ignore me. I guess because like you said, I'm skinny and weak."

"You have health problems?"

"I was born with a defective lung. They took it out when I was a baby. The doctors said it would grow to fill the space, and I wouldn't have that much trouble, but they were wrong. It's hard to breathe with too much exertion."

"That's why they don't all attack you. Xenotrife are hunters. A lot of people don't know that. They kill people because they were made to kill people, but at least some part of it is a sport to them. The stronger ones won't bother with you. The weaker ones might."

"Aren't they all the same?"

"Are you and me the same?"

"What are you going to do with me?"

"Good question. I didn't come out here for you. I heard noise in here and thought you were a trife. I'm going to kill them all."

"By yourself?"

"Damn right by myself. Guardian Alpha, he's too weak to get it done. The rest of the crew? They'll die."

"You won't die?"

"Nope."

"Why not?"

"I have super powers."

"Like Spiderman?"

"Do I look like a spider to you, Stringer? I'm like Wolverine. But don't tell anybody."

"Why not?"

"It's a secret. I'm not even supposed to know. That bitch Valentine thinks I was too out of it to know what she was doing to me. She thinks I'm an idiot. She thinks all us Marines are idiots. Maybe Caleb and his lap-dogs. I'm Pratt by the way, Sergeant Sean Pratt."

"Nice to meet you, Sergeant Pratt," David said. "What did they do to you?"

"Injected something into me. Me and Private Ning. I don't know what or why. Anyway, I have to find some trife. You're welcome to come along. Or you can stay here."

"Isn't there somewhere safe I can go?"

"Metro is locked down. You can head to Deck Twenty-nine and see if the Marines will let you in. Or Deck Eighteen. That's where Valentine is. She's liable to stick you with something too."

"What's Metro?"

"That's where the civilians are. A city in a starship, if you can imagine that. You can't get in there. The only people who have a key are already inside, and they aren't about to risk opening up for you."

"So Deck Twenty-nine is my best chance to survive?"

"Could be. Or your best chance might be staying put here. You don't have to go in the sink though. There's a head three doors down. You…" Pratt trailed off, turning around. "Stay behind me, Stringer."

David started to calm after talking to Sergeant Pratt, but now his heart began to race again. He reached absently for the revolver that wasn't there. He could see it closer to the front of the mess. Why did the sergeant have to kick it away?

"Here they come," Pratt said. He sounded happy about it.

The hatch slid open. David could barely see around Pratt's armored shoulder, but he noticed the inky black flesh of the trife. It hissed as it rushed Pratt.

The weapon the sergeant carried fired silently, a red bolt snapping from the end of it, and hitting the creature in the chest. It fell to the floor at the Marine's feet.

"Come on!" Pratt shouted. "I know you're coming! Let's do this!"

There was a crash to David's left. His head snapped around to watch the vent cover hit the ground and bounce away. A dark form came in behind it, climbing from the vent along the ceiling toward Pratt.

The sergeant spun and fired, hitting the demon in the chest. It collapsed to the floor, but more trife were coming out of the vent and through the hatch.

"That's right," Pratt shouted. "Come get some!" He turned back to the hatch and did something with his weapon. When he fired again, a ball of blue and red fire lashed out, hitting the trife in the doorway and melting them to ash almost instantly. "Ha-ha!"

The trife at the vent used the redirection to dive toward the sergeant. It hit him in the side, claws raking along his arm. David saw them cut through the black part of the armor and into the man's flesh, blood spraying from the wound. Pratt rocked to the side, taking a step to regain his balance. The trife bit his arm, claws continuing to slash at him. Another demon came out of the vent, and three more charged in from the passageway.

Pratt growled and turned his body, grabbing the trife on his arm and hurling it at the others. It howled and crashed into one of them, slowing it down. The other two both leaped at Pratt, while the one from the vent climbed overhead.

The sergeant punched the first one in the head, breaking its neck with a sharp crack. He took the second one on the side, its claws angling for the less-protected space on the side, connecting and cutting through. Pratt held his gun awkwardly and fired into the creature, the blast of superhot gas cutting into his armor too. He gritted his teeth against the heat, looking up as the third demon dropped toward him.

He çaught its head in his hand, turning and throwing it into the wall with a strength David couldn't believe. The maneuver sent the sergeant off-balance, and Pratt found himself with two trife on his back with more still coming.

"Get off!" he howled, spinning harshly and then throwing himself back into the long counter. The trife were crushed between him and the metal, and he bounced back in time to fire his rifle again, shooting three more of the creatures in rapid succession. Then he stood fixed and still. Waiting.

No more trife appeared. The fight was over. Pratt ten, trife zero.

"That's right," the sergeant said, turning back to David. "I told you, Stringer. They can't hurt me. I'm like Wolverine." He turned sideways, feeling at the slice in his armor. He ran his finger along it. He should have been bleeding out. Instead, his finger came back clean.

"I don't believe it," David said. People didn't heal that fast. It was impossible.

"You can't see past the visor, but I'm smiling right now." He walked over to where David's revolver lay and picked it up. "This is yours. You're going to need it." He tossed it to David, who fumbled the catch. It hit the floor near his feet.

"Civilians," Pratt said. "Good luck, kid." Sergeant Pratt turned around.

A loud, hard crack sounded, followed by a second and then a third. David froze, watching as Pratt's head snapped back, fragments of bullet, helmet, bone, and brain exploding out from the back of it. The same thing happened to his chest and stomach, three rounds tearing straight through the combat armor and continuing through his body. His arms flailed out as he tumbled backward, coming to rest on top of one of the dead trife.

David stared at the sergeant for a few seconds, half-expecting him to get back up. The blood continued to flow, the wounds too massive to recover from. David looked up at the woman standing in the doorway. She was wearing armor that made her look like a robot had swallowed her. Hundreds of interlocking alloy strands and bands wrapped around a fitted black bodysuit similar to the ones the Marines wore, though her version didn't leave as many exposed areas for the trife to cut through. It was sleeker and more fitted, giving him a good look at her athletic frame. She didn't have a helmet on, and he stared at her heart-shaped face, forgetting himself when he looked into her blue eyes. She was beautiful.

And she had also just murdered Sergeant Pratt.

She stared at David, her face hard and cold. Then she laughed to herself, as though his existence was a joke to her. Maybe it was. She was a goddess. He was a peasant.

"Uh. I'm David Nash," he said.

She lowered the gun she had used on Sergeant Pratt. It was relatively compact and mostly rectangular. She snapped it to the side of her armor, replacing it with a pistol. She started walking toward him.

"You're the one who turned the water on?" she asked.

"That was me."

"I thought Pratt was here alone."

"You killed him."

"I had to. The sample didn't take."

"Sample?"

She had almost reached him. He never considered pointing his gun at her. Maybe he should have?

"I thought I would have more time to work on it, but this is war. Do you understand?"

"No."

"If I hadn't killed him, he would have gone after the rest of the Guardians. The acceleration can cause mental instability."

"I still don't know what you mean."

She came to a stop in front of him. "You aren't supposed to." She put her free hand up, reaching out and touching the side of his face. It had been so long since anyone had touched him in any way, he leaned into the momentary comfort.

He heard a small thunk and felt a sudden warmth on the other side of his neck. He looked over as the woman pulled the pistol away from him.

"Goodnight, David."

David tried to say something, but he collapsed before he could finish opening his mouth.

Riley caught him before he hit the floor, lifting him easily with the added strength of the exosuit. She switched her grip and draped him over her shoulder.

"Craft, do you copy?"

"I hear you, Doctor Valentine."

"Send Mackie to my position for escort back to Research. I've got a new test subject, and we didn't even have to go into Metro to get him."

Chapter 37

The Guardians reassembled in the CIC. The preparations for Caleb's plan were gathered near the hatch leading out of the module in the form of a dozen containers, each of them containing various amounts of urine donated by the members of the team.

If the trife were drawn to human smell, he was going to give them a smell.

He was also going to give them sound, or rather a lack of it. While he was still too weak to walk around without his combat armor, Washington and Show were both strong and agile enough to manage it. They had removed the armor-plated, rubbery black armor in exchange for simpler and less protective bodysuits – essentially the same spider-steel garment that made the base of the SOS. Caleb had heard from other Marines that the bodysuits hadn't always been so easily sliced by xenotrife claws. They had evolved and adapted to the protection, their nails growing harder and sharper over generations until they could slice through the material a little too easily.

"Craft, are you there?" Caleb said through his comm, checking his link with Research. He still wasn't sure how Hacker Harry — as the Marines had taken to calling the scientist — had managed to connect Research to their ATCS, but he had.

"Roger, Alpha," Doctor Craft replied.

Valentine had been gracious enough to loan them the engineer to help operate the mission and keep them appraised of trife movements through the live zones of the Deliverance. Of course, she had promised Caleb he owed her one for the loan. He couldn't imagine how she was going to ask him to pay her back.

"Guardians, comm check," Caleb said. "Name and designation. Sergeant Caleb Card, Guardian Alpha, check."

"Private Yen Sho, Vulture Two, check." She said it out loud, her lack of SOS meaning she wasn't wearing an ATCS. It was an obvious drawback to the idea, just like losing the extra protection of the heavier armor. Caleb had to believe the sacrifice would be worth it; otherwise he had already signed off on her death and Washington's as well.

"Corporal Gilab Hafizi, Vulture Three, check."

Washington waved to the group and then raised his thumb.

"Private Jonas Washington, Vulture Four, check," Caleb said for him.

"Corporal Herman Wagner, Raptor One, check." Caleb nodded. He had sent Ning to replace Wagner, helping Master Sergeant Gold with the modifications to the pipes, preferring to keep the sick Marine out of the action as much as possible. He expected Gold and Ning to join their teams once the module work was done, but he imagined they would have completed the first approach by that point. With any luck, it would turn out they wouldn't need the two extra hands.

Then again, luck hadn't been on their side yet today.

"Private Toshi Yasuka, Raptor Two, check."

"Private Karl Shiro, Raptor Three, check."

"Private Mariana Flores, Raptor Four, check."

"Guardians online," Caleb said. "ATCS is fully networked, save for our two ninjas."

"I never thought I would be a ninja," Sho said.

Caleb reached over and tapped on the primary terminal's control surface, bringing the sensor grid up on the main display. He tapped an area near the stern, pinching his fingers and spreading them to zoom in on it until it showed the schematic of a large room surrounded by secondary compartments and corridors. The area was in the dead zone, leaving the life form readings blank.

"This is the interchange," he said. "Where the power from the reactors is converted to energy for the ion thrusters. Three percent of that power leaks out into this space, which according to Valentine and her team is enough to fuel about ten-thousand trife."

He heard the gasps from the Marines who hadn't been present when Valentine elaborated on her earlier statements about the interchange.

"Ten-thousand?" Flores said. "How the hell do we stop that?"

"There aren't ten-thousand right now," Caleb said. "We're estimating the remaining trife at around six hundred."

"Alpha, you do realize there are ten of us?" Flores added. "Eight without Master Sergeant Gold and Private Ning."

"I'm aware of that, Private. We're all aware of that.

But we're still out here, and we're preparing to go to war. Do you have a problem with that?"

"No, Alpha. I just like to point out the obvious." Flores laughed, drawing a few smiles from the other Guardians.

"Six hundred," Caleb repeated. "The biggest problem is that we don't know where all of them are. Scratch that. We don't know where most of them are. Only about fifty are still in a live zone. We're pretty sure the trife can sense the sensors, which is how they know to avoid them."

"We didn't know that before this?" Private Shiro asked.

"There's a lot about the trife we still don't know," Corporal Hafizi said. "We've been too busy dying to do any real in-depth studies."

"Not today, *mi amigo*," Flores said. "Not today."

"Amen to that," Wagner said. "Speaking of which, if anyone is interested in a prayer before the coming battle?"

"Right now, I'll take all the help I can get," Yasuka said.

"I was a Chaplain before the war started," Wagner said. "Bow your heads."

The Guardians all lowered their heads. Caleb was lukewarm about religion, but like Yasuka he wasn't going to deny any potential edge, no matter how unlikely it might seem.

"Dear Lord, grant us strength and wisdom as we gird our loins for battle against Satan's minions. Give us the courage to stand firm in the face of adversity, and allow us to be instruments to Your mighty power as we seek to protect the lives of thousands of innocents. Amen."

"Amen," the Guardians said.

"And please don't let us die," Flores added.

"Amen," the Guardians said.

"As I was saying," Caleb said, picking up where he left

off. "Our first move will be here." He pointed to the edge of the dead zone on Deck Fourteen, two decks up and fifty meters distant from the interchange. "Vultures will take point, with Raptors on bounding overwatch. Hafizi and I will place the first piss-trap here." He zoomed in on the space, a Y-junction with a good line of fire to the center. "We'll back off and see what they do. If we can't bring any of the bastards out, Hafizi and I will go back in and make some noise, while Raptors fall back to here." He pointed to another section of the corridor a fair distance from the trap. "We'll hold position to draw them in, and then Washington and Sho will cut them down."

"Alpha, one question?" Sho said.

"Go ahead."

"Won't the trife wise up to the move after we use it? They won't fall for the trick again."

"That's a definite possibility," Caleb agreed. "We know the trife on Earth can communicate with one another across distances, though we still have no idea how they do it. Some scientists believe they pass a pheromone through the air. Others have suggested ground vibrations, and a few think the queens can communicate telepathically. The important thing is, if we bring them in we have to kill them all. We can't give them a chance to carry what they've learned back to the others."

"Kill them all," Flores said. "Got it, Alpha."

"Once we've established that we can pull the trife away from the nest, we'll start a secondary run here, with the goal of drawing at least twenty percent of them away. We'll also start placing Dragonflies in the access passageways and vents near the interchange to start mapping and monitoring the secondary transport paths. If that goes well, we'll head here, only fifty meters from the interchange. It's the engineering module. The doors are wide. The terminals offer good cover, and it's the closest point to the nest where we can shoot freely without risking critical damage to the ship. The trick to this is that we have to get all of the remaining trife chasing us here, including the queen, and we have to get them massed densely enough they won't be able to back away or run from the barrage."

"How do you presume we do that, Alpha?" Hafizi asked.

"Two contact points. Engineering has the same drainage as Marine and Research. That's where we put whatever piss-traps we have left. We won't have backup from the operator in there, so we need to be alert and pay attention to the ATCS."

"What if they run?"

"We chase them. But if we wind up in the interchange, it's knives only, no matter what happens. One bad shot hits the exchangers, and this whole ship and everyone on it is gone faster than I can snap my fingers."

"No offense, Alpha, but I don't love this plan," Yasuka said. "It's risky."

"Standing here is risky," Wagner said. "I think it's a good balance between aggressive and defensive."

"This is the plan," Caleb said, cutting them off. "If you don't want to participate, maybe you can catch up to Sergeant Pratt." The Sergeant had vanished into one of the dead zones and hadn't come back out. Had he found a path to the trife? More likely, the trife had found him.

"I'm with you, Alpha, Wagner said."

"We're all with you, Alpha," Yasuka added.

"Doctor Craft, we're ready to—"

"Guardian Alpha? Anyone, can you hear me?"

The voice came through the main terminal commlink.

Caleb recognized Sheriff Aveline's voice immediately. She was breathless and agitated.

"Sheriff?" Caleb said. "This is Guardian Alpha. I copy."

"Alpha," she said. "I'm standing in the Law Office in Metro. Deputy Lacuna is with me. He has the corpse of a trife in his arms."

Chapter 38

Caleb's heart sank. "What?" he whispered stiffly, uncertain he had heard Sheriff Avaline correctly.

"We've got half the office combing the engineering passages behind the city and the other half walking the streets. It killed thirty-three passengers before we caught up to it. We've been calling out to you for over an hour. We were starting to think you were dead. "

"I've been here the whole time," Caleb said. "I don't understand why you weren't getting through."

"I swear, half this ship is already busted and we just launched. We've been in here half a day, and we're already getting calls about broken lifts and stuck doors like that's a major concern with everything else going on."

"Cats in trees, remember Sheriff? Where's Governor Lyle in all this?"

"He's with the engineering team. They're trying to figure out how the trife got in."

"Just the one?"

"That we know of. It's a small one, so preliminary guess is it may have found a gap in a stuck air vent or something. We can't take chances on more getting through."

"How can we help you with that?"

"Besides killing them all? Engineering is working with us to isolate the entry point and get it fixed. But we need some backup from the outside."

Caleb's jaw tightened. He barely had enough Marines as it was, but how could he turn down the request? "What's the location?"

"Deck Twenty, near the stern," she replied. "We think. We're following the trail of casualties backward."

Caleb checked the grid. The location was reasonably close to the interchange, just barely outside of the dead zone. The sensors were clear, not that it meant much. If he changed up their strategy a little, maybe they could keep an eye on the vents leading into Metro and stay on track with the original plan.

"We'll be there soon. We were headed that way, anyway. Do you think you can manage until we get there?"

"We'll do our best. Thank you, Alpha."

"If you run into trouble, reach out to Doctor Craft in Research. He can relay a message down to us."

'We'll just have to make do. Hurry, Caleb."

"Roger that, Sheriff. We'll be there ASAP."

"Thanks. Sheriff out."

"Lily, wait," Caleb said before the comm link went dead.

"What is it?" she replied.

"Maybe we can talk again soon. Once the trife are gone. Even if you can't come out here."

"You get all the trife off the ship and we can talk as often as you like."

He could sense the smirks and soft chuckles from the Guardians in the CIC with him. He didn't care. He had already prayed because he would take every edge he could get. Having something to look forward to wouldn't hurt either of them.

"Confirmed. Talk to you later, Sheriff." The link fell silent.

"Doctor Craft," Caleb said. "We're moving out. Guardians, let's go. Make sure you grab a trap on the way."

"Oorah!" they replied in unison.

Caleb picked up his MK-12. His P-50 was already stuck to the back of this SOS, a blaster clasped to his hip. The other Guardians followed his lead, grabbing their weapons and moving into line.

They approached the hatch leading out of the module and it slid open. He paused to grab one of the containers of urine, snapping it to his hip opposite the pistol. Then he entered the passageway, scanning it quickly. There were scratches on the walls and floor, claw marks from the trife who had been banging on the door earlier. There was no sign of the demons themselves.

"Once more into the breach," Sho said behind him.

They started along the corridor, trailing away from the Marine module toward the stairwell that would take them up to the higher decks. The Marines behind him were silent and focused. Washington moved to the left of Caleb as they walked, his plasma rifle leveled and ready. Shiro was bringing up the rear, also armed with a P-50.

They advanced at a steady pace, making it to the stair-well without confrontation. Caleb could tell his body was regaining its strength, the pain medicine beginning to wear off slightly as they continued. His legs felt stronger and lighter, and less like they had lead weights tied to them.

Craft continued to maintain comm silence as they started the ascent. He had only planned to speak if he saw anything unusual happening on the sensor grid, and thankfully there was nothing to report.

The Marines rose quickly, making the trip from Deck Twenty-nine to Deck Twenty within a few minutes. The Guardians were expecting to stop there, but Caleb didn't slow as they reached Twenty. He went right past it, continuing the climb.

"Alpha, aren't we supposed to be helping Metro?" Hafizi asked.

"We will. The more trife we take out on this side of the seals, the fewer can sneak in through the vent."

"Roger that."

They kept climbing to Deck Fourteen, coming out near the central lifts. Craft still hadn't said anything about the trife, leaving Caleb to assume the area was clear. Of course, the doctor couldn't see in the walls or vents any better than the Guardians could, so they still moved cautiously, maintaining their formation as they made their way to the first choke point.

"Raptors, split here to take a position on both sides of the fork," Caleb said as they neared the Y-intersection. "Flores, load a pair of Dragonflies in these two vents. Be ready to run when we call for you."

"Roger that, Alpha," Corporal Wagner said. "We've got your back."

"Roger, Alpha," Flores said, unslinging her hard pack, the one with the Dragonflies inside. She laid it on the ground and flipped it open to take out two of the small robots and release them into the vents.

"Vultures, let's go. Stay alert." Caleb led the Vultures forward, coming from the left corridor of the intersection toward the choke point. "Sho, Washington, wait here."

"Roger that, Sarge," Sho said.

Caleb and Hafizi continued forward, entering the

intersection. Caleb took the container of urine from his hip and unscrewed it, turning it over and dumping the contents out onto the floor. Hafizi opened his and splashed it onto the walls.

"Do you think they'll fall for this?" Hafizi asked.

"We're about to find out. Let's move back."

They retreated to where Sho and Washington were waiting. They would find out if the smell of urine was enough to bring the trife to them or if they needed to be physically present to entice them.

"Raptor Four, do you have anything?" Caleb asked.

"Negative, Alpha," Flores replied. "Vents are clean. No visual, no… wait. Onboard microphones just started picking up sound. Gathering telemetry. Standby."

Caleb shouldered his rifle, waiting for Flores' report. He still didn't hear or see anything. "Craft, nothing?"

"Negative, Alpha," Doctor Craft said. "I would have told you if there was movement from the group in the aft."

"Alpha, I have it," Flores said. "We have motion through the vents, approaching the intersection."

"They must have been close to get there so fast," Sho said.

"Alpha, they stopped," Flores said. "Twenty meters back of the intersection."

"Check the map, is there a vent back there?"

"Standby." A moment later. "Confirmed. "They probably have line of sight."

"And they can see nobody is there," Caleb said. "I'm going in. Hafizi, wait here. Let's see if we can draw them out with one piece of bait."

"Alpha, it should be me," Corporal Hafizi said.

"Negative. My plan. My risk. Sho, Wash, get ready."

"We're ready, Sarge."

Caleb started forward, heading back to the intersection. He walked into the area, rifle up and ready, turning slowly and pretending he was searching for the trife.

"They're moving, Alpha."

"Alpha, I've got movement in the corridor ahead," Craft said. "About twenty trife."

"They think you're alone," Hafizi said.

"Good. Haffy, have Wash and Sho move in closer."

"Roger."

Caleb looked back toward the Vultures. Then he started to sing. *"From the Halls of Montezuma to the shores of Tripoli…"*

His voice echoed in the corridors. His ATCS picked up the trife, and he turned back around to face them.

A single demon charged him from the corridor. He shot it in the chest, sending it sprawling, still singing.

"We fight our country's battles in space, air, land, and sea.."

"Alpha, I'm picking up audio from the second vent," Flores said. "It's getting loud."

"They're sending a lot of bugs your way, sir."

"Good. Don't let me down."

"We've got you covered, Alpha."

Caleb stood in the middle of the intersection, trying to watch all of the avenues of attack at once. He could hear the trife in the corridor now, sharp claws clacking and clattering against the floor. They were going to rush him en masse, and use their vastly superior numbers against him.

Except their numbers weren't as superior as they thought.

"We are proud to claim the title Of U.S. Space Force Marine."

"Watch the vents, Alpha," Flores said, giving him warning. Caleb looked over. He could swear he saw the yellow eyes looking back at him.

"Haffy, send Washington in," Caleb said, stopping his singing and starting to backpedal away from the corridor.

The trife came around the corner in the distance, moving on all fours, a scrambling black slick of aliens with only one motive — erasing him from the universe.

He reached the right fork, crouching against the wall and shooting, taking out the lead trife. Most of the demons behind the leaders leaped over, but a few stopped to put their hurt brethren out of their misery.

It didn't matter. Washington emerged from the tunnel, P-50 at the ready. The demons hissed as he came into view, taken by surprise by the quiet Marine dressed in black.

Their hisses turned to screams, the superheated gas of the plasma rifle washing over them and burning them to death. Nearly twenty trife had come after him. They died in seconds.

But what about the creatures in the vents?

"Alpha!" Flores shouted. "They're on the move, headed back toward… shit! The Dragonfly is out. We're blind."

"Fall back to the rendezvous point," Caleb said. "Now!"

He heard more claws in the corridor ahead. "Craft, what the hell is happening?"

"They're coming, Alpha," Craft said. "They're still coming."

"Why didn't you say anything?"

"I'm in communication with Metro," Craft replied, his voice stiff. "The trife are attacking them too."

"How many?"

"I don't know. All of them?"

Chapter 39

Caleb continued to back up, joining Washington in the corridor. What the hell was happening? The plan was to draw in a few of the trife, not bring the whole damn nest running. Of course, they weren't all chasing after him and the Guardians.

They were heading for Metro.

Lily had said the one they caught came in through a jammed vent, the space too small for most of the trife to get through. But what if the hole was larger than they thought? Or what if the creatures were able to dislodge it? Somehow, they knew that one of their number had made it inside, and they wanted to do the same. Did they know how many people were hiding in there? Did they know how many they could kill?

There were somewhere near thirty law officers in Metro. That wasn't nearly enough. They might be former Marines, but they didn't have armor, they didn't have assault rifles, and they definitely didn't have plasma.

"Craft, location?" Caleb asked. He heard a crash behind him, and his ATCS lit up as Hafizi's sensors picked up the demons emerging from the vents. He heard gunfire a moment later, and then the hiss-whine of plasma.

Washington started shooting beside him, switching his P-50 back to bolt mode. The red-blue lines of heat sank into the incoming slick of trife, blasting through the front lines.

"Alpha, Metro requests immediate assistance," Craft said.

"A little busy," Caleb replied. "Maybe you can go help them out?"

"We don't have any weapons here. We're scientists, not Marines."

"Have to do everything myself," Caleb muttered. He glanced over at Washington, making a quick decision. "Fire in the hole!"

He squeezed the secondary trigger on his MK-12. A loud thunk followed, and a silver ball launched from the barrel into the crowd of trife ahead.

It exploded a few seconds later, the detonation shaking the corridor and rending metal, tearing the incoming trife apart and leaving the path behind them clear.

Washington smiled and flashed his upturned thumb as they turned around and sprinted along the corridor. His ATCS was registering more of the demons closing on the Raptors, who were trying to make their way to the rendezvous point -- an adjoining corridor half a klick back.

"Raptors, this is Alpha. Vultures are headed for the stairwell. We're heading to Deck Twenty to support Metro. Cover our movement."

"Roger that, Alpha," Wagner said. "We've got them."

Caleb heard the gunfire echoing through the corridors. He could see the targets vanishing on his ATCS, cut down by the Raptor's fire. The trife were coming on hard, but the combination of advanced weaponry and enclosed space gave the Guardians an edge, and the demons were out of tricks.

He hoped.

The trap he had tried to lay had failed, not because the trife were wise to the plan, but because they were able to sense living humans beyond the scent of urine or sound. He didn't know how. It couldn't be that their hearing was so acute, or Washington wouldn't have taken them by surprise. The same went for registering vibrations on the floor or having extra-fine vision. And yet they knew all of the Guardians were there. Not only there, but where they were within the confines of the ship. They had known about the bridge, the Marine module, and maybe Research. Valentine probably wouldn't tell him if the trife had attacked; it might give him some satisfaction.

So what was it about those things that separated them from Washington in his current ninja state?

His thoughts were interrupted as he caught up to Hafizi and Sho. There were dead trife all around them, both burned by plasma and shot with conventional rounds. The two Vultures were standing in the middle of the scrum. Sho was bleeding from a large gash across her face, which Hafizi was in the process of patching.

"Sho," Caleb said, rushing over to her.

She turned to look up at him. Her left eye was gone, torn out by a demon claw.

"Too many," she said. "Bastards."

"Hold still," Hafizi said, holding the patch up. It had a strong smell of its own, a chemical cocktail of healing agents that would stop the bleeding and begin repairing as much of the damage as it could.

Washington put a hand on Sho's shoulder to comfort her. She reached up and squeezed his wrist. "I'll be okay," she said. "Ugly, but okay."

He motioned to his own face, more heavily scarred and malformed than hers would ever be.

"But you're a man. Nobody cares about an ugly man. And you didn't lose your eye."

"You won't come out ugly," Caleb said. "Just stay alive and you'll see."

"Roger that, Sarge."

"This is going to hurt," Hafizi said. He used his free hand to pinch Sho's face, bringing the cut skin back together. At the same time, he pressed the patch against it, holding it there while it reacted with the blood and skin, fusing to it.

Caleb was impressed when Sho didn't make a sound. He knew how much the patches hurt. He shifted his attention to his HUD. The Raptors were closing on the rendezvous point, managing the trife coming after them. Another group of the demons was headed toward his team, closing from the corridor they needed to go down.

"Alpha," Craft said. "What the hell are you doing? Metro needs assistance, asap."

"We're on our way, damn it," he snapped back. "It isn't exactly a picnic up here."

"I'm good to go," Sho said, wrinkling the undamaged side of her face. "Wash, keep my right side covered, will you?"

He nodded.

"We've got to go through them to make it to the nearest stairwell," Caleb said.

"Roger that," they replied, moving into position with Sho in front. Caleb didn't love putting her forward like that without a SOS, but he would be able to cover her bad side more easily.

They continued ahead, a small boat powering into a

rushing tide. Sho adjusted her P-50, switching to stream mode as they closed on the demons.

"Be careful not to slag the corridor," Caleb said. "We still need to get through."

"Roger," Sho replied.

"Fifty meters," Caleb said, giving her the position. There was a slight angle to the corridor ahead. "We need to get around the corner before they do."

"On it," Sho said, sprinting forward. Caleb sped up after her, feeling the pushback from his body immediately. He wasn't so far removed from his injury that he could go all-out without complaint.

It didn't matter. This was his duty, and he would fall flat on his face and die before he would let Sho make that turn alone. He growled softly as he pushed harder, his slightly wobbly legs supported by the combat armor's artificial muscle.

They reached the corner, turning only a few seconds ahead of the trife. The demons were so close to Sho that Caleb had a moment of terror, certain they were going to cut her down.

Gas spewed from her P-50, washing them in heat that burned the skin from their muscle and the muscle from the bone. Twenty trife dropped in a second, the others hissing and screaming and trying to back away. Caleb raised his rifle and fired into their backs, cutting them down before they could escape.

"Alpha, we're closing on your position," Wagner said. "Picking up trife coming out of the walls behind you."

Caleb checked his HUD. The trife had approached from an access tunnel, trying to ambush them from the rear. Didn't they know the Raptors were further back?

"Raptor One, hold your position!" Caleb shouted. "Wedge up; you're in the crosshairs."

"Say again, Alpha?"

"They're boxing you in. Wedge formation, full retreat. Circle to the central lifts and take them down to Deck Twenty, we'll rendezvous at the mess outside Metro."

"Roger that. We're... Raptor Two, watch your six! Flores, coming your way!"

Caleb quickly brought up the vitals of the Marines under his command. Raptor Two had gone red. Damn it!

"They're tearing us apart," he said. The trife were outmaneuvering them at every turn, using their ability to accurately locate them in the maze of corridors to pick them off. He had thought the confines and corridors were giving his Guardians the advantage, but now he realized his mistake.

As deadly as the trife had been in the open spaces on Earth, they were much more deadly in here.

Chapter 40

"Should we help them?" Hafizi asked.

"Negative," Caleb replied. "We need to get to Deck Twenty. If the trife overwhelm Metro, it's all over for all of us."

"Roger that."

They regained their formation, rushing toward the stairwell. Caleb kept his attention on the HUD, monitoring the Raptors' retreat. He opened the feed from Wagner's helmet camera just in time to watch the team run past a suddenly opening hatch to their left. Wagner spun around, shooting the first trife out of it before spinning back. Muzzle flashes and the sound of gunfire echoed off the walls. Wagner ran full-ahead, Raptors Three and Four behind him, getting ahead of the ambush.

"Raptor One, you have permission to use secondary ordnance," Caleb said.

"Roger that, Alpha," Wagner replied. "Raptor Four, blow them to shit."

Wagner spun back again, giving Caleb a view of the destruction as Flores pulled the secondary trigger and sent a silver ball into the midst of the trailing horde. He felt the vibrations in the floor as the round went off, putting a quick end to the chase.

"You called it, Alpha," Wagner said. "How did you know?"

"Intuition, I guess. Meet us on Deck Twenty."

"Affirmative, Alpha."

The Vultures reached the stairwell, pushing through and onto the steps. "Sho, switch positions with me. Wash, swap with Haffy. Armor in front and rear."

"Roger," they replied, updating the formation. Caleb eyed the tactical, waiting for targets to come into sensor range. They started down the narrow stairwell single-file.

"Craft, we're dropping to Deck Twenty. What's the situation?"

"Sheriff Aveline is reporting a broken seal in one of the engineering maintenance corridors. They're doing their best to hold the trife back, but they're losing ground. They're going to solder the secondary hatch between the city itself and the passage, but it can't stay that way forever. The corridor leads to the water filtration units."

Caleb didn't need Craft to explain what that meant. He already knew. If the units were to break and the engineers couldn't fix them, the entire city would die anyway.

"We're almost there," Caleb said, dropping to Deck Seventeen.

The Vultures kept going, racing downward. Caleb's tactical updated with new targets as he reached Deck Fifteen, the trife joining them on the stairwell from two decks above.

"Haffy, watch your tail," he warned.

"On it, Alpha," Hafizi replied. "Don't slow down."

Caleb didn't, dropping the last set of risers to the hatch on Deck Fourteen. He glanced at his HUD. The trife were pouring into the stairwell like water, from each of the doors above them, at least a hundred of the demons in all. How many of the creatures were in here? They had estimated the number at six hundred, but it seemed like there were more.

A lot more.

Caleb grabbed the handle of the hatch, turning and pushing it. His shoulder slammed into the door when it didn't open.

"What the?" He turned it and pushed again. The door was jammed. "Shit!"

Sho nearly collided with him, expecting him to be through the hatch and into the corridor. "Alpha?"

"Haffy, we're jammed up here. Hold the rear. Wash, hold the rear. Switch to conventional."

Caleb heard the bullets start flying a moment later, a long burst that cut into the trailing trife. He turned back to the door. Why was it stuck? He was starting to feel like the Deliverance had it in for them.

The firefight intensified behind him. He took a step back, and then lunged at the door, kicking it right above the handle. Something cracked and snapped, and the door flew open.

"We're through!" Caleb said, moving into the corridor. His ATCS lit up to his right, a massive blob of red. Craft hadn't been kidding when he said all of them. He quickly checked on the Raptor's position. They were nearing the central lifts.

"Alpha, there are too many," Hafizi said. "Where are they all coming from?"

"We're clear," Caleb said. "Get down here, and we'll seal the stairwell. Move it, Marine!"

Caleb turned in the direction of the trife. The demons were facing away from him, toward what he assumed was the corridor leading to the broken hatch. They started shifting as he moved aside. Sho shouldered up next to him with her P-50.

"How many are there?" she asked.

"Too many," Caleb replied, glancing back. There was a corridor a few meters behind them. "We can go around."

Washington came out of the stairwell with them.

"We need to wait for Hafizi," Sho said.

The trife began their charge, rushing them from thirty meters away.

Caleb looked at the stairwell and then checked the tactical. Hafizi should have been right behind them, but he was still in the stairwell. His vitals were orange from a wound to his leg. He had gotten hit and hadn't said anything.

"Shit, Hafizi's down," Caleb said. "Break down the corridor and wind your way back. Use the urine to throw them off. You need to get back to the seal – "

"Alpha, I'm down," Hafizi said. "Leg is done. Can't run. Get out of here."

"Haffy, I'm coming."

"No you're not. Fire in the hole!" Hafizi shouted.

"Run!" Caleb shouted, turning and sprinting away from the stairwell, Sho and Washington right behind him.

Caleb heard the explosion, felt the vibration and then the heat as the grenade went off, blasting out the side of the stairwell and into the chasing trife. They hissed and screamed and died, their brethren behind them momentarily distracted as they stumbled over their dead and dying. Caleb lowered his head, only able to spare a moment to mourn the loss of another fellow Guardian.

The three remaining Vultures ran along the adjacent corridor. Caleb kept an eye on his HUD. Some of the trife were still coming, but others had turned back to focus on getting into Metro.

"We can't even get close," Sho said as they neared another intersection, turning left and continuing along the corridor. "They always know where we are."

"They didn't know where you were before. They tracked Hafizi and me."

Washington came to an abrupt stop.

"Wash, what are you doing?" Caleb said, stopping and turning.

The big Marine thrust his finger out at him, shaking it forcefully.

"What?"

Washington approached him, tapping on his helmet, and then on his back where the ATCS power supply was located.

Caleb stared at him. Of course. He was an idiot. The battery pack was using energy. Creating heat. Not to mention sending all kinds of radio signals. The trife were picking up one of those things, or maybe both of those things. They were drawn to the SOS. They would be similarly drawn to the CIC, the bridge, or Metro.

He looked past Washington, raising his rifle as the trife approached, firing into them. He cut them down in a long burst, killing nearly a dozen and leaving them free and clear, at least for the moment.

"Raptor One, sitrep."

"We're in the lift, Alpha," Wagner replied. "On our way to Fourteen."

"Roger that. I've got new orders, and they're going to sound a little crazy, and it's going to make things even more challenging, but it may be the only chance we have."

Chapter 41

Sho and Washington helped Caleb out of his combat armor, leaving him in only a pair of boxer briefs and a t-shirt, both of which were already soaked with sweat from the exertion of the fighting. It was impossible to keep wearing the SOS without it powered up, the armor plating too heavy for him to carry without the assistance of the artificial muscles. The boots were part of the SOS as well, and his bare feet quickly grew cold on the metal floor.

If there was any good news, it was that his headache was returning, which also meant his finer motor control and strength was coming back with it, the medication he had taken earlier wearing off.

He missed the ATCS immediately, both in his inability to communicate with the Raptors and the loss of the positioning of the trife within the sensor grid. He wasn't thrilled to lose contact with Craft either, but there was no other choice. They had to take the trife by surprise, and they couldn't do that when their equipment was telegraphing all of their movements. He could picture the Raptors standing in one of the lifts stripping out of their

SOS. He had heard of Marines who went naked beneath the combat armor. He hoped none of them fit into that profile.

Caleb finished undressing and then grabbed the MK-12 and the P-50, slinging the plasma rifle over his shoulder. He had no way to carry the laser pistol, so he left it in the small storage compartment they had slipped into.

The door slid aside, offering them exodus back into the passageway. Caleb took it slow, pausing in the frame and scanning both sides of the corridor, MK-12 up and ready. He missed the targeting reticle of the ATCS too.

"Clear," he said, moving out into the hallway. He had checked tactical before shutting down, and he knew which way they had to go. He led the Vultures down the passage to the next intersection and turned left, followed that one past three adjacent corridors and turned left again, stopping at the corner.

The trife assaulting Metro were gathered there, still hissing at one another as they waited for the group up front to pierce the city's defenses. Craft had said the engineers managed to get the secondary hatch sealed and fused, stuck closed until they undid their work, which would only happen when someone in the Guardians gave the all clear.

Sho handed him one of their urine traps. He unscrewed the top and threw it straight across the intersection. A dozen heads turned the moment it hit the ground and spilled.

Caleb ducked back, and the three Vultures retreated a few meters down the hallway, waiting for the trife to start turning the corner.

They didn't wait long.

A group of ten demons moved to the intersection, turning in the direction of the urine, hissing to one another when they saw there was no one there.

It didn't matter. It was already too late for them. Sho and Washington both fired their plasma rifles, cutting the aliens down.

"Clear," Sho said.

Caleb ran forward, watching where he placed his bare feet as he stepped over the freshly killed trife, their melted bodies still steaming hot. More of the demons turned away from the Metro hatch, reacting to the death of their brethren. Louder hisses rose from the group, and a larger mass charged Caleb.

"Get ready," he said, firing a few potshots into the group. Then he broke to the right, toward the spilled urine, hopping athletically over it.

Sho and Washington pressed against the sides of the hallway, and they waited for the group of trife to turn the corner and begin chasing Caleb before moving into the open. They fired their plasma rifles into the backs of the demons, killing them before they had any idea what was happening.

Caleb stopped and turned around, shooting one demon who managed to escape the plasma stream. He waved to Sho and Washington, who flashed him a thumbs-up. Clear again, all three of the Vultures moved back into position near the intersection, looking down toward the outer hatch.

The trife were gone from the passageway, the group waiting in the back already dead. Caleb could still hear their hisses echoing from ahead of the primary seal, but they were fading moment by moment.

"They're on the move, Sarge," Sho said.

"Trying to find out what's going on without staying in the open," Caleb said. "Wash, are you keeping time?"

Washington nodded.

"How long?"

The big Marine let the plasma rifle hang from its strap and put up both hands, lowering his fingers one at a time. A few seconds after he reached zero, a whistle sounded from the other side of the corridor.

The Raptors.

"Full assault mode," Caleb said. "Hard and fast. This is going to get ugly. There's no way around it."

"Roger that, Sarge," Sho said.

They had gotten as many of the trife as they could to break ranks. While the demons were currently moving into the vents and access tunnels, they would come back once they saw what they were dealing with. The unarmored Guardians would be surrounded, and they would have no other option but to fight their way out of it.

In a sense, it was their last stand against the creatures. Except it wasn't. Even if they survived, they still had the queen to deal with.

Caleb whistled back, signaling the Vultures were ready.

"Here we go, Marines," he said.

"Oorah!" Sho replied while Washington pumped his fist.

Then they charged.

Chapter 42

The Vultures joined with the Raptors as they reached the outer seal, which had been lifted away from the ground by the trife, using a strength Caleb couldn't believe they possessed. Claw marks scored the narrow slot in the floor where the hatch rested when lowered closed. Even with the malfunctioning locking mechanism refusing to engage, the demons had done what the strength of a hydraulics couldn't. They had clawed at the bottom of the hatch until they managed to force their claws beneath it and lift its great weight. It was an unforeseen failure for a relatively simple design. But it didn't matter now. What was done was done.

They just had to undo it.

The six remaining Guardians moved through the broken hatch without comment, quickly organizing into a formation with a pair of plasma rifles front and back, and two MK-12s in the middle. They were expecting the corridors immediately beyond the passage to be crawling with trife, but they were surprisingly clear.

It was so surprising that the Marines slowed to a stop a few meters in, looking both ways down the passage.

"Where the hell did they go?" Wagner asked.

"Wait," Caleb said. "Listen."

The Marines stood in silence, listening for the trife. Caleb could hear clinking and thunking in the walls in both directions. The trife had moved into the ventilation shafts, but where were they going?

"Which way to Metro?" Shiro asked.

Caleb took a moment to recall the layout of the ship. "I'm pretty sure Metro is that way," he said, pointing to the right.

"What's that way?" Wagner asked, motioning left.

"Craft said the city was cut off from water filtration," Caleb said. "It must be in that direction."

"Do you think the trife know what will happen if they destroy the city's water supply?" Sho asked.

"They can't be that smart," Wagner said. "They're stupid bugs, like roaches."

"They aren't stupid," Sho said.

"We can't risk it," Caleb decided. "Come on."

"You're sure it's this way, Sarge?"

"Fifty-fifty chance. Move it, Guardians."

They turned left, running along a curving corridor that sloped downward. They passed a few hatches leading into other areas marked as water control, emergency cutoffs, and waste filtration. They slowed at each to see if the trife were there.

They weren't.

The Guardians continued down the corridor, following it to an open hatch labeled as water filtration. A trife was standing guard directly inside it, and it hissed at them as they came into view.

A single bolt from Sho killed the trife, setting off a chain reaction of hisses in the room behind it. Caleb looked down as a trail of water came around the corner and spilled out along the floor. He looked up again, able to make out the shadowy forms of multiple water tanks in the background, the trife slashing at them with their impossibly sharp claws.

"Son of a bitch," Wagner said, noticing the water. He raised his rifle.

"Wait!" Caleb said. "You can't shoot in there. If you put more holes in the tanks, we won't be able to recover."

Wagner glared at him. "Are you kidding, Alpha? How the hell are we supposed to fight them?"

They needed to figure it out quick because the trife were organizing, a group of them breaking away and charging toward them.

"Plasma, stream only," Caleb said. "Short bursts. Don't melt the tanks."

"Confirmed," Wagner said, flipping modes on his rifle. He hit the leading demons with plasma, dropping them.

Caleb dropped his MK-12, retrieving his plasma rifle and switching its mode.

"Spread out, watch your fire. Don't hit your fellow Marines!"

They charged into the filtration room. There were close to sixty trife inside, and as they entered Caleb could hear the vents behind them crashing to the ground.

"Washington, cover our asses," he shouted.

Washington stopped and turned, holding his P-5o with his right hand and pulling his service knife from its sheath on his hip with the other.

Caleb charged ahead, breaking to the left. There was a larger machine resting on the floor, with a small raised metal platform beside it, offering access to a control station connected to it. A trife vaulted the platform, headed for the controls.

Caleb fired, his plasma rifle still in bolt mode. The blast hit the demon in the back and knocked it forward. It slumped over the controls and tumbled to the ground.

He charged the position, eager to defend the system from the demons, who clearly knew how they could hurt the humans without attacking them individually. He saw Sho out of the corner of his eye as she let loose a stream of gas that killed three of the trife on the leftmost tank. That got the attention of more of the demons, and they abandoned the tanks to attack.

Caleb reached the steps to the platform, scaling it and turning toward the rest of the room. The water was coming from the tank closest to him, which had enough of a gash in it that it was losing water in a hurry.

He turned to the control panel, quickly wiping the trife blood away and tapping on the surface. Could he shut down individual tanks?

A hiss got his attention, and he sidestepped as a trife landed on the platform beside him, claws slashing toward his face. They missed him and slammed into the railing, the trife backhanding with them and nearly tearing into Caleb's unprotected chest. He managed to jump back, switching the plasma rifle to stream and squeezing the trigger. The stream lasted for only a moment but it was long enough to melt the front of the trife. It screamed and fell away.

Caleb heard a scream from the other side of the room. He looked in time to see a trio of trife tackle Wagner, dragging him to the ground and tearing into him.

He winced and looked back at the control surface. The controls were simple, and he hit the emergency cutoff on the closest tank, stopping the flow of filtered water to it.

Someone started shooting, the sound of bullets echoing in the room.

"Who the hell is firing?" Caleb screamed, vaulting the platform to the floor. He looked back toward the entrance, where a woman in the oddest combat armor he had ever seen was quickly emptying their rifle into the trife, one perfectly-aimed round at a time.

He only watched for a second, and then he returned his attention to the remaining trife. A pair were rushing him, and he blasted them with a short stream of plasma. He heard a hiss over his head and looked up in time to see the armored Guardian shoot the trife over him. Caleb stepped aside as it tumbled to the floor.

The intensity of the fighting began to subside; the trife were suddenly overwhelmed despite their superior numbers. They stopped trying to attack and began making for the nearby vents, eager to get away from the carnage.

"Don't let them get away," Caleb said. "Stay on them!" Now that the trife were away from the tanks, he switched the plasma back to bolt mode, firing individual rounds at the retreating trife. The other Guardians followed his lead, cutting them down before they could make it to the relative safety of the tunnels.

They were all dead within minutes.

Chapter 43

Caleb made his way to their interloper. He knew she was female by the way the strange armor wrapped around her body, sitting tight against her breasts and hips. Her helmet was equally sleek, fitted against her head, the visor black over her eyes and the mouth covered by what appeared to be an air filter.

"Lily?" he offered when he reached her, wondering if she had broken protocol and left the city to help them defend it. This woman was about the right size and shape to be Sheriff Aveline.

She reached up with her free hand, gripping the helmet and sliding it away from her head. She took a moment to shake her hair loose before smiling at him.

"Sorry to disappoint you, Alpha," Doctor Valentine replied.

"What the hell?" Sho said, approaching the pair. "Where did you come from?"

"Research, obviously," Valentine replied. "You did ask for our help, didn't you, Sergeant Card?"

"I did. To be honest, I wasn't expecting any. You could have punctured the tanks shooting in here like that."

"Please. The guidance systems on the Cerebus wouldn't let that happen."

"Cerebus?" Sho said.

Doctor Valentine shook her arm. "The armor. It's a prototype. A product of my work, but not the work itself."

"Whatever that means."

"You're lucky this part of the ship is on Metro's internal network. Sheriff Aveline – Lily – saw you go in here and she begged us to do something. Contrary to what you might think, I don't want any of you to die."

"Then you should have been here sooner," Flores said, coming over to them with Shiro. Washington approached from the rear.

"You stripped to your skivvies for a reason, Private," Valentine replied. "It was good thinking. I hadn't considered the transmission potential of our radio signals in here. We were bringing the damn things right to us. You figured it out, Alpha. I'm impressed."

Caleb glanced at Washington, who raised his eyebrows expectantly.

"It wasn't me," Caleb admitted. "Washington had the idea."

Doctor Valentine turned to Washington. "Nice job, Private."

Washington flashed his thumb.

"This area's clear, Alpha," Valentine said. "But there's still the elephant in the room. Or rather, on the ship."

"The queen," Caleb said.

"She won't have had time to produce offspring yet, but unless you want to start over we don't have a lot of time to waste. We need to hit her now."

"Do we look like we're in any shape to launch an offensive?" Caleb asked. Besides Sho's wounded face, Flores had a gash on her arm, and Shiro looked like he was ready to collapse. Only Washington seemed unfazed by the effort they'd all just expended.

"The trife don't care if you're tired," Valentine replied.

"Maybe you can go back there and take care of it for us?" Sho suggested. " You're the one with superhero armor."

"Which the trife will know is coming from a mile away. Fortunately, I didn't need to sneak over here."

"So take it off and come with."

"You asked for help, and I gave you help. That's the best I can offer."

"Are you kidding?" Sho said, obviously frustrated. "Do you see how many of us are left here, Doctor? We need every able-bodied fighter we can get, and it's clear you're both able-bodied and a fighter. You've seen combat before, and I don't mean some mop-up drop into a relatively safe zone. Why don't you admit you're special forces and quit the charade?"

"It's not a charade, Private Sho," Valentine replied, remaining calm. "I'm a geneticist. You can look it up on the manifest. Yes, I used to be a Marine. And yes, I spent some time in MARSOC. You're astute enough to have picked up on it, though I have no idea how. That was before the trife. Things changed."

Her voice cracked when she said the last two words, showing a sudden vulnerability Caleb would never have expected from her. Everyone had their own trife apocalypse story to motivate them, from the murder of Washington's wife to the loss of his own parents. He could only imagine what was motivating her.

Her expression stiffened back to stone. "I'm sorry, Alpha, I can't go after the queen with you. I have orders from Command, a vital mission of my own to accomplish. I can't risk my life."

"But you can risk ours?" Flores said.

"Command considers you more expendable than I am. That's a fact. I would have been well within rights to let you die out here. The water tanks would be more important if we were making the full trip."

"But Proxima's a lot closer," Caleb said. "Does that have anything to do with your work, Doctor?"

"Yes, in part. That's all I'm going to say about it. Caleb, take your team back to the Marine module and reload. Don't waste any more time. A queen can produce as many as three hundred trife per day given enough consorts and enough energy, and the interchange is producing plenty of energy."

Caleb sighed. He knew she was right, but damn he was tired, and he knew his team was tired too. "What are you going to do?"

"I'm going to close the hatch and let Sheriff Aveline know its safe to move in and reseal it."

"What about the vents?"

"These vents are isolated from the outside."

"Then how do you know more of the trife didn't get into the city?"

"Because you killed them all before they escaped."

"Are you sure?"

"The Law Office has the tools they need to monitor the situation. As long as the stragglers are cut off from the nest and a strong power source, the best the trife could hope for would be to kill a few more civilians."

"You make that sound so acceptable," Sho said.

"What's done is done. We stopped them causing complete mayhem in the city. Now you need to stop them outside the city."

Caleb nodded. "We're wasting time. Guardians, let's go. Washington, take point."

Washington nodded and started toward the door, the other Guardians following him. Caleb stayed behind with Valentine.

"Are you sure you're on our side, Doctor?" he asked once they were gone.

"I'm on humanity's side," she replied.

Her wording wasn't lost on him, even if he didn't know exactly what it meant right now.

"Thanks for the save," he said.

She gathered her hair with one hand and slid the helmet back over her head with the other.

"You're welcome," she said, her voice muffled by the helmet's filter. "Good hunting, Alpha."

Caleb stared at her black visor as she passed him by on her way to safety. He sighed heavily and rejoined what was left of his Guardians.

Once more into the breach.

Chapter 44

"This is going to hurt a little," Private Shiro said, leaning over Sho.

"I can take it," she replied.

"I'm sure you can."

Shiro took the edge of the patch and slowly peeled it away from Sho's face. Caleb winced as he saw the damage underneath. That patch had stopped the bleeding, pulling the extra blood to the edges, and started knitting the wound closed. It was long and deep, a pair of scars that would remain long after the damage was fully healed, running from her forehead, across her eye, and down her cheek.

"How ugly am I?" Sho asked, looking over at him.

"I don't think you're ugly at all," Shiro said. "I think you're a brave Marine."

"Thank you."

"It isn't that bad," Caleb said. "Maybe when we get to Proxima they'll be able to get you a replacement eye and do some work on the scarring to make it less noticeable. If you want that."

"The eye? Maybe. The scars? We all have scars, don't we?"

Caleb turned around and bent his head. Shiro had already patched up Yen and then removed the patch on his own neck, revealing a long, pink scar from his most recent wound. He had others on his body, especially on his hands and arms. It was the price to pay for fighting the trife.

"I'm going to replace your eye patch," Shiro told Sho. "You'll be as good as new soon."

Sho laughed. "Yeah, right. As good as new, my ass," she scoffed, playfully punching him in the arm. "Put the damn patch on and be done with it. We've got work to do."

Shiro smiled and smoothed the patch over the healing wound before turning to Caleb. "That's it, Alpha. We're as healthy as we're going to get."

"Roger that," Caleb said, glancing over at the other rack in the sickbay. Private Ning was there, asleep. Whatever had happened to him, his fever had gotten bad enough Shiro had recommended sedation. "We'll worry about Ning when we're done with the queen. "Let's head for the CIC. We don't have any more time to waste."

"Affirmative, Alpha," Shiro said, following Caleb from sickbay, crossing back to the CIC. Caleb had already traded his t-shirt and boxer briefs for a fresh pair and layered a bodysuit over it, offering at least a little more protection than the zero he'd had without his armor.

Flores was already in CIC, along with Master Sergeant Gold. While Flores had her own combat armor, the Module didn't have a bodysuit sized to fit the private, who was mostly small and petite except across the chest. It wasn't a point of attraction for Caleb, but rather a technical challenge he had set Gold to solving. The Master Sergeant's solution had been to cut two of the bodysuits in half and carefully melt them back together. The top half was intended for a larger man and hung away from her arms and lower torso while still flattening her breasts. The bottom fit pretty well.

"It's still better than wandering around out there in a bra and panties," she said, noticing Caleb's survey of the solution. She had taken a deep cut across her arm because of the earlier lack of armor.

"Roger that," Caleb replied. "It's good work for such short notice. Where's your knife?"

Flores turned around. She had strapped two sheathes across her back, each one containing the long blade that had become standard issue for fighting the trife close in.

"Gold, patch me into Research." Caleb watched Master Sergeant Gold tap on the terminal controls and then give Caleb a nod to go ahead. "Craft, is Valentine back yet?"

"Not yet, Alpha. She's on her way."

He wanted to ask Craft if the good doctor was the only trained special forces in their group, but he had a feeling he knew the answer already. He was grateful Valentine had decided to help them rather than let them die, but the fact she was wearing some kind of advanced armor while they were getting chewed up didn't sit well with him. How much was she hiding that could have helped him keep his people alive?

"We're moving out as soon as my last two Marines are ready," Caleb said. "Ning's condition is getting worse. Are you sure you don't know what happened to him?"

"If he's sick, he was sick before we left Earth," Craft insisted.

Caleb didn't respond. It was the same answer – or lie – he'd gotten before, word for word.

Washington entered the CIC, nodding to Caleb as he joined Flores near the exit.

"Shiro and Sho will be along in a minute," Caleb said. "Gold, can you bring up the grid for me?"

"Of course, Alpha," Master Sergeant Gold replied. A moment later, the ship's grid appeared on the primary display.

"Zoom into the target area again." As Gold zoomed them into the interchange Caleb waited a minute until Shiro and Sho came into the room, joining Flores and Washington before walking over to them. "Guardians. A-TEHN-SHUN!"

They came to attention, still and straight. Caleb walked across the line, checking their armor and weapons, making sure each of them had at least one knife. They couldn't shoot inside the interchange, and it was better for all of them to die than for the whole ship to be destroyed. He had reluctantly banned ranged weapons for the mission, save for a single P-50 that Washington would carry to finish whatever the queen had produced in the last hour, whether they were eggs, embryos, larvae, or any other type of disgusting baby trife.

"At ease," he said, satisfied with their preparations. They relaxed slightly, and he pointed to the grid. "I know we looked at the interchange before, but things have changed a little over the last two hours. For one, we lost Hafizi, Wagner, and Yasuka. Three more fine Marines, dead to the trife. I've got their names written on my heart with the rest, and I'll be trading those names for the lives of some of the demons."

"Oorah!" the Guardians shouted in reply.

"I know things look bleak. I know we aren't where we were hoping we would be right now. But take a look at yourselves. Take a look at one another. You're all warriors.

You're all Guardians. You're all survivors. We stick together. The queen is already as good as dead. The nest is already destroyed."

"Oorah!"

He retreated to the terminal, taking over at the controls. "Based on our prior recon, we expect the enemy to have placed sentries along a perimeter outside the nest." He set markers around the interchange. "These are the most likely locations. Since the whole area is outside the visibility of the sensors, we're assuming the trife will be in the corridors, rather than tucked into the ventilation shafts or the maintenance passages. We're going to use their playbook against them. There's an access area here." He marked it on the grid. "Flores, you're small enough you should be able to get inside, and make your way across to here, behind the interchange." He marked the endpoint. "Scout the space and make your way back to us."

"Roger that, Alpha," Flores replied.

"Once Flores comes back, we'll split into pairs, and take a wide approach around the main corridors to these secondary passages here." He marked the three locations on the map. "They're essentially service shortcuts to get from the interchange to the thrust units."

"You should know," Craft said, listening into the briefing. "That area is going to be pretty hot and hard to breathe in. Engineering uses special suits to work in that area."

"Good to know," Caleb replied. "Prepare to sweat. And don't linger back there. It's vital that we coordinate our attack, and we'll synchronize after Flores' report."

"Alpha, why don't we send a Dragonfly in?" Flores asked. "Do you think the trife will know what's up?"

"We have no way to be sure, and that makes it too risky."

"What if the bastards know I'm in the access passage? What if they come after me? We can't use comms down there."

"You'll have ten minutes to get in and get out. If you don't come back, we'll have to assume you didn't make it."

Flores' face paled slightly. "Roger that."

"Are there any questions?" Caleb asked.

Sho raised her hand. "Sarge, do you think we'll be heroes if we pull this off?"

"You're already a hero to me, Yen. All of you are."

"Oorah!" they replied.

Chapter 45

David woke up.

That alone was a minor miracle. He definitely hadn't expected he would. Not after the woman in the strange armor had knocked him cold, injecting him with who knew what. She had said she hit the other guy, Pratt, with some sort of sample or something.

Had she done the same to him?

His heart began racing at the idea. He didn't want to die. He didn't want her to hunt him down and shoot him half to pieces.

He wanted to open his eyes, but he wasn't sure if he should. As long as he kept them closed, he could deny he was in trouble. He could deny everything. Ignorance was bliss after all, right?

"I'm telling you, John, the sample was close. The healing factor was working the way we had hoped. I put half a dozen rounds in him to keep him out."

"You shouldn't sound so excited about killing a man, Riley. Especially an innocent Marine. It's a little frightening."

"This is war. You don't win a war by being afraid to do the hard thing. You heard Pratt on the comm. He would have hit Sergeant Card the first chance he got."

"I'm not convinced of that."

"I don't care. It's not your job to question my job. We have a responsibility to all of humankind. If that means we kill a few Marines, you know what? They were going to die anyway."

David kept his eyes closed. He recognized the voice of the woman. She was the one in the armor. Obviously, she wasn't here alone.

He heard the hiss of a door. He was tempted to open his eyes, but he thought better of it.

"You wanted to see me, boss?"

"Harry, yes," Riley said. "I want to know what the hell went wrong with our seal? The only thing that was supposed to be able to get into that part of the ship was us."

"I don't know. Did you get a look at the hatch?"

"Yes. The trife were digging under it like they thought they were moles."

"They might have damaged the blocker that kept the seal from fully engaging. That would explain it."

Riley sighed. "It's like they knew there was a space under the door, even if it was only three millimeters."

"Smart bastards," John said.

"Please," Riley replied. "You know better than that. They're acting on feel. Instinct."

"I'm not sure I believe that anymore."

"It doesn't matter. I helped the Guardians fix the problem, and I reset the blocker. Once Sergeant Card finishes clearing out the bugs it won't be a problem anymore."

"Do you think he'll be able to do it?"

"I guess we'll find out."

David swallowed hard. He wasn't completely sure what Riley was talking about, but it didn't sound legal. What had he gotten himself into now?

"What about him?" John asked.

David shook in response to the words. He tried to get himself under control, hoping they hadn't noticed his lack of control.

"He'll buy us some time before we have to start plumbing the city. If we get lucky, he may even turn out to be the one."

"This whole thing is crazy, Rye," Harry said. "We barely escaped Earth in one piece, and now we're using the people we swore to help as science experiments."

"Not you too. For the greater good, Harry. You do know what that means, right? You don't have to like it. You just have to do it. That's the job. Speaking of which, have you taken care of your other job?"

"It's done. I still think it's a bad, bad, bad idea."

"That isn't for us to say. The orders came straight from Command."

"We should just go to Earth-6. We can settle down with the colony. We can have a semi-normal life, maybe have a few babies."

"With you? Not in a million years."

All three of them laughed.

"Seriously, we have our orders; we follow our orders. It's that simple. Now, I'm going to get out of this thing, and then we'll start processing the next sample. I want to make a few tweaks to the genome based on the success we had with Pratt."

"What about Ning?" John asked.

"Apparently the sample made him sick, and that was it. It was a dud."

"At least it didn't kill him," Harry said.

"You two are dismissed," Riley said. "John, start prepping the lab. Harry, get back to work on the translations."

"Yes, ma'am," Harry and John said.

David heard their feet moving to the hatch, and then the hatch sliding open and closed again. He remained still, keeping his eyes closed and doing his best not to move.

"You can open your eyes, David," Riley said. "I know you're awake."

David's heart nearly burst. How did she know? He opened his eyes. He was disoriented at first because he thought he had been lying down. Instead, he was strapped into a chair in a large room. A few different machines were resting against a nearby wall, along with a terminal and display, and what appeared to be a refrigerator. Riley was standing in front of the fridge, an amused expression on her face.

"Who are you?" he asked.

"Doctor Riley Valentine," she replied. "I'm a scientist."

"You're doing experiments on people."

"Yes."

"Why?"

"To make better people. People who can survive the trife."

"Super soldiers?"

"It's a tired term, but essentially, yes. We lost our home world. All of us, including you. But maybe you can help us get it back."

"I'm not a soldier."

"No, but you're a living human. That's all we need right now."

"Because you have orders."

"You heard that? Good. Yes, because I have orders. Because I don't accept that some alien race is going to take our Earth from us. I'm not going to lie to you David. I'm going to give you something, and you may not survive it. Not because I want to. Because I have to."

"You don't have to do anything you don't want to."

"Who told you that, your mother?"

David's face flushed with embarrassment.

"For argument's sake, let's say I want to," Riley said. "In the sense that I want to save our planet, I do want to. I'll do anything I have to. Do you think that makes me a bad person?"

David hesitated for a few seconds before shaking his head. "No."

Riley smiled. "Not the answer I was expecting. You're smarter than half my team."

"Thanks, I guess."

Riley walked behind him and he heard her doing something he couldn't see. She reappeared a moment later, holding a needle in her hand.

"You said you needed to make some tweaks," David complained.

Riley laughed. "This? It's just another sedative. You weren't supposed to have woken up already. Sweet dreams, David."

She stuck the needle into him.

He opened his mouth to object.

He was unconscious before he could make a sound.

Chapter 46

Caleb shifted and reached for the knife on his thigh as the small hatch to the access corridor slid open. Eleven minutes had passed since Flores had entered the area, and he was within seconds of accepting she hadn't survived the recon. Then she emerged from the darkness, sweating but intact, though her expression told him she didn't have great news.

"Alpha," she said. "Mission accomplished."

"What did you see?" Caleb asked, the other Guardians filling in around the two of them.

"I saw the queen. I've never seen one before. She was bigger than the others, height and girth, like she lifts weights. Muscled. She had some kind of stuff running down from between her legs, a thick gel."

"Did it look like ejaculate?" Caleb asked.

"Sort of, but thicker, and it was black, not white."

"Gross," Sho said.

There were trife all around her. At least three hundred of them. They were pressed tight against her and one another. They had sticky stuff on them too, that looked more like ejaculate."

"Serumen," Caleb said. "That's what Doctor Craft called it. Reproductive secretions. I bet the black stuff contains the eggs."

"Probably. I couldn't see to the floor where the black ichor was running, but I think they may be making new trife already. The whole thing was just like a twisted alien orgy."

"And you said three hundred of them?" Gold said.

"At least."

"Alpha, we can't stab that many before they kill us."

"The upshot is they don't seem very aware of their surroundings," Flores said. "They just want to reproduce."

"They aren't so different from us after all," Shiro joked.

"So we go in, hit them with the P-50, and call it a day," Sho said. "Does that sound about right?"

"We can't keep the plasma active for more than a few seconds inside the interchange," Caleb said. "If we melt any of the transfer circuits, the whole ship will either explode or lose power. Either of those things would be catastrophic."

"So what are we going to do, Sarge?"

"The queen is the primary target. We have to take her out, and we can't do that with that many– what did Valentine call them – consorts in there. We need to lure them away."

"That's a good idea, but how do we do it?"

Caleb closed his eyes, recalling the part of the grid he had committed to memory and then opening them again. "The main hatch to the interchange is about two hundred meters down that corridor. There are going to be sentries stationed there. We take them out, and we go in."

"Through the front door?"

"Not all of us. Sho, you and Shiro will take the main entrance. Kill the sentries, go inside, and blast the nest to get their attention."

"That sounds like fun, Sarge," Sho said sarcastically. "And then what?"

"If they chase you, run."

"That's your plan? Run?"

"If they chase you."

"What if they don't?"

"Keep shooting them, but be careful – extra careful – until they come after you, because they will...eventually. If we can get them far enough away from the interchange, you can blast them without worry. Washington and Gold, you'll go in through the entrance I marked earlier, past the thrust units. You need to be in position when Sho and Shiro launch their assault. Monitor the reaction from the consorts and then hit the trife who refuse to leave. See if you can get them to focus on you."

"What if the queen focuses on us?" Gold asked.

"Even better. Flores, head back through the access passage and wait on the other end. If the queen goes after Wash and Gold, you'll come out and try to stab her in the back."

"Roger that, Alpha," Flores said. "What if she doesn't?"

"I'll come in through the second passage. If Washington and Gold don't get her attention, then it'll be on me to distract her."

"The sentries will move in when we attack," Sho said.

"If they get in your way, you need to fight through them," Caleb replied. He paused a moment. "Let's be honest. There are a million things that can go wrong. There may be another hundred sentries guarding the nest, and just too many of the demons overall for us to overcome. I don't know where they're all coming from. It seems like there are more of the things than I saw in the hangar before we launched. But we have to deal with where we are. We volunteered for this because we care what happens to the people in Metro. We give it our best shot, and if we die, we die knowing we tried."

"Roger that, Sarge," Sho said. "I'm ready."

"Me too," Shiro said.

Washington gave his thumb up, and Gold did the same.

"Let's kick their ass," Flores said.

"Start counting ticks on my mark," Caleb said. "Don't hit the nest until you reach three hundred."

"Affirmative," Sho said.

"It's been an honor serving with all of you."

"You too, Alpha," they replied in turn.

"Here we go. Mark!"

Caleb started counting the seconds in his head, the same as the rest of the Guardians would. He broke from the group with Washington and Gold, heading down the corridor leading to the thrust units. Flores moved back toward the access passage, while Sho and Shiro moved slowly down the corridor toward the main hatch leading to the interchange.

When they came together again – if they came together again – the Deliverance would finally be free of its demons.

Chapter 47

Washington and Gold split from Caleb at the corridor leading into the thrust units. They were as far aft as they could get, half a kilometer from the large external ion thrusters that were pushing the Deliverance to an ever-increasing velocity, one that would top out at close to seven-tenths the speed of light in a couple of years. The corridor was placed over the top of the thrust units, with hatches leading into the back of the massive, modular engines on one side, and to narrow corridors allowing access to critical parts of the design on the other.

Like Craft had warned, it was hot. Hotter than Caleb was even expecting. He started sweating the moment the hatch to the rearmost passage opened. By the time he entered the engineering space and descended the metal stairs to the base of the unit, he was wiping perspiration out of his eyes.

He approached the quick access hatch leading to the interchange, still counting the seconds in his head. He was at two hundred eighty, leaving him twenty seconds to wait for Sho and Shiro to make their move.

He tapped the control panel to the hatch. It slid open, revealing the nest to him for the first time. It was positioned slightly off-center within the interchange equipment, which were a series of two-dozen large, dark columns arranged in a grid that filled the room. Each circuit had a heavy conduit running into it from above, and another hidden line running out of it below the floor, where they merged and fed back into the thrust units. The cabling was nearly two meters in diameter, rising out of the floor behind Caleb and plugging into the unit. He could feel the electrical field generated by the sheer volume of power being fed into the units, and it would have made the hairs on his arms stand up if they had any room to move beneath his bodysuit.

The queen was only partially in sight from his position, rising out of the scrum of consorts as a bigger, more powerful version of the aliens he had come to know and despise. She was barely moving, her mouth open, her eyes closed. The other trife writhed and pressed against her and one another, soft hisses escaping them as their thick serumen was passed forward. Caleb didn't understand the full trife reproductive process, and he didn't care to understand it. He was more concerned about the way the demons were wrapping around the interchange. Would Sho be able to hit them hard enough to get their attention and not destroy the ship in the process?

His count reached two hundred ninety-five. It was about time to find out.

He put his hand on the handle of his knife. The trife hadn't yet noticed the hatch open. Between his lack of electronics and their distraction, they had no idea he was standing there.

He reached three hundred at the same time he noticed the shadows change in the room, the main hatch sliding open out of his sightline. There was no reaction from the trife for the first few seconds, and then Caleb heard the rise in pitch of their hissing on the other side of the room and saw flashes of fire reflected on the metal walls.

Sho hadn't put the P-50 into stream mode, smartly realizing she might do irreparable damage to one of the columns. She fired bolts into the trife, one of them hitting the trife right beside the queen.

Her eyes opened as her mouth snapped closed. The consorts around her began to shift, trying to untangle themselves from one another. Sho kept shooting, sending four more bolts into the group. The rounds seared through one trife into another, some of them probably striking the floor. She had to be careful she didn't hit the conduits beneath the columns, or she might disable the connected thrust unit. Proxima would take twenty years at full burn. Losing one thruster could double the length of the journey."

The queen stayed where she was, but the consorts began to move, the front lines rushing for the door and the two Guardians standing in it.

"Here we go," Caleb said softly. He had chosen Sho because he knew she was a fast runner. Hopefully Shiro could keep up.

The consorts filtered from the room, hissing loudly as they trailed Sho and Shiro. Caleb continued watching, at least half of the demons abandoning the nest to give chase. One of his plans had finally borne some fruit. He moved from the doorway, carefully crossing to the first column and pressing himself against it. He looked over to his left, finding Gold moving in. He looked the other way, searching for Flores. He had to assume she was there somewhere.

"Hey, uglies!" he heard Gold shout, the older Marine's

voice echoing in the space. The queen's head whipped around, looking for the source. The other consorts began to spread away from her, winding around the columns in the direction of the sound.

Caleb saw Gold waving his arms as he backed up toward the closest doorway. He was trying to lead them back to use the hatch as a bottleneck and control the flow of demons if they tried to attack.

Some of them did follow, nearly fifty in total. It was a ridiculous amount of trife for the two Marines to try to fight on their own, especially armed only with knives. There was a good chance they were sacrificing themselves to draw more of the creatures away.

Caleb wasn't about to let such a selfless sacrifice go to waste.

He waited for a few more seconds, watching the queen. It had its eyes locked on Gold, but it wasn't moving. Caleb circled the column he was behind, moving closer to the lead trife. He caught sight of Flores as he did. She was out of the hatch and approaching the queen from the back.

The consorts moved into the room with Washington and Gold. He couldn't see or hear them. He didn't know how long they would last. There were still a couple of dozen consorts at the feet of the queen, but he had to make his move. He had to get her attention and draw it into position for Flores to make the killing strike.

And he had to do it now.

He broke from his cover, intending to position himself directly in front of the queen, to draw her attention and give Flores the chance she needed.

Only it didn't happen that way.

The plan didn't go according to plan.

The trife queen spun back around before she saw him.

Then she bolted away, leaving her nest behind to chase the human with the gun.

Chapter 48

"Shit!" Caleb shouted, loudly enough that some of the trife nearby turned their heads, noticing him for the first time.

He couldn't believe it. Why had the queen suddenly abandoned her nest to chase Sho? Why hadn't she gone after her in the first place?

Had the Guardian killed enough of its consorts that it was pissed at her? He almost smiled at the thought, but a hiss too close for comfort suddenly drew his attention. He turned and brought his knife up, holding it near his forearm. A trife he hadn't noticed slashed at his face. He ducked under the demon's claws, pivoting and slashing the blade across its chest, cutting it wide open. He shouldered it aside, shouting again as he changed his grip, stabbing a second trife in the stomach and falling to one knee to avoid its bite.

He heard movement behind him and turned on his knee, swinging the blade. Flores barely jumped back in time to avoid the strike.

"Damn, it's me, Alpha!" she cried out.

Caleb sprang up, pushing her aside as a trife came up

behind her. He jammed his knife into its open mouth and up into its brain, yanking the blade away.

"You're welcome," he said.

She smiled and nodded, and they stood together. Flores had a blade in each hand, though her left-handed grip seemed awkward.

"What do we do now?" she asked.

Caleb looked back to where the queen had been. There was a hard, thick, semi-translucent gel where the serumen had mingled with the crap coming from between the queen's legs. He could see something wriggling and squirming within it.

Trife. Dozens of trife.

"That thing is going to slaughter Sho and Shiro," he replied.

"Go," Flores said. "We'll take care of these."

"Three against one hundred?"

She smiled. "They're just bugs, Alpha. And we've got Washington."

Caleb looked back to the doorway. He could see the big Marine behind it, slashing out with his knife, cutting into the trife before they could get within arm's reach of him. A pile of dead aliens already lay in front of him, and he was smiling like he was having the time of his life.

"Go," Flores repeated, shoving him on his way.

Caleb sprinted across the interchange, winding around the columns to avoid the few consorts still in the room. One of them nearly tackled him as he closed on the exit. He dropped and rolled, catching the demon with his knife and almost cutting it in half. He got back up, sparing a momentary glance back at his other Guardians.

Flores had closed on the trife from behind, catching them off-guard and using her twin blades to dig into their backs, stabbing two of them in the short time he watched them. The ranks were already thinning, the Marines getting the best of the consorts, who seemed sluggish from their reproductive efforts.

Then he was out of the interchange and running across the ship. Sho and Shiro were supposed to lead the trife back as far as they could get them, but how far would that be?

He had only covered a dozen meters when he came across the first dead trife killed by a plasma bolt. He followed it to another and then another, and kept running, using the dead aliens as breadcrumbs to track both the queen and the two Marines.

He ran as fast as he could, his heart pulsing, his breath heavy. He was exhausted before they started this mission, which had gone from perfectly executed to a potential disaster in seconds. At least they hadn't punctured a circuit or damaged a thrust unit.

He came to a stop when he reached a thick pile of dead trife close to the central lifts. Dozens of trife consorts had been burned by a plasma stream, leaving them looking like the smoldering remnants of a bone-filled bonfire. Was this what had caused the queen to leave the nest?

He stepped carefully through the mess, still fresh enough to be giving off heat. Finding the P-50 that had done the damage on the deck a few meters further on, he picked it up and checked its cell charge. It was out of fuel.

Caleb continued ahead, a little more cautious now. Sho and Shiro had made a beeline for the lifts. Did they know the queen was after them? Had she already caught up to them?

He heard scratching and hissing a moment later and then the sound of claws on the metal floor coming back his way. He couldn't face the queen head on alone. He scanned the corridor, running back to a nearby hatch. He hit the control panel and ducked inside, barely making it through before the queen turned the corner ahead. A moment later, her large, dark form scampered past.

Where was she going?

Caleb considered following her but decided against it. He didn't think she was going back to the interchange. She had lost Sho at the lifts, and the nearest operational stairwell was back aft.

He came out of hiding, running to the lifts. There were more dead trife there as well as a line of human blood. Was Sho hurt again? Or was it Shiro? He traced the blood to the lift and tapped the control panel. Deck Six. Was she headed for the bridge?

Caleb went to the next lift over, tapping the controls to summon it. It was four decks up and only took a few seconds to arrive. He ducked inside, reaching for the controls.

"Come on," he said, ordering the lift to ascend. The ride felt like it took forever, even if it lasted only a dozen seconds.

The lift doors slid aside, and Caleb nearly fell out the door, catching himself on the side of the cab. Regaining his balance, he sprinted away from the shaft, headed for the bridge.

Why would Sho go up there?

He had a feeling he knew why.

He ran down the corridors, trying to remember the layout of the deck. He knew he was heading in the right direction when he passed Private Gurshaw, one of Pratt's men who had died defending the area. He wasn't surprised to notice that Gurshaw's sidearm was missing.

He jumped over the dead Marine's drying blood, his padded feet slapping the metal floor in a rapid-fire cadence. There, at the intersection up ahead, he'd wait for the queen. He knew it led back to the stairwell he believed she was ascending. Had he gotten here ahead of her?

His knife held at the ready, he crouched down and crossed the intersection, looking to the left to scan the long corridor. It was empty, dark and silent. No electronics, nothing to give his position away. The softer soles of the bodysuit didn't make much noise either.

The queen hadn't made it up the steps yet. The bridge wasn't that much further. He had to make it there.

Something hit his feet, catching his ankle from behind and tripping him up. He sprawled face-first hard on the floor, sliding half a meter before flipping his legs over and gaining purchase. He awkwardly got back up and faced the way he had come.

A trife's tail vanished into an open compartment. A large head emerged to replace it.

The head of the queen.

Chapter 49

Caleb stood motionless as the trife queen emerged from the small storage space. As quiet as he had tried to be, it was clear the creature had heard him and prepared accordingly.

She was smart. Smarter than the other trife he had encountered on Earth. Was that a result of becoming the queen, or had she been selected because of her intelligence? Was this the trife that had coordinated all of the attacks against them?

Was this the trife that had gotten so many of his fellow Marines killed?

Caleb gripped his knife. The queen was at least two full heads taller than he was, forcing her to crouch in the human-sized corridor. Her long arms were thicker than a normal trife's, her claws longer, her legs more muscled. Her leathery black flesh glistened from the dried black ichor that had run between them. Her head was wider than an ordinary trife's, her mouth and teeth larger. He would have preferred to stay away from her, to shoot her from a distance.

But it wasn't one of his options.

He could turn and run, or he could stand and fight. He wasn't sure running was one of his options, either. The smaller corridors might slow the queen. But would it be enough to keep her from catching him?

The trife queen opened her mouth even wider. Caleb expected a hiss. Instead, he got a loud, ear-piercing scream that sent a shiver down his spine. The queen lowered herself, following up the cry with shorter bursts of sound that echoed in the passageway.

The challenge made up his mind for him. He wasn't going to run. He owed it to his dead brothers and sisters to accept the fight and prove their worth as much as his own.

"You want it?" he said, stepping toward the queen. "You got it."

The queen screamed again and then burst toward him, faster than he could believe. Still, he was able to duck beneath a giant claw, its tips so close to slicing his face open he could feel the displaced air against his cheek. Throwing himself sideways, he barely avoided her snapping teeth. He bounced off the side of the corridor and took a back-handed swing at her head with his knife.

The queen's tail whipped around and hit him in the chest, throwing him into the corridor again. He rolled up on his feet, bringing his forearm up in defense as the queen's mouth came at him a second time. Two dozen teeth pressed into the bodysuit and then through, biting deep into Caleb's arm. He held back his scream, refusing to show her his pain as she refused to let him go. He used her head as leverage, pulling himself sideways and driving his knife toward the queen's eye.

She saw the knife coming at her in time to let go of his arm and back up to avoid it. She was on him again in an instant. Caleb barely twisted away from her claws, taking a glancing blow that nearly knocked him down. He swung his damaged arm in response, hitting the queen in the face and leaving a trail of both his and her blood across her snout.

She screamed again, this time right in his ear, the noise so forceful he could feel the moisture of her breath on his eardrum as it succumbed to the screech. He threw himself to the floor, bringing his knife up over his chest in a desperate effort to defend himself.

The queen stomped up and leaned over him, her head swaying back and forth in an effort to escape the stabs of Caleb's knife.

Caleb couldn't feel his left arm. He was losing too much blood from it, and he wasn't carrying a patch. Not that it mattered. He figured he was about to get his face bitten off.

"Just do it," he screamed, his eyes filled with the fire of his anger as he glared up at the queen. He had tried, and he had failed. He was resigned to paying the price for his failure.

"Get the hell away from him!" Sho shouted.

Caleb heard the report of the rifle Sho had taken from Gurshaw an instant before the queen's head snapped back. She screamed and turned toward Sho. Caleb tilted his head to look over at Sho a dozen meters away, still shooting at the queen. The creature took three rounds to her torso and then turned and ran.

Not away from the gunfire.

Toward it.

Sho continued to shoot, sending four more rounds into the queen before her rifle was empty. She dropped it and grabbed for her knife, but the queen was almost on her.

Shiro let loose a guttural cry as he jumped out of the adjacent corridor and plowed into the queen, stabbing her in the shoulder. The queen screamed, throwing her arm out and batting Shiro away.

Caleb forced himself to his feet. His left arm was limp at his side, his vision blurry. It didn't matter. He had lost Banks, Habib, Rodriguez, Hafizi. He wasn't losing Sho too.

He sprinted at the queen, who slashed at Sho, driving the other Vulture back. Caleb and Sho made eye contact as she saw him coming up behind the demon.

"Come on you bitch!" Sho shouted, lunging forward and stabbing at her.

The queen caught the blade between her teeth, yanking it from Sho's hand. Long claws raked the Marine's chest.

Caleb leaped toward the queen, his knife gripped in his good hand. The queen started to turn to defend against Caleb's attack, but she was too big and too slow. She struggled to maneuver, and that struggle cost her.

Caleb sank his blade into her back, right below her thick neck, burying the metal up to the handle. The queen screamed, flailing from the wound and knocking Caleb off her back. He tumbled to the floor, leaving him to scramble away from the queen's wildly swinging tail as she took a step toward Sho. Sho rose up in front of the queen and stabbed her in the eye.

She screamed again and fell at Sho's feet.

Dead.

Chapter 50

Caleb rested his head against the wall of the passageway, doing his best to stay conscious. His eyes shifted as Shiro vaulted the dead trife and rushed to his side, taking account of his wounds.

"Sho," Caleb said. "Take care of Sho."

"I'm okay, Sarge," Sho said, getting past the queen. She was bleeding from her chest, but the bodysuit had managed to absorb at least some of the damage. "It isn't deep."

"That needs treatment," Shiro told Caleb, looking at his arm. "I don't know if we're going to be able to save it."

"Figures," Caleb said. "My kingdom for a patch. I'm going to bleed to death out here."

"Ask and you shall receive, Alpha," Shiro said, producing a patch.

"Gurshaw?" Caleb asked.

Sho nodded. "He didn't need it."

Shiro retreated to the queen, pulling his knife from her shoulder and wiping it as clean as he could on his bodysuit. Then he used it to cut away Caleb's sleeve.

"That was some battle cry," Caleb said. "Aaahhhhh." He mimicked it softly, smiling when he was done. "You could have been a Vulture if you didn't scream like a cat in heat."

Shiro and Sho both laughed. "Good to see you have your sense of humor, Sarge," Sho said.

"We need to check on the interchange." Caleb responded. "Gold, Washington, and Flores are still down there."

"You're in no shape to help them," Shiro said, opening the patch and placing it at the top of his wound. He wrapped it tight around the arm to stop the blood loss.

"We can check on them from the bridge," Sho said. "It isn't far."

"Help me up," Caleb said, holding out his good arm. Shiro helped him to his feet, and they made their way past the queen. Caleb stopped in front of it, staring into its open-eyed death gaze. This thing had nearly cost them the entire ship, and maybe all of Metro with it.

"She's dead, Sarge," Sho said. "Come on."

He followed them, down the corridor to the end and then to the right. Another short passage and they were back at the bridge. The hatch was sitting open. The smell was horrible. There hadn't been any time to clear out the dead, human or otherwise.

"How are we going to see them here?" Caleb asked. "There are no sensors in the interchange."

"Right," Sho said. "But also wrong. The terminal in the Marine module is subnetworked into the main ship's computer. The bridge has access to the full network, which includes hundreds of internally mounted cameras in sensitive areas of the ship, all hardwired into the system. No wireless comm needed."

"But the subnetwork doesn't have access?"

"The module networks don't."

"How do you know about this?"

"We got up here ahead of Miss Bitch back there. The terminal was already active, and set to one of the feeds."

"What do you mean it was already active? Who activated it?"

"I don't know. The ghost you and Wash saw, maybe?"

Caleb didn't like the answer. He didn't like any answer. Someone had been on the bridge, possibly watching them. Could it be the man he had seen being chased by the trife? Who was he?

They entered the bridge. The terminal was still on, a smaller display in front of it showing a camera feed from what looked like the top of Metro. The angle gave them a wide view of the city, which seemed downright peaceful. The atmospherics were in full daylight mode, and there were people out in the park, others walking the streets, and still more visible through open windows into their cubes. Caleb had been concerned about any trife hiding in the ductwork and getting into Metro, but it seemed law had everything under control.

Sho tapped on the control surface, and a list of cameras streamed across the display. She tapped on the one that said INTERCHANGE-PA.

The display changed, showing the interchange. There were plenty of trife still on the floor inside, but none of them were moving. There was no sign of the Guardians.

"They were in with the first thrust unit," Caleb said. "Do we have a camera there?"

Sho checked the list and switched to THRUST UNIT 1.

More dead trife. No sign of Washington, Gold, or Flores.

"They didn't die in there at least," Sho said.

"See if you can get the sensor grid up on the display."

"Roger that, Sarge." Sho manipulated the control surface, flipping through screens until she found the sensor grid. Caleb studied it for a moment. There were no life signs in any of the live zones.

"Damn it, where are they?" Caleb said.

"Behind you, Alpha," Flores said.

Caleb turned around. Washington and Flores were standing in the doorway to the bridge. Flores' bodysuit had cuts along both sides and down one of her legs. Washington's already scarred face had taken another hit, and he had another wound on his arm.

"Where's Gold?" Caleb asked.

Washington shook his head.

"He fought well for an old man," Flores said. "Went down swinging."

"I didn't see him in with the thrust unit."

"We retreated up the steps and back into the corridor. You'll find him there."

Caleb lowered his head. Six surviving Marines out of hundreds.

"You're hurt, Alpha?" Flores asked.

"It's nothing," Caleb replied. "I'll probably lose the arm. I can't even feel it."

"We don't have replacements out here. You'll have to go into Metro."

Caleb shook his head. "No. I'm staying out here. Even Washington couldn't drag me away."

Washington made a face as if to say, are you kidding?

"The queen is dead," Sho said.

"But we still have a lot of work to do," Caleb replied. "Most importantly, we need to be completely sure the ship is clear. One trife can turn into thousands in the right environment."

"Roger that," Shiro said. "We should get you properly treated first, Alpha. All of us could use medical attention."

"I can't argue that. Let's head back to the module. Stay alert, Guardians. We can't be sure we're free and clear just yet."

The six remaining Guardians moved into formation and headed out. They crossed the corridors to the lifts without incident, taking it back down to Deck Twenty-nine. No trife attacked them on their way to the module, and they made it home without any sign of demons.

"Do you think we got them all, Sarge?" Sho asked.

"I don't know. I hope so. If not? We will. I won't rest until we do. One-armed or not."

"You're a badass, Sarge."

"Oorah!" Shiro and Flores barked in response.

Chapter 51

Caleb stood on the bridge of the Deliverance, looking up at the black expanse of space as projected through the high-definition cameras mounted along the bow. He had been back here plenty of times in the sixty days since the Guardians had destroyed the trife nest, killed the trife queen, and set about finishing up the first leg of their mission by ridding the ship of the demonic aliens. He had come up more often with each passing day as the work the Guardians had to do to get the ship back to where it should have started continued to diminish. He enjoyed looking out at space. He found it comforting to know they were headed to a place where the trife couldn't reach them, even if that place wasn't the one he had initially expected.

He reached down toward the primary terminal control surface with his left hand. He hardly thought about that hand anymore, growing more accustomed to the sensations from the artificial limb. Doctor Valentine had warned him that the standard mechanical replacement took about a month to integrate and fully synchronize with its organic host, and what she had given him was anything but standard.

She called the unit experimental, an offshoot of the technology that had produced her Cerebus armor. It was composed of hundreds of rings of alloy wrapped around a base gel material where the wires, actuators and micro-motors were positioned. It was about the same weight as his original flesh and bone arm, but it was much stronger, and way more durable. According to Valentine, there hadn't been a trife yet that could even dent the advanced material.

Of course, she wouldn't say what it was made of, or where she had gotten it. Research maintained their secrets as fully as ever, in spite of the thaw that had occurred between their team and the Guardians, and especially between Caleb and his counterpart. He and Riley had come to an understanding and a level of mutual respect that he would never have thought possible the first time he met the doctor. She didn't make the best first impression, but she wasn't as bad as he had thought.

That was something, anyway.

He tapped the comm controls, opening a link to Metro.

"Sheriff Aveline, this is Guardian Alpha, are you there?"

"Caleb Card," Lily said, responding to the comm. "You're late."

"I know. Sorry, Lily. One of the Dragonflies picked up a random audio fluctuation and sent us running to investigate."

"A day in the life of a Guardian, I suppose."

"Yes, ma'am. How's your day going?"

"No cats today."

"No cats ever. We didn't bring any with us."

"True. It's quiet. A good quiet. People in Metro seem happy enough, and Engineering is getting a handle on some of the teething problems."

"Please don't use that term," Caleb joked. "It brings back bad memories."

Lily laughed. "I thought you liked your new hand?"

"I do. But I'd still rather have the original." Caleb paused. "Lily, now that things are more settled, we're planning on initiating the original Guardian protocols as they were designed. We'll be doing alternating rounds of stasis cycles to prolong our lifespan until we arrive at our destination. The loss of so many of our people means we'll only keep one Guardian active per shift."

"You're going to be out there alone?"

Caleb hesitated. Doctor Valentine had suggested they not say anything to anyone in Metro about their redirect to Proxima, so as not to get anyone's hopes up with the news. It was bad enough Governor Lyle and Vice-Governor Jones knew the truth, but they had promised to keep it to themselves in solidarity with the idea. Better to let the passengers be resigned to dying on board and pleasantly surprised when they lived to see their destination, instead of having them get over eager to arrive. They all agreed the population would be easier to manage that way.

"It has to be that way. As it is, I'll be seventy-two years old when we get there."

"And I'll be long dead. I'll make sure my descendants know who you are so they can thank you for what you did. In the meantime, you can always talk to me if you get lonely. Any of you can. I don't mind doing my part. Just don't expect me to wait for you." She laughed, but it was tinged with sadness.

"I'm sorry things worked out the way they did. I had a

good feeling about you when I met you. I think we could have had something."

"Me too. But what can you do, right? I know duty comes first to people like you. I respect you more than I can say for the sacrifices you've made."

"I have another one to make. Guardian protocol limits our communication with Metro to Engineering. The idea is for most of the residents, Sheriffs included, to think about the fact that they're on a starship blasting through space as little as possible."

"That makes sense." She paused. "So, did you call to say goodbye, Caleb?"

Caleb swallowed hard. "I did. I wanted to hear your voice one last time before I go into the pod."

"You're going into stasis now?"

"In about two hours. Private Shiro's taking first watch with Private Ning, just long enough to help get him back to full health."

"You still don't know what was wrong with him?"

"No, but he's improving every day. He just started walking again. Anyway, as long as things stay quiet I'll be hibernating for the next year."

"I hope things stay quiet, for my sake as much as yours."

"Me too. Take care of yourself, Lily. It was a pleasure getting to know you."

"The honor was mine, Caleb Card. Thank you for everything."

"You're welcome."

"Sweet dreams, Sergeant."

"Bye."

Caleb closed his eyes, forcing himself to disconnect the link. He opened them again and took a deep breath, staring out at space. He would only have to do four cycles to get to Proxima. It would be lonely, but he would manage. They all would. They had found a vast store of movies on the ship's data stack. Between that, the gym, and their duties roaming the ship, it would help pass the time.

He let his gaze linger for a minute, and then he shut down the displays and headed off the bridge.

Chapter 52

"Nervous?" Sho asked.

"Should I be?" Caleb replied.

"I am," Flores said.

They were standing in one of the Marine module's two stasis chambers. It was the first time any of them had been in the compartment, tucked away behind a blast door at the back of the armory. It was a strange place for the room, but Doctor Valentine had explained how the chambers had been added late in the module's development, and that was the only area where they could add them without significant cost overruns.

Government efficiency at work. Not that it mattered all that much where the chambers sat. They were going to be in cryogenic sleep; their bodies shut down to the most base level they could be and still survive.

All of the Guardians had been through the training on both how to operate the pods inside the chamber and what to expect from their use. It was a misinterpretation of the technology to believe they wouldn't age while in stasis. Their bodily functions wouldn't stop completely, but rather slow to a glacial crawl. For every year in a pod, they would grow approximately one week older. That meant they would each be about four years and three months older when they arrived, counting the time they would cycle out of stasis. Not bad when everyone in Metro would gain twenty years.

Caleb tried to imagine Lily in her fifties, with gray hair and wrinkles, a husband, and a teenage son or daughter. There was a part of him still disappointed he wouldn't have the opportunity to join her in the city, but only a little. He knew his place was here.

He would have preferred to take the first duty cycle. He wanted to be the one to kick things off and to keep an eye on the ship during the earliest stage of the journey. While they were as confident as they could be the trife were all dead, it still didn't sit that well with him that they had never found the man he had seen running from the trife. They had checked every room, every vent, every access panel, every corridor. They had monitored the sensors and the cameras. They had used all of their Dragonflies. They had spent hundreds of hours going over every area of the vessel. No trife. No stowaway. He knew it hadn't been his imagination. Hell, Washington had seen the man too. But he was gone.

Just gone.

They had found Sergeant Pratt. Or rather, they had found his body. It had been severely damaged, sliced and torn by the trife, a few demon corpses nearby. A large group must have found him out there and jumped him, ending his singular war against them before it ever got started. Riley continued to insist the sergeant had cracked. Caleb still struggled to accept it.

Shiro had volunteered for the first cycle because Ning was still recovering from his mysterious ailment. The private had turned out to be a valuable part of the group and seemed to enjoy his default role as the team's doctor.

He was dedicated to seeing Ning back to health, even if nobody knew exactly what had happened to him, including Ning. All he remembered was helping Pratt batten down Research and coming back to join the fight before starting to feel nauseous. It was strange, and Sho continued to insist Research knew precisely what had happened to both him and Pratt.

Doctor Valentine denied it of course. There was no way to prove or disprove the theory. He had decided to accept he would never know the truth for certain.

"They told us in training you only have good dreams in the pods," Caleb said. "Something to do with the cryogel and REM patterns at that level of neural and chemical activity."

"Yeah, they said that," Flores replied. "But they aren't going to tell us we'll have nightmares the whole time. They wouldn't get any volunteers."

"I don't think we'll experience much of anything," Sho said. "Go to sleep. Bam! I'll wake up two years later. What do you think, Wash?"

Washington shrugged noncommittally. He didn't care one way or the other.

"I guess we'll find out," Flores said.

"I want to say, it was an honor to fight alongside you," Caleb said. "All of you have made me incredibly proud, and I have every intention of calling out your skill and bravery to Command when we arrive on Proxima."

"Thank you, Sarge," Sho said.

"Yeah, thanks, Alpha," Flores said.

Washington flashed his thumb.

"Let's do this," Sho said.

Caleb nodded, taking a moment to embrace each of

the members of the Guardians, and giving them a moment to say goodbye to one another. If they saw each other again before they reached Proxima, it wouldn't be for anything good.

Caleb walked over to the last pod in the row. They were all identical, all large enough to fit a man of Washington's stature, with glass lids on top and wires and tubes running into them below. A display rose from the side of each, a control terminal below it.

He tapped on the control surface and then entered his identification into the pod. His image appeared on the display, along with his vitals and the current Earth date and time. He adjusted the clock, setting the thaw for a year ahead.

He pulled off his sneakers, shirt, pants, and underwear, the cool air in the room causing his skin to prickle. It felt weird to be naked. The stasis process demanded having every last hair removed, from the top of his head to the bottom of his feet, including his eyebrows and pubic hair. It had something to do with the ability of the sensors to take measurements through the gel.

For some reason, having no hair made him self conscious. He resisted the urge to cover himself and folded his clothes, putting them beside the pod before lifting himself in.

"Damn, that's cold," Sho said. He looked over. She was sliding into her pod.

He turned and began sinking into the seat. It was cold all right – damn cold. He shivered slightly, coming to a rest in what turned out to be an extremely comfortable position.

He reached over with his right hand, tapping the control ring at the top of his left shoulder to power off his artificial limb. It grew heavy against him, and he could sense the gel padding he was resting on adjusting for the new weight and keeping him balanced. The lid of the pod began closing above him.

"See you on the other side, Sarge," Sho said.

"Roger that," he replied.

The lid closed. He had gotten so accustomed to the random sounds in the ship he was shocked when they vanished into a wall of silence. He let his head rest back, closing his eyes.

They had been trained that the hardest part of cryosleep was trusting the system. After all, it was human nature to panic when the head became submerged under liquid. For as much as Caleb promised himself he would be one of the few who could handle it without anxiety when the cryogel reached his face and began to cover his mouth, he tilted his head and sucked in a breath, his heart rate increasing. This was the only time in the process an increased pulse wouldn't open the seals, and it didn't matter if he panicked or not. The pod would continue to fill.

He started to calm as he pulled the gel into his mouth and down into his lungs. The material was formulated to carry everything the body needed. All he had to do was relax and let it work.

He couldn't breathe, and it took about thirty seconds for him to realize he didn't need to. He wasn't becoming oxygen deprived. He wasn't dying. The gel was rising over his eyes, thick and warm, and he realized it was pretty comfortable after all.

He had fought and survived.

He had fought and saved thousands of lives.

He had fought and earned his sleep.

Everything was going to be okay.

Chapter 53

Caleb's eyes opened. He was cold. So damn cold. His body shivered violently, working hard to warm him.

He couldn't see at first. He still had cryogel in his eyes. He tried to reach up to wipe it away, forgetting his left arm was offline. He used his right, at the same time fighting not be overwhelmed by the resumption of sensation, the sounds of the Deliverance hitting his ears for the first time in a year.

Why was it so damn cold? He had thought the cryogel would warm before waking him, but that didn't seem to be the case. It was like being dumped out of an ice bath into a refrigerator.

He got the gel out of his eyes and then took a moment to adjust to his senses. He reached over with his right hand, tapping the control on his left shoulder and powering his artificial limb back up.

Sho had been right. He didn't remember much of anything. No nightmares. No dreams. One moment he had been fighting the panic of drowning in the gel, and the next he was awake.

He reached out, taking the sides of the pod and pulling himself to a sitting position, dragging his feet up and then standing in the device. He looked over at the line of pods. The glass lids had crystals covering them, making it impossible to see inside. They were all active, the occupants alive. Not that he expected anything else.

He jumped onto the floor, pleased to find his muscles felt as though he had only laid down a few minutes earlier. He stretched his arms and legs and then grabbed for his clothes, the gel already evaporating.

Once he was dressed, Caleb padded over to Sho's pod, looking down into it. The gel was kept nearly frozen while the pod was active, the crystallization of the layers leaving his view of her like an impressionist painting, her body reflected and broken into kaleidoscopic shards.

He tapped on her terminal control surface and glanced at the display when it turned on. Her vitals were good. He left her pod and went to the next, checking Washington and Flores in the same way. All green. All good.

Satisfied, he made his way to the hatch. He would find Shiro and Ning and make the handoff, getting a quick briefing on anything that happened over the prior year and helping them prep for stasis. They would go to sleep, and then he would be alone for the next year. It was a strange thought, considering there was a city of forty-thousand people on the other side of a six-inch thick seal.

He reached the hatch and put his hand to the control panel, tapping on it to open the door.

The panel made a short beep, the light on it flashing green.

The door didn't open.

Caleb smiled. "I don't believe it." There had been plenty of malfunctions while he had been awake. Why was this a surprise?

He tried it again. It still didn't budge. He wasn't worried. He tapped the control panel, bringing up the menu and opening a comm link with the module's command center.

"This is Guardian Alpha, Caleb Card," he said. "Private Shiro, are you there?"

He waited a few seconds for a response. None came.

"Private Shiro? Are you in the CIC?"

No response.

Caleb still wasn't worried. The original Guardian protocols had called for ten Marines to be awake at one time, with one of them in the CIC around the clock. Obviously, they couldn't do that now. Shiro was probably finishing up his final patrol.

Caleb repeated the message. Waited a few minutes. Repeated it. He continued the process for another hour.

Then he started to worry.

What if something had happened to the private? Shiro was supposed to stay in communication with Research at all times and with Metro Engineering in the event of an emergency. If something had gone wrong, they would have woken him.

He tried the comm again, and then he tried the door again. It was flashing green, but it wasn't even trying to move. Was the motor dead? Was there something else wrong with it?

His calm was fading. He hadn't thought he would wake up only to find himself trapped in the chamber. What the hell was going on out there?

Relax. He had to relax. Start at the basics.

He went back to his pod and activated the terminal. Maybe something had malfunctioned with the pod and woken him too soon, and Shiro wasn't expecting him. It could be he would have to wait a few more hours to get in touch with him. No big deal.

It took him a minute to find the log. It contained outputs for each significant event and a line with a status summary for every twenty-four hour period. He could use it to find out exactly what had happened, and when.

The first line showed when the pod was activated, the next few diagnostics of its startup process and then the status as he entered it and was put to sleep.

He started scrolling through the status lines. His heart began to race. What the hell? It didn't take long for him to realize there were more than three hundred lines. He used his finger to scroll the log. It kept going, past three hundred, line after line with a timestamp of the date and time along with the status:

ALL SYSTEMS NOMINAL

He had been under for more than a year. Much more than a year. The log seemed to go on forever.

He scrolled it, the lines flying past his eyes as rapidly as his heart was beating, a different kind of panic settling in. How could he have been asleep for so long? Why hadn't anybody woken him?

As he passed the twenty-year mark, a new question caused a fresh panic. Why the hell hadn't they reached Proxima yet?

He kept scrolling, line after line after line. Thirty years, forty, fifty. He reached one hundred, and he wasn't even near the end. He could barely breathe. He could hardly think. This couldn't be real. This couldn't be happening.

The dates rolled past. One hundred fifty years. One hundred seventy. One hundred ninety. He blinked his eyes and stared at the timestamp. Maybe it was writing the log every hour? Maybe he had gotten that wrong?

He confirmed the year was increasing. Two hundred. Two hundred ten. Two hundred twenty.

Finally, the screen bounced as it reached the bottom. Caleb's eyes drifted to the last message in the log.

REMOTE THAW COMPLETE. SUCCESS!

Remote thaw? Had someone woken him from outside the chamber? He didn't even know that was possible. He calmed slightly, but only slightly. It was hard to be relaxed when one year had become two hundred thirty-six.

He leaned back against his pod. Someone had woken him, but the door was still closed. Nonfunctional. He was locked in. Did anyone know it?

Someone must have.

The door slid open.

Thank you for reading
Deliverance

I hope you've enjoyed the first entry in the Forgotten Colony series. If you did, please take a moment to show your support for this book, and for the series as a whole, by leaving a review on Amazon now (mrforbes.com/reviewdeliverance).

By showing your support, you can not only help me gauge interest in the series, but you can provide social proof to others that this is a book/series/author worth reading.

In any case, I know there are a lot of books out there, and I'm grateful you chose mine. Thank you, thank you, thank you.

Want more M.R. Forbes? There's a more complete description of my first-in-series in the next section of this book, or even better you can check out my backlist at mrforbes.com/books.

Again, thank you so much for your support. If you have Facebook, please stop by my page sometime at facebook.com/mrforbes.author. I'd love to hear from you.

Cheers,
   Michael.

Other Books By M.R Forbes

Some things are better off FORGOTTEN.

Sheriff Hayden Duke was born on the Pilgrim, and he expects to die on the Pilgrim, like his father, and his father before him.

That's the way things are on a generation starship centuries from home. He's never questioned it. Never thought about it. And why bother? Access points to the ship's controls are sealed, the systems that guide her automated and out of reach. It isn't perfect, but he has all he needs to be content.

Until a malfunction forces his Engineer wife to the edge of the habitable zone to inspect the damage.

Until she contacts him, breathless and terrified, to tell

him she found a body, and it doesn't belong to anyone on board.

Until he arrives at the scene and discovers both his wife and the body are gone.

The only clue? A bloody handprint beneath a hatch that hasn't opened in hundreds of years.

Until now.

Earth Unknown (Forgotten Earth)
mrforbes.com/earthunknown

A terrible discovery.

A secret that could destroy human civilization.

A desperate escape to the most dangerous planet in the universe... Earth.

Two hundred years ago, a fleet of colony ships left Earth and started a settlement on Proxima Centauri...

Centurion Space Force pilot Nathan Stacker didn't expect to return home to find his wife dead. He didn't expect the murderer to look just like him, and he definitely didn't expect to be the one to take the blame.

But his wife had control of a powerful secret. A secret that stretches across the light years between two worlds and could lead to the end of both.

Now that secret is in Nathan's hands, and he's about to make the most desperate evasive maneuver of his life -- stealing a starship and setting a course for Earth.

He thinks he'll be safe there.

He's wrong. Very wrong.

Earth is nothing like what he expected. Not even close. What he doesn't know is not only likely to kill him, it's eager to kill him, and even if it doesn't?

The Sheriff will.

Starship Eternal (War Eternal)
mrforbes.com/starshipeternal

A lost starship...

A dire warning from futures past...

A desperate search for salvation...

Captain Mitchell "Ares" Williams is a Space Marine and the hero of the Battle for Liberty, whose Shot Heard 'Round the Universe saved the planet from a nearly unstoppable war machine. He's handsome, charismatic, and the perfect poster boy to help the military drive enlistment. Pulled from the war and thrown into the spotlight, he's as efficient at charming the media and bedding beautiful celebrities as he was at shooting down enemy starfighters.

After an assassination attempt leaves Mitchell critically wounded, he begins to suffer from strange hallucinations that carry a chilling and oddly familiar warning:

They are coming. Find the Goliath or humankind will be destroyed.

Convinced that the visions are a side-effect of his injuries, he tries to ignore them, only to learn that he may not be as crazy as he thinks. The enemy is real and closer than he imagined, and they'll do whatever it takes to prevent him from rediscovering the centuries lost starship.

Narrowly escaping capture, out of time and out of air, Mitchell lands at the mercy of the Riggers - a ragtag crew of former commandos who patrol the lawless outer reaches of the galaxy. Guided by a captain with a reputation for cold-blooded murder, they're dangerous, immoral, and possibly insane.

They may also be humanity's last hope for survival in a war that has raged beyond eternity.

(War Eternal is also available in a box set of the first three books here: mrforbes.com/wareternalbox)

Hell's Rejects (Chaos of the Covenant)
mrforbes.com/hellsrejects

The most powerful starships ever constructed are gone. Thousands are dead. A fleet is in ruins. The attackers are unknown. The orders are clear: *Recover the ships. Bury the bastards who stole them.*

Lieutenant Abigail Cage never expected to find herself in Hell. As a Highly Specialized Operational Combatant, she was one of the most respected Marines in the military. Now she's doing hard labor on the most miserable planet in the universe.

Not for long.

The Earth Republic is looking for the most dangerous individuals it can control. The best of the worst, and Abbey happens to be one of them. The deal is simple: *Bring back the starships, earn your freedom. Try to run, you die.* It's a suicide mission, but she has nothing to lose.

The only problem? There's a new threat in the galaxy. One with a power unlike anything anyone has ever seen. One that's been waiting for this moment for a very, very, long time. And they want Abbey, too.

Be careful what you wish for.

They say Hell hath no fury like a woman scorned. They have no idea.

Man of War (Rebellion)
mrforbes.com/manofwar

In the year 2280, an alien fleet attacked the Earth.

Their weapons were unstoppable, their defenses unbreakable.

Our technology was inferior, our militaries overwhelmed.

Only one starship escaped before civilization fell.

Earth was lost.

It was never forgotten.

Fifty-two years have passed.

A message from home has been received.

The time to fight for what is ours has come.

Welcome to the rebellion.

Or maybe something completely different?

Dead of Night (Ghosts & Magic)
mrforbes.com/deadofnight

For Conor Night, the world's only surviving necromancer, staying alive is an expensive proposition. So when the promise of a big payout for a small bit of thievery presents itself, Conor is all in. But nothing comes easy in the world of ghosts and magic, and it isn't long before Conor is caught up in the machinations of the most powerful wizards on Earth and left with only two ways out:

Finish the job, or be finished himself.

Balance (The Divine)
mrforbes.com/balance

My name is Landon Hamilton. Once upon a time I was a twenty-three year old security guard, trying to regain my life after spending a year in prison for stealing people's credit card numbers.

Now, I'm dead.

Okay, I was supposed to be dead. I got killed after all; but a funny thing happened after I had turned the mortal coil...

I met Dante Alighieri - yeah, that Dante. He told me I was special, a diuscrucis. That's what they call a perfect balance of human, demon, and angel. Apparently, I'm the only one of my kind.

I also learned that there was a war raging on Earth between Heaven and Hell, and that I was the only one who could save the human race from annihilation. He asked me to help, and I was naive enough to agree.

Sounds crazy, I know, but he wished me luck and sent me back to the mortal world. Oh yeah, he also gave me instructions on how to use my Divine "magic" to bend the universe to my will. The problem is, a sexy vampire crushed them while I was crushing on her.

Now I have to somehow find my own way to stay alive in a world of angels, vampires, werewolves, and an assortment of other enemies that all want to kill me before I can mess up their plans for humanity's future. If that isn't enough, I also have to find the queen of all demons and recover the Holy Grail.

It's not like it's the end of the world if I fail.

Wait. It is.

Tears of Blood (Books 1-3)
mrforbes.com/tearsofblood

One thousand years ago, the world was broken and reborn beneath the boot of a nameless, ageless tyrant. He erased all history of the time before, enslaving the people and hunting those with the power to unseat him.

The power of magic.

Eryn is such a girl. Born with the Curse, she fights to control and conceal it to protect those she loves. But when the truth is revealed, and his Marines come, she is forced away from her home and into the company of Silas, a deadly fugitive tormented by a fractured past.

Silas knows only that he is a murderer who once hunted the Cursed, and that he and his brothers butchered armies and innocents alike to keep the deep, dark secrets of the time before from ever coming to light.

Secrets which could save the world.

Or destroy it completely.

About the Author

M.R. Forbes is the creator of a growing catalog of science fiction novels, including War Eternal, Rebellion, Chaos of the Covenant, and the Forgotten Worlds novels. He eats too many donuts, and he's always happy to hear from readers.

To learn more about M.R. Forbes or just say hello:

Visit my website:
mrforbes.com

Send me an e-mail:
michael@mrforbes.com

Check out my Facebook page:
facebook.com/mrforbes.author

Chat with me on Facebook Messenger:
https://m.me/mrforbes.author

26480352R00199

Printed in Great Britain
by Amazon